PRAISE FOR *THE*

"Rich with hope and romance, and readers will love it."

—Shondaland

"Funny, poignant, and wickedly clever—I'll be hunting for everything Eden Appiah-Kubi writes from here on out."
—Courtney Milan, *New York Times* and *USA Today* bestselling author

"Appiah-Kubi's unique retelling of Austen's *Pride and Prejudice* gives it a modern spin with surprising twists and empowering storylines."

—*Library Journal*

"The cast of characters is diverse—EJ is Black, Jamie is a recently out trans woman, Tessa is Filipina, and Will has both Chinese and Korean heritage—and hearing EJ, Jamie, Tessa, and the other women who populate Longbourn discuss ambitious career goals, healthy sex lives, and more with unabashed frankness is refreshing."

—*Kirkus Reviews*

"An inclusive reimagining of *Pride and Prejudice* that Jane Austen fans are sure to fall in love with."

—POPSUGAR

"It's really wonderful to read a book filled with a diverse cast of women characters, and have them have dreams and ambitions outside of getting married or falling in love. There is romance within these pages, don't be mistaken, but for the most part, you get to follow along as EJ, Jamie, and Tessa discover what they desire out of life."

—*Real Simple*

Her Own
HAPPINESS

ALSO BY EDEN APPIAH-KUBI

The Bennet Women

Her Own HAPPINESS

EDEN APPIAH-KUBI

Published by Montlake, Seattle

www.apub.com

Amazon, the Amazon logo, and Montlake are trademarks of Amazon.com, Inc., or its affiliates.

ISBN-13: 9781542030472 (paperback)
ISBN-13: 9781542030489 (digital)

Cover design by Faceout Studio, Spencer Fuller

Cover illustration by Taylor McManus

Printed in the United States of America

To my fat, Black, and different women/femmes: you are enough, you are never too much, and the world needs your light, even though it doesn't often deserve it.

You must be the best judge of your own happiness.

—*Jane Austen,* Emma

AUTHOR'S NOTE

Dearest Reader,

This novel is not about the pandemic; however, the events of this story take place in the spring and fall of 2021 and do not ignore the big and small ways lives changed during this time. While there are no on-page descriptions of death or illness, this may be a hard time to revisit. So I encourage you, if something in this book is stressful or triggering, please pause, take a breath, or skip pages / skim until you feel like your feet are on solid ground.

This story contains discussions of sizeism/fatphobia, sexism, racism, depression, and suicidal ideation. If you can't engage, for any reason, please don't make yourself try. Be gentle with yourself where you can.

Love and hugs,
Eden

SPRING 2021

3/20/21

Dear God,

Today sucks, please make it suck less. Thanks.

Also, Amen.
Maya

Maya

The prayer was today's entry in her Just One Line journal, a gift from her sister. Maya had made the mistake of telling her she was thinking of getting into journaling (which is a thing you say when you're going through a crappy time but don't want to talk about it anymore). This led to her mom, her sister, and her cousin all sending her some kind of journal for Christmas. She wondered where this enthusiasm had been when she wanted to try out burlesque—pasties could get expensive.

The journals had been sitting in a pile collecting dust until the sudden loss of her group house was followed by the sudden loss of . . . well, everything she'd been working toward for the past seven years. She was packing her life into her two beat-up suitcases when she uncovered the journals beneath a layer of debris on her desk. With a shrug, she shoved all three into her faithful FUCK THE PATRIARCHY tote bag and promptly forgot about them. For weeks, she hadn't spared them a thought, but now, sitting at her departure gate, she was in desperate need of something to do.

She'd already wrung all the thrills she could out of Gate 13 of the Honolulu airport: perusing the Hudson News; securing a seat where she could neither hear nor see the constant stream of bad news pouring from the television; staring in blank confusion at a vending machine full of notebooks and beach towels. Maya's phone had lost its appeal when her cousin "Gigi the JD" sent her a link. She was one of several lawyers on Maya's dad's alarmingly accomplished side of the family, and was constantly on the hunt for inspirational speeches and aspirational figures. So Maya wasn't surprised to see that her cuz's link led to a TED Talk (ugh) called "Girlbossing for Good" (boooo!)—she was just disappointed.

"Hard pass," she groaned, shoving her phone into her tote bag with some force. She briefly fantasized about throwing her phone across the room. But of course, she couldn't afford a new phone—or an old phone, or even one last poke bowl in the main terminal.

Okay. She was starting to wallow. Time to do anything else. Maya felt around her tote bag again and pulled out the journals.

I am definitely bored enough to try this, she thought, picking up the most colorful journal of the bunch. It was the one from Momma: *Flourish! A Black Woman's Guided Journal of Reflection and Prayer.* Maya had tried to stay connected to her church and her faith for the last two years, but prayer had stopped being a source of comfort and started to be one of frustration—it would have been more comforting to believe in nothing.

She couldn't say that she'd lost her faith entirely, but it was distinctly uninteresting at the moment. These days, she rarely experienced awe or wonder; she felt salty.

Maya thumbed through the journal absently, then looked at the cover illustration: a line drawing of a bronze-skinned woman with an Afro, eyes closed, head bowed in prayer. Swirls of color and streaks of gold floated above her head as if this woman were communing with the divine. Pretty, but it didn't match Maya's mood—and she found the content a touch (okay, a lot) too hetero for her taste. She was not "preparing for her Boaz" or looking to "preserve the union after he cheats."

"Blech," Maya said, running a hand through her shoulder-length microlocs. "I'm a Christian, but I'm not 'prayer-journal Christian.' That's . . ." She gestured vaguely. "Another level."

She selected the journal from Gigi. The journal itself was spiral bound and covered with daisies. The words *Yes She Can* screamed from the cover in an exuberant yellow font.

"This gives me MLM," she said, tossing it in her bag without opening it. All its "seize the day" / "you go girl" energy did was remind her how little she had going on in her life.

Finally, there was her sister's Just One Line journal. It was navy blue with shimmering foil stars. Maya opened the front cover and found a note.

Hey Mai,

If you want to start a new habit, start small. Got one of these for college graduation and it's the only journal I've ever kept up. Hot tip: journals are a good place to be angry or sad. I was angry and sad a lot last year. This helped.

Love,
Ella

"This wins," Maya said. She turned to the first page, then paused and sighed heavily, steaming her pride flag–printed face mask.

I don't want to write anything about today—this day sucks. Suddenly, like a bolt of lightning, Maya got the idea to write a snarky little prayer as entry number one. It at least reflected her true feelings of the day. She went to fill in the day's date.

Wait. It was her birthday! In the middle of everything, she had forgotten.

Birthdays were a big deal to Maya, especially her own. She was a queer, fat, Black woman who had been an openly queer, fat, Black, artistic teenager. She'd learned earlier than most *not* to accept other people's ideas about her body or her success. That's why making it another year was always something to celebrate. She wasn't sure if she'd ever get married or have kids. Like most millennials, she didn't expect to be able to retire—ever. There was no sense in saving her joy for big milestone events. Sometimes that meant throwing a rager or going all night at booth karaoke; other times it was a game night or a classy dinner party. She contained multitudes.

"I'm thirty-one today," she said thoughtfully, leaning back in the squeaky plastic chair. "Huh."

Maya didn't drink much and didn't smoke, and she always thought drugs were more expensive and less fun than advertised. Her belief and trust in herself were her great rebellion. That's why she didn't care that it had taken her six years to get her BA. It's why, generally speaking, aging into her thirties wasn't a source of panic . . . until now, after things had fallen apart so spectacularly. She ran her finger up and down the tattoo on her left wrist, the way she always did when she was trying to calm herself down. The fact that she had forgotten her birthday meant that things were truly bad in a way she couldn't quite deal with.

Even last year during lockdown, in the scariest part of the *panini press*, she'd still found a way to celebrate by breaking in her brand-new Nintendo Switch and her brand-new vibrator—both courtesy of a generous care package from her younger sister. She'd also made her first pavlova, and it was really good.

It's my freaking birthday and I don't even have a cookie! The one thing Maya truly required on her birthday was a delicious dessert, usually one that she made herself. She had always loved baking and delighted in making something new and elaborate every birthday. If she made it for herself, it didn't matter that it came out "a bit pear-shaped," as her sister liked to say. (Ella hadn't gotten just her master's in the UK—she'd picked up all the idioms.)

"What a stupid day to be without a cookie," Maya grumbled to herself. She sank a bit in her plastic bucket seat, dangerously on the verge of pouting. "Okay, now I'm whining—and hungry." Her phone buzzed, a welcome interruption to her thoughts.

> Come down to the snack bar!
> I've got NACHOS! 😋

She smiled. Ant always managed to text her when she needed an escape from her own head. Maya looked at her surroundings and sighed. She could use a change of scene anyway. Airports were depressing once you got past security. The decor was an aggressively bland blue-gray pattern of GATE-GATE-STARBUCKS repeated with such regularity you felt like you were living in a simulation.

She moved quickly down the wide hallway, deftly dodging groups of tourists clumped around kiosks, mailing themselves pineapples or buying themselves forty-dollar leis, trying to hold on to their memories as long as they could. Out the corner of her eye, Maya spotted a middle-aged man in a brand-new aloha shirt, coughing like he was about to hack up a lung—his required mask well below his chin.

Maya sighed a different sigh this time, an angry one. She prayed Mr. Hacking Cough was departing Hawai'i and *not* arriving for a fun-filled vacay to infect her friends who had their first or second jobs at Honolulu hotels and restaurants.

Before she could shoot the guy the side-eye he deserved, Maya spotted Ant. It was easy since he was a head taller than most folks and better dressed. At present he was wearing matching "marigold" sweat-shirt and joggers, a bright yellow that matched the piping and laces on his sneakers. Just the right shade to complement and not clash with his tawny brown skin. The shoes had a name like a spaceship and truly did "pull the look together," as he'd insisted they would when he splurged on them a few months back.

Early in their friendship, Ant told Maya he was on a personal mission to show that the big and tall could be stylish. His goal: to look effortlessly cool—which took a lot of work. (Maya could only imagine. It was hard enough finding cool plus-size women's clothes.)

His wide smile drew her in like a lighthouse in a violent sea. She forgot everything else, quickened her pace, and met him at a café table near a small snack bar.

"Get in on these," he half sang, turning to proudly display a plastic tray of round tortilla chips, flanked by a small rectangle of watery salsa and a container of nacho cheese.

Maya withheld a scoff. Those weren't even bowling-alley nachos— they were *roller-rink* nachos. On another day she would have mocked the snack for its profound basic-ness, but now she didn't have the energy. She settled on "Thank you," and put her hoodie and bag on a hook beneath the table.

Ant raised both eyebrows and wiggled his wire-frame glasses. "Oh, she has manners today?"

It was an old joke between them. Knowing someone for seven years offered lots of opportunities for inside jokes. Maya tossed her locs and sniffed. "I'm always polite. I even sent your mom a thank-you card for the plane ticket this morning." It was literally the least she could do.

Losing her house, then the job she loved was awful. Doing both in the middle of "these unprecedented times" meant that she couldn't couch-surf or barter her way through this crisis. Maya realized she had no choice but to move back home with her parents—the worst-case scenario. She'd been working up the courage to ask her baby sister for help buying her ticket home (which was all too humiliating, but she was *not* asking her parents).

Then, like a miracle, Ant revealed that he'd landed an internship with the Smithsonian and could rent a deeply discounted room with his aunt in Takoma Park. Maya'd never been so happy to be from the Maryland suburbs. Yes, her life was awful right now, with no end in sight, but she'd have something to hold on to: her best friend would still be less than half an hour away. Little miracles like that kept her from losing her faith altogether.

So when Ant asked if she could be his "emergency support human" for the flight—a combination of claustrophobia and a general fear of flying made traveling miserable for him—Maya said yes without a second thought. It was her way of saying thank you for the miracle. Then God, the universe, or whatever responded with another miracle: Ant's navy-doctor mom covered her ticket to DC.

"Okay, Miss Manners, will you please partake of this bounty? I'm tired of holding back."

She selected a chip and dipped it into the cheese. As it emerged, a small tendril of steam hissed from the yellow goo.

"It's warm! Nice," she exclaimed before taking a bite.

Ant gave a crooked smile of satisfaction. "I asked the lady to nuke the cheese for a full thirty seconds. Had to wait until her line was clear, but I think it was worth it." He fished around the pockets of his hoodie. "I also snagged a hot sauce packet for the salsa." He gave a knowing look—no, a smirk. As they both knew, Maya thought that any salsa milder than "spicy" was just unchilled gazpacho.

His evident self-satisfaction was too much for Maya. "I'm going to say thank you, and only thank you, because your head's too big already."

"You sure you're not an Aries, Maya? You stay loud and wrong," he blandly retorted, squirting the hot sauce into the salsa. "Also, my head is the perfect size. I have received many a compliment on how generally well proportioned I am." He winked, twinkling brown eyes fringed by full, dark lashes. He was the only person Maya knew who was good at winking.

Maya stuck out her tongue. "The stars don't tell me who I am, unlike some people I could name."

"And on paper Christianity is about as weird as astrology," he replied languidly. "It's like how Canada has a real messed-up history, but it's not as messed up as the US, so people don't notice."

Maya rocked on her stool thoughtfully. "I can't argue with either of those points." She shrugged and returned to the nachos.

They ate in companionable silence until Maya looked up and noticed that people were standing up and starting to get in line.

"We should get over there," she said quietly.

Ant nodded with determination but made no move toward their gate. Maya noticed his hands begin to shake. She rose and took a step closer to him, gently slipping her hand into his.

"You should know that I'm not just an emergency support human—I am also a witch, specializing in the magic of holding hands." She gave his hand a squeeze. "Instant bravery and a little bit of comfort."

He smiled at her again; it was smaller and a little nervous, but it was there.

"Oh hey, I got this for you, too. It was the last one they had." Ant reached into his pocket and produced a black-and-white cookie wrapped in plastic. "I asked the snack bar lady if they had anything sweet, told her it was your birthday. She actually went to the back and found this."

Maya felt her eyes well with happy tears. "What have I ever done to deserve you?!" She threw her arms around Ant's neck and gave him a long squeeze. Then she picked up the cookie and held it like the treasure it was. "This has pulled today right out of the gutter for me. Thank you."

There was a crackle over the speakers. Boarding was about to begin for real.

"I'm glad to hear it, Maya. Let me put this stuff in the trash," he said, nodding to the nacho debris. The plastic tray rattled a little in his hands.

Maya gathered her stuff, then casually took Ant's arm. "Hey," she said softly. "I'm gonna be here the whole time."

He took a deep breath, slipped his mask back on, and nodded. Arm in arm, they walked over to their gate.

"I feel bad for the person who has to sit next to us and listen to us talk about manga or N. K. Jemisin for five hours."

Ant stopped short. "What do you mean?"

Maya tilted her head. "The other person in our row." She could see his face break out in a grin, despite his mask.

"Oh, my mom is swimming in miles. We're flying first class, all the way to DC. Happy birthday!"

Maya blinked. She must have been truly out of it, since she'd missed that detail. Then again, she did spend the entire time in the security line trying to not cry.

Now she was flying first class *and* she had a surprise cookie? Her birthday was truly starting to look up.

∽

The flight was blissfully uneventful. Courtesy of her friendly reminder to take his antianxiety meds while they boarded, Ant was much less nervous by the time they were cruising. After the first hour he was able to let go of her hand and play some *Animal Crossing* on his Switch, and she spent most of the flight surfing through in-flight entertainment options that were much more enticing when they came with her *first-class* seat.

She couldn't remember falling asleep but woke during the plane's descent. Maya had to resist the urge to wake Ant, too, as their plane whizzed by the monuments. Instead she took a beautiful photo of sunrise over the Washington Monument before their plane dropped them at DCA, which was actually in Virginia.

How long had it been since she'd had this view? Four or five years at least—since Ella's graduation from undergrad. DC seemed to be welcoming her with a golden spill of sunlight over the monuments, tiny buildings, and bridges she named to herself without thinking. From up here, everything was reassuringly familiar.

That feeling did not last past the arrivals gate. National Airport (she'd never call it "Reagan") had apparently gotten a serious renovation since the last time she flew through. Stepping off the Jetway, Maya might as well have landed in any other city in the country. Nothing looked like she remembered it, from the restaurants to the security checkpoints.

The only face she recognized at all was the "girlboss" from Gigi's TED Talk with the carroty-red hair. Her name, as screamed from the cover of *Washingtonian* magazine, was Emme Vivant.

"DC apparently got a new queen while I was gone," Maya said to Ant as they rode down the escalator.

Emme was everywhere. Her Meghan Markle complexion glowed in three-foot-high digital ads for her book, the ludicrously titled *(Ad) venture Capital: Girlbossing for Good.* She power-posed on the covers of *Black Enterprise* and *DC Life.* She even appeared in cardboard-cutout form near the baggage area for reasons that weren't readily apparent.

Ant paused before the cardboard figure, taking in her modern business glam. "Nice sneakers," he said with a nod. "Call me a sucker, but I want to buy her book just to know what the fuss is about."

Maya snorted. "Nothing on earth could make me read anything by a person who identifies as a 'girlboss' in the year of our Lord 2021. Besides, I think her dad is or was an evil developer—according to my dad, at least. He used to be a housing organizer back in the day."

Ant raised impressed eyebrows. "Go, Mr. D. How did he like it?"

She chuckled. "He likes to say he got into teaching because it was better pay and better hours, so . . ."

Ant laughed again, but by some silent agreement let the conversation drop. Maya felt a sudden chill from the early-morning spring air coming through the sliding doors—or was it from a creeping sense of desolation? There'd been no miracle at the buzzer, no sudden change of heart from her old boss or her old landlord. Her Hawaiian dream was over. Now all she had was the rest of her life.

That thought made her eyes fill with sudden hot tears. She blinked and looked away, hoping that Ant didn't notice. Thankfully, when she glanced over, he seemed to be locked in his own mental spiral.

Ant was rubbing the place where his glasses met his KN95. His eyes were wide, bouncing around the baggage area. "It's so weird . . . I've lived in three different countries, but I've never done such a big move by myself. I think this is the biggest change I've ever made. The bigness of it is suddenly making me a little dizzy."

Maya took Ant's hand and gave it a firm squeeze before any more panic could creep across his face. "Hey," she began gently. "You're gonna be okay. No matter what happens out here, you're gonna grow, and that will be worth the trip. Plus, no matter what, you're gonna have me to eat pizza and binge-watch random movies with."

Her words had the desired effect, and Ant's shoulders relaxed. She gave a small smile seeing him breathe easily again. He squeezed her hand in return. "Thank you, Maya."

"Anytime, Antonio." She pulled him into a hug and gave him another tight squeeze. If only her little pep talks worked as well on herself. Suddenly everyone in the baggage area jumped at a god-awful buzzing noise that came from a nearby machine. The yellow light on top of it flashed and its conveyor came to life. The suitcases were coming, the very last step in their arriving. It was time.

Ant

Though they hadn't talked about it much, Ant knew Maya was worried about how her parents would react to her sudden return. From everything she'd said, he'd thought there would be sarcastic sighs and condescension. Instead, there were just tears. Maya's mom cried, "My baby!" from about forty feet away while they waited for their suitcases. She ran to Maya, sweeping her into a cloud of hugs and kisses. Then Maya was crying, too.

It was a beautiful thing to behold, but he knew Maya well enough to guess that she'd feel embarrassed about such a vulnerable display later. Ant looked away to give them a bit of privacy and noticed that their last suitcases were right next to each other—and about to take a second trip around the conveyor belt. He raced over to grab both bags.

When he reached Maya and her mom again, they'd broken apart, eyes damp and masks askew, but still held hands. It had taken Maya's mom a moment to notice Ant. She bobbed warmly in his direction.

"Hello, young man." She chuckled. "I've only got dose one of my Pfizer, baby, so you'll get your hug next time. I can't wait! Haven't so much as shaken hands with anyone but her father since last March."

He nodded and tried to look understanding.

Maya released her mom's hand and pulled him in for another hug. The one that meant goodbye. He didn't let go until he absolutely had to.

"Hey," she whispered. "You're gonna be okay."

"I know," he lied.

She smiled at him, more brave than happy, and gathered her suitcases. Maya's mom sprang for one of those cart things that could hold five bags at once. Ant helped load everything up, then watched his best friend walk away until she disappeared into the elevator, ready to wave in case she looked back.

He was finally alone, with himself and with the truth: Ant's reason for being on the mainland had just wheeled her suitcase out of the airport, and he didn't know when he'd see her again.

Ant patted his cheeks and rubbed his face. It was mid-morning, but he certainly didn't feel awake. He wasn't sure whether he was drowsy or reeling with the unreality of traveling five thousand miles over sixteen hours. You never got great sleep on a plane, even in first class. Ant adjusted his backpack and draped his messenger bag over one of two large, wheeled duffels—his whole life for at least the next few months. He'd really done it. He had left home, left Hawai'i, and was starting something completely new. He was ready, he had to be—it was happening now.

His phone buzzed, shaking Ant out of his thoughts. It was Auntie Kay.

Hey Ant, I'm 5 minutes away
I'll be pulling up at arrivals soon

Great! See you soon

Most of the time Ant felt like he moved through the world with a touch of grace for someone as tall and big-boned as he was, but nothing made him feel more like a Heffalump than trying to wheel the two massive suitcases that he'd been traveling with since his family came back to the States. Once he got to Hawai'i, he never really went anywhere else. He had tagged along with his mom on a work trip to LA when he was sixteen, but no other destination had seemed worth getting on a plane for five hours (minimum). Luckily, he loved Hawai'i.

But standing outside in the cool March air, Ant took in the train and then the highway. It was all connected by land. He could drive between states instead of flying between islands—once he got a car, anyway. Suddenly, he wanted to sit down with a map and start plotting road trips.

Ant inhaled deeply. The whole world suddenly felt bigger. He was going to try not to feel stupid after being ruled by his fears for so long and enjoy this moment. *He was going to do road trips.* He had a non-work-related goal, the kind of thing that made such a huge move worthwhile.

He twisted the new black ring on his middle finger, his ace ring. Those who recognized it would know he was ace instantly. Those who weren't familiar would give him the opportunity to practice opening up about his identity. It was the only choice he'd made about his new life that had nothing to do with Maya. Ant had finally gotten comfortable enough with himself to lean in to his ace identity. To be open about it. And as Maya said, when you're someplace new, queer people are almost always looking for other queer people. He hoped that was still true during a global plague.

Ant looked up at a friendly honk. There was Auntie Kay, flashing her lights in greeting. Now his adventure was beginning.

༄

Auntie Kay wasn't technically his aunt. Ma had a complicated relationship with her blood siblings, which had resulted in him seeing them maybe three times in his twenty-five years of life. By contrast, Auntie Kay—his mother's best friend—had opened her home to them after his dad died, and even flew out to Hawai'i for his high school graduation. That was the last time he'd seen her in person, but they'd FaceChatted a lot in the last month, so Ant was able to recognize her friendly, round face through her car's windshield. She stopped in front of him and pulled her medical-grade mask over her nose. Though it had been a minute since they'd met in person, he was fairly certain that he liked her.

"Living my Uber-driver fantasy." She laughed as he slid into the back seat. She guided the car onto the highway and played tour guide for the first half of the ride, pointing out landmarks: the Washington Monument, an interesting-looking bridge, the Capitol Building. When she wasn't showing him the sights, she was apologizing for the traffic.

"Everyone complains about everyone else's driving. Marylanders think Virginians are the worst; Virginians think Marylanders are the worst. DC drivers have to put up with everyone. But half the people who live here didn't grow up here, so most of the time when you see some absolute bullshit on the highway, it's someone from Maryland who learned to drive in Ohio or Virginia who are actually from Bucks County, Pennsylvania. We get a lot of Pennsylvanians.

"We're all united by how much we hate the traffic. It's always bumper-to-bumper somewhere. You get in your car at two in the morning and get stuck staring at the Mormon temple so long you'd have time to climb out of your car and paint *Surrender Dorothy* on the overpass." She must have caught his confused stare.

This made Auntie Kay chuckle for reasons that weren't entirely clear, but she had that kind of energy that made everything she said entertaining. Ant warmed to her instantly. He and Auntie Kay were going to be buddies; now he just had to charm the rest of his housemates.

Ant slumped back and puffed his mask with a sigh. The only thing more daunting than moving thousands of miles from home was going from living with his mom to living with someone he kinda knew plus two complete strangers—two and a half if you counted Auntie Kay's girlfriend, who didn't technically live there but sounded like she was around more days than not. Auntie Kay had reassured him that Rio and Sylvie were lovely and considerate—but he simply didn't know how to *be* around them. And with the pandemic still in full force, he was probably going to be around them a lot.

He could at least practice his polite conversation with Auntie Kay. So far, not awkward. That was something.

"You're from here, right?" Ant half shouted to make sure he could be heard over the breeze from the windows. Traffic was finally loosening up.

"Born and bred, that's why I get to talk smack about everybody else. Folks here get off lucky: You can call yourself a Washingtonian after three years and a Marylander once you eat some crabs and go to an Orioles game. I went to college in the Midwest. You can't say you're from there until your grandchild graduates from *your* high school. That's why I moved back. Well, that, and all the snow." They were at a stoplight, so she turned and offered some reassurance. "We get some, but not *that* much. Winter's cold and long, but it's not spiritual torture."

That made Ant snort so hard he dislodged his mask. "You really didn't take to the weather then." He paused, watching the trees along the highway. Half were bare, but the other half were starting to sprout white blossoms. "There are a lot of flowering trees here! They're going to be so beautiful soon."

Auntie Kay pursed her lips. "We pay the price in allergies, though. Everyone who comes here starts having allergy problems. All these trees mean we've got a lot of floral sperm floating around."

Ant half laughed, half choked at that. "Sperm?!" he squeaked out.

"Because it screws up your nose," Auntie Kay offered with a high giggle.

Ant shook his head. "You are leaning in to this Uber-driver role."

It wasn't long before they pulled off the highway and onto the main street of what looked like a cute small town.

"Only this block is like this," Auntie Kay explained. "The rest is suburbs. The folks here like to think they're crunchy granola, but these days everyone does yoga and recycles, so they're yuppies. Do you want to stop for lunch? I'll buy and you can tell me about your famous 'five-year plan.'"

Ant tried to communicate his smile with his eyes. "Sounds great."

And now he would have to lie to his aunt. Like he had lied to his mom. It was a small lie: that he was planning to move to DC shortly after graduation in May, then work in public-service gardens/parks for five years, until he could go back to Hawai'i and get a job with Honolulu Parks and Rec or the botanical garden. It was a good plan, a reasonable plan. The kind that he could have come up with if he had been thinking about it hard enough. The truth of the matter was, this plan had kicked into motion when Maya sobbed on his shoulder, saying there was no way she could stay in Hawai'i. He'd realized, rather quickly, that he didn't want to be in Hawai'i without her.

The question became "Why would Ant go to Washington, DC?" And the answer was the same as it was for most transplants: a prestigious internship. So he started applying. He also shared this plan with his mom, who was . . . much happier than he'd expected. Apparently, she'd been really worried about him "failing to launch." Whatever that meant.

She wanted to make sure nothing stood in Ant's way, hence the call to Auntie Kay. Now his new landlord was taking him to lunch, and he was going to share boring stats about horticulture careers, public gardens, and other stuff that sounded saner than "I came out here because I thought I'd miss my best friend too much."

He wasn't in love with her—let's be clear on that. But one nice thing about realizing he was asexual and then finding the ace community: he found people who valued friendship the way he did. People understood moving for your S.O. or someone you planned to marry, but it made just as much sense to move for your best friend if they were a big part of your life—and Maya was.

"How does Middle East Cuisine sound?" Auntie Kay led them to a restaurant with outdoor seating and enticing smells. "It is both the food and the name of the place."

Ant smiled. "Sounds great! I could eat a horse." Maybe if he stuffed his mouth with falafel, he could keep his true motives from spilling out. Ant knew he was a terrible liar, but it was either keep up the ruse or sound completely insane. And as ruses went, there were worse ones.

Maya

It took Maya four days to stop waking and expecting to be in Honolulu, her eyes casting about her room, looking for the shadows of palm trees or the particular bright gleam of the island sun. Few things were worse than thinking you were in Hawai'i and finding yourself somewhere else.

Even after waking, Maya couldn't shake the new heaviness from her limbs, couldn't ease the stiffness in her movements. She couldn't seem to get out of bed at all. It was exhausting to try. She slept but didn't rest. She barely ate. She didn't respond to her mother's quiet concern or her father's much louder encouragement. There was a sucking weariness at the center of her soul Maya simply couldn't dislodge. She named it "the octopus" because it felt like she was wrapped in tentacles pulling her down, down, down. She remained in bed, feeling every part of her great loss: her home, her career, the life she'd rebuilt for herself over seven years—all gone in a matter of weeks. Sleeping or waking, she was constantly buffeted by memories.

⁂

Maya didn't have to close her eyes to remember the email from her landlord. The memory of opening her laptop to that screen was seared in her brain with all her other waking nightmares. In three terse sentences he'd written that he was selling the house Maya shared with two other social work majors in a month's time (meaning they had thirty days to move—turned out that wasn't *technically* illegal, despite Hawai'i's eviction moratorium). She'd spent one week arguing with her friends about trying to fight for the house. Then three more days fighting to keep her friends from trashing the place and losing their deposit. They were all UH seniors, but Maya was the only one planning to stay in Hawai'i after graduation. For her roommates the experience was awful but not earth-shattering. For Maya it was a major crisis, until something worse made the stealth eviction seem minor in comparison.

Two days before she moved onto Ant's mom's couch, Maya saw footage of the Ohana Center engulfed in flames on the morning news. She watched a charred section of the roof crash down onto the lanai, where they had homework club while the schools were still virtual. The mural that she'd designed as part of her AmeriCorps project was scarred by fire. Auntie Lenora—her boss, her mentor, her second mother—ended up having to move, too. The fire had spread from the center to her neighboring tiny house, taking out most of the roof. It was too much.

Soon Maya was on the phone, trying to brainstorm ways of starting again, but Auntie Lenora stopped her. "I'm sorry, Maya. It's over. I'm too old to start again."

Though her voice was rough with tears, Maya knew that Auntie Lenora's answer was final. She was the kind of sweet-faced Native Hawaiian "auntie" who was a force of nature. When it came to the center, her word was the law. And just like that, Maya had lost her home, her reason for being in Hawai'i, and her career. She'd been working at the center since she decided to stay in Honolulu.

She was the program manager then, but their plan had always been for Maya to take over the center one day. It was why she'd majored in social work—hell, it was why she'd even gone back to school in the first place. Her sister had wisely pointed out that their parents still had her college fund sitting around and would help with room and board if she were in school.

Now the center was rubble. Ms. Lenora was moving in with her brother on the Big Island and there had been nothing for Maya to do but go back to Maryland and, apparently, take to her bed until the world ended.

⌒

Her parents exhibited immense restraint and hovered just enough to make sure she ate and occasionally showered. She scrolled through her phone, not really seeing anything but welcoming the escape from her head. Somehow, she found herself actually watching the Girlboss's TED Talk, which started with white letters on a black background.

"DID YOU KNOW THAT YOU ARE LIGHT?" —REV. GINA ELTON-DIMARCO

The view changed to a stage. A tall, light-skinned woman stood at the center of it (red hair, halo braid), looking like Athena in a heather-gray jumpsuit.

"That's the first line to the poem 'Lightbearers,' which I found exactly when I needed it, when my dreams and plans were rudely interrupted by life. I'd just graduated with my MBA, ready to take on the world, when my father got a very scary diagnosis that kept me at home to look after him. My world was shrinking, and I was struggling to see a point to anything. Then I stumbled on this poem, and it reminded me that I am light, so the point is to shine. To illuminate. And so I use the resources I have as an angel investor to illuminate the work of BIPOC, women, and LGBTQ entrepreneurs."

Maya paused the presentation and opened a browser to search for the poem.

Lightbearers Rev. Gina, she typed quickly on her phone. Finding this poem felt vital. Rev. Gina's words felt like the first glimpse of light after weeks of crawling through a dark tunnel. She needed to find the source like she needed to breathe.

"A YouTube channel?" Maya had been expecting a book she could buy or something less social media–y. But she clicked the "Lightbearers" link anyway. It appeared to lead to a two-minute video of the sun rising over a still lake.

"Did you know that you are light?" The feminine voice was warm and younger than she'd expected, with a slight rasp. The camera moved over the water. "Did you know that you shine by simply being? That you feed those around you? They photosynthesize your presence."

Maya sat up in bed, watching that camera move through the tree line, caressing the leaves and branches. Something caught in her throat. "Did you know that your existence is enough?" The camera settled on a tiny flapping yellow bird singing its song from the high bough of a tree.

Suddenly tears fell from Maya's eyes, but for the first time in weeks, they weren't full of pain. She felt like God had just given her an engraved invitation back to the world—and just in time, too. Up until this moment she hadn't wanted to leave her room—or even her bed—but she was starting to be afraid of what would happen if she stayed there.

Maya smiled at her phone screen and clicked the link to Rev. Gina's YouTube channel. She found a playlist of more poetic affirmations and forced herself out of bed. It was time for a bath, and maybe a little yoga afterward.

∽

After a couple of days that started with a Rev. Gina affirmation, morning yoga, and a shower, Maya felt ready to brave the world beyond her former bedroom—starting with the kitchen. For the past month of her incapacitation, her dad had brought her coffee and two boiled eggs in the morning, and her mother had brought her dinner. It hadn't taken her long to notice a pattern: three days of the same soup, punctuated by a hearty salad—chili-chili-chili, chicken Caesar, then gumbo-gumbo-gumbo, salmon salad. A small part of Maya wondered if her parents were trying to drive her from her room through sheer culinary boredom. If that was their plan, it was brilliant. Maya *hated* repeating food. As a kid, she'd been the only one who complained about leftovers. It got so bad that when Maya was fourteen, her mom said, "Well, you cook then!"

And she did. That's how Maya was. With the help of a few episodes of *America's Test Kitchen* (thanks, PBS!), Maya whipped up a barbecue-flavored twist on a South African meatloaf that got raves from her sister and dad and grudging respect from her mother. After that, cooking became one of Maya's chores and probably the only one she loved. When she left home, Maya still didn't have much patience for repeating food, but she had a lot more culinary skill than the average high school senior—a skill she called upon as she stared into her parents' fridge once again.

To her dismay, the fridge was about 80 percent occupied with meal kits, stacked three per shelf. Maya had a frugal person's aversion to meal kits, or anything that seemed overly convenient and expensive. These were values she'd *thought* she got from her parents, but the *panni* had changed a lot of things. Mentally, she pushed the meal kits to the side and searched for more ingredients. There was oat milk, soy milk, mushrooms (fine), eggs (yay!), and some cheese: half a tube of goat cheese and a small rectangle of goat mozzarella—something she hadn't known existed until that moment. Further investigation revealed a bag of fresh spinach, half a Vidalia onion, and a massive jar of chopped garlic.

"The gateway drug to meal kits," Maya muttered, shaking her head. She spread the viable ingredients on the counter and stared at them, willing them to make sense as a meal to her. "Speak to me!" she said, stepping back from the counter. Nothing—of course, because food doesn't talk. She tilted her head to the side and thought.

Wait, was there butter? Maya opened the fridge again and practically dove into the side door.

"Butter!" she cried victoriously. The presence of butter was always grounding. She set it on the counter, and then an idea came in a flash. "Savory crepes!"

Now the cooking came easily. Making the batter, then chilling it in the fridge. Dicing onions, sautéing the onion and garlic. Getting a sear on the mushrooms and wilting the spinach. It was a little past noon when Maya heard the door of her mom's sunroom office open and her parents' footsteps come down the steps.

"What smells so good?" they exclaimed in unison as they came into the kitchen. Her parents were so cute and married sometimes. They were both working from home today. Maya beamed as she took down three plates from the cabinet.

"I've made spinach and mushroom filling for some . . ." She glanced at the oven clock. "Lunchtime crepes."

Her mother came over and gave her a warm side hug. "Well, now I'm happy that parent conference ran long. Fix me up a plate, baby."

Maya's mom and dad had worked from home during the whole of the pandemic. Her mom was a guidance counselor for a high school in the county, while her dad was the principal of a DC charter school for boys. Neither of them was playing with Miss Rona. Maya's mom had had asthma since she was a kid, and her dad had been diagnosed with "mild diabetes" the previous year. Plus, they were both chubby Black people. They were the kind of people this disease liked to kill.

Her mom gave Maya another squeeze and went to get down some glasses. Her dad sidled up to her and peered into the pans. "This sounds amazing, Sprout, but there's no cow milk in any of this, is there?"

Maya worried her bottom lip thoughtfully. "There's goat cheese, soy milk, and regular butter," she replied, adding said butter to a waiting pan. "I've never made crepes with soy milk, so we're gonna see what happens."

He patted her arm. "Butter is fine—that sounds fine. When you cook, the food always turns out good. I'm being careful about dairy. For some reason my lactose intolerance ain't tolerating nothing but butter. Can't even do a splash of your mom's half-and-half in my coffee." He shook his head. "There's something about puking when you're over fifty years old that's traumatizing."

Mom made a noise somewhere between a grunt and groan. "Matthew, we're about to eat!" She shook her head as she put the ice into glasses. "Please do something useful and get the silverware?"

Dad shrugged. "I'm giving Sprout the lay of the land. Things are different around here."

Maya shot a meaningful glance to the closed fridge. "Like the meal kits," she said with a smile.

Her mom was folding napkins as she sat at the dinette table in the kitchen. "Which are from a local Black-owned company—and they saved our marriage. I heard about them on the *Kojo* show, the one with Emme Vivant. She seems to really be about what she talks about. Her whole book's about helping other people start businesses."

The girlboss! "Did she mention a book coming out, something about 'Adventure Capital'?"

Both her parents nodded. Maya had to chuckle. "That lady has been inescapable since we touched down in DC. I swear every billboard in the airport had her face on it."

Her dad snorted. "The Vivants love plastering their name on things, so that tracks. In my day it was whole neighborhoods."

"She ain't her daddy, Matthew. We all know how you feel about Emile Vivant."

"More like E-Vil Vivant," he muttered. "A.k.a. Mr. Gentri-FIRE!"

Maya and her mom exchanged a look as her dad went full "true-crime podcaster," laying out how and why Emile Vivant burned down one of his company's apartments when the tenants tried to buy the building. He sounded every bit the impassioned young organizer he once was. All that was missing was his flattop fade.

Momma was less than charmed by this trip down memory lane. "Matthew, Maya's out of her room. Can we please live in the present?"

Daddy exhaled and nodded sheepishly, and Mom brought the conversation back to the twenty-first century.

"Anyway, in the before-times, we'd only eat together a few days a week. But 'cause of the Rona, we found ourselves having to ask each other 'What do you want for dinner?' *every night.*"

Her dad seemed to shudder at the memory. "It was a nightmare," he added, putting the forks and knives in their place. Maya started to laugh but then looked at his expression. He wasn't kidding.

"But they are ex*pen*sive!" her mom continued. "I have to stretch one box for three days to justify the cost."

Maya smiled as she added the goat mozzarella to the crepes. Her parents were the same people after all.

She dished up two crepes per plate and assessed. They weren't as crispy as she normally got them—that was probably the soy milk—but they remained crepes. She tore a small piece off the nearest corner.

And damn good ones! she thought.

"Here comes lunch!" Maya said, using her former waitress skills to balance one plate on her forearm. She set a plate in front of each of her eager parents and set the last one down for herself. "Let's eat!"

And they ate. Her mom and dad exclaimed over the crepes (profusely, but sincerely) and talked of little but the meal. Once all plates were clean, her mom leaned back and patted her belly—her noticeably smaller belly.

"Momma, have you lost weight?" Maya asked reflexively. She immediately regretted the question because there were all sorts of terrible reasons to lose weight during a pandemic. Maya had probably lost a chunk of her own quarantine weight by being overwhelmed with depression since she'd been back in Maryland, battling "the octopus." Also, fuck diet culture. Also, a little rude. "Sorry, that's not a thing to ask."

Her mom patted her hand. "It's all right, baby. I did lose a bit of weight. It's been a hell of a lot of work, so I'm glad you noticed. I can do a split now, too!" She shimmied her shoulders and smiled her familiar, warm smile. Maya noticed that her mom's face was a bit slimmer, too. It made her look closer to her age, in a way Maya found distressing. In her mind her mother was forever twenty-eight. She knew she should get over that since she herself was in her thirties now.

"These days your momma usually drinks her lunch," Maya's dad added. "And I'm not talking 'three-martini'—I'm talking smoothies. Goopy and green. *Every day.* We got a blender just for smoothies." He gestured to the small rocket ship on the rear kitchen counter. "This is the first real lunch you've had since September."

Momma rolled her eyes. "He's grumpy because I work out during lunch now instead of talking to him. Like we have enough to say for two sit-down meals a day." She gave a small chuckle. "Since I'm fully vaccinated, I'm not as scared at the prospect of going back to in-person school in the fall. It'll give me a chance to miss him."

Maya blinked. *Momma's fully vaccinated now. What else did I miss while I was wallowing in bed?*

She focused on her mom again, who was looking at her plate a little sadly. "I would have been big mad if I missed these. I forgot what a gift you have!"

Maya gave a sheepish half smile. She knew that wasn't a dig, more of a wince at how long it had been since she'd been back home. "I'm glad y'all think I still have the touch."

They were all quiet for a moment. Maya could tell they were treading lightly. They'd been so sweetly gentle with her, she could only be grateful. She swallowed and broke the silence. "Thank you, for everything since I've been home. And before. This was all such short notice. And I spent most of April in a sadness cocoon . . . thank you."

"Of course, baby," her mom said, springing up to wrap her in a hug.

"We're always here, and everything we have, you have," her dad said, squeezing her from the other side. They held the hug until tears came to Maya's eyes. Happy ones this time. She quickly wiped them away as they took their seats again.

There was a silence, not so much awkward as anticipatory. Her mom had her hand on her dad's forearm, probably keeping him from jumping in with any painful questions. They looked at her and waited. They wanted her to lead.

She sighed. She didn't know where to begin.

"I don't know what to do now." She sighed. "I was preparing for a very specific life that is gone. The Ohana Center was everything to me. I was a leader there. I watched so many kids grow up . . ." She trailed off, swallowing. The grief was still too much.

"I earned my degree in December, and they're mailing it out here. In a normal year I would walk in May," Maya started again. She saw her father's eyes brighten. "It's social work with a minor in deaf studies. If the Ohana Center was still standing, I would have slid right into an assistant director position, but . . ." She scrubbed her face with a hand. "I need a new plan, but I'm tired just thinking about it."

Maya groaned internally. What she really needed was a career fairy to make her Hawai'i résumé relevant—maybe even impressive— here. Her BA in social work felt about as useless as a third leg back in Maryland. You needed a bachelor's to answer phones in most places out here.

The DC metro area was one of the most educated parts of the country. Great news for bookstores and theaters, but bad news if you weren't interested, at all, in pursuing a master's. Maya was pretty sure she didn't want to do that. In fact, all she knew was what she *didn't* want to do: no nursing homes, no CPS, no hospitals. She'd heard too many disheartening stories about bureaucracy and burnout. Listening to her parents, even on good days, made her wary of public schools. And her heart was still too stuck in Hawai'i for her to even think of doing youth work out here. Her head and heart were too filled with "no" to make room for any ideas.

"We don't want you to make any big decisions right now," Momma said somberly.

Maya raised her eyebrows. "Momma, my whole life, you're the one who said, 'Broke in your twenties is an adventure; broke in your thirties is a crisis.' This is a crisis! I have to act with some urgency."

Daddy held his hands up placatingly. Maya noted that he was showing remarkable restraint, not rushing in with his opinion. He probably didn't want a repeat of their old fights, either. "We understand, Maya, but it's probably going to take a minute to get into the rhythm of this area again. That's gotta be the biggest adjustment."

"The vibe is almost antithetical," she agreed.

"So I'm gonna ask you to listen to your mom on this. She's been talking to a lot of her former students who are also in crisis—and their parents. The year we've all had killed a lot of dreams. You aren't alone in starting over. But this can be your rebuilding year. You can have your old room for as long as you want. You can have free access to my car. We'll even put you back on the family plan, Sprout, so you don't have to worry about your phone bill, okay? We want you to be able to think past your basic needs. No conditions. And no unsolicited advice." Her dad gave the floor a quick, uncomfortable glance. "No one wants a repeat of your high school years."

"Especially me," Momma said with a snort. Then she focused on Maya and squeezed both her hands. "And we know you're grown. We plan to treat you like our adult daughter. Promise."

Maya's eyes filled again, and she had to let some tears fall. She was so *relieved*. Before she knew it, her dad was crouched at her side, dabbing at her damp face. She dared to look at him and saw the tears in his eyes, too.

"We're so happy you're home and safe," he said. His voice was hoarse with emotion. "Get settled. Try and connect with some friends. We can get through the rest together."

And for that moment, Maya was able to pause the anxiety spiral that had been trying to swallow her in the middle of all her sadness. She let out a deep sigh she hadn't known she was holding.

Nothing needed to be figured out right now. She could take baby steps back out into the world.

In or Out with Emme Vivant
Marley St. James
Washington Post Magazine

If you've made a friend, met your least toxic ex, or started an online a cappella group, then you know about connection app the Spark. However, you may not know the driving force behind the app, Emme Vivant. Heir to a massive real estate empire in DC, polished, beautiful Emme could be buying mega yachts like the rest of the super-rich. Instead she's become one of *Forbes'* 40 under 40 (and our favorite angel investor) by only backing projects developed by women of color, queer folks, and the kind of people who typically can't get a meeting in Silicon Valley. Emme recently hopped on a Zoom with us to do a round of IN or OUT.

MSJ: Since your first big project is the Spark, what do you say to ghosting? In or out?

EV: Regrettably: in. Ghosting should be reserved for creeps—clear and present dangers, right? But otherwise, if you just don't like someone, you should say so. Everyone should get better at hearing no and saying no.

MSJ: How about the opposite of ghosting: Weddings?

EV: I'm never getting married, so I have to say "out," right?

MSJ: Why don't you want to get married?

EV: I'm a bisexual woman over 30, so I marched/pro-tested/donated for marriage equality until it was legal. It is a right. But personally, I don't need it for stability and don't require it for love. Plus, once I learned Oprah didn't get married, I realized it was truly just an option. One that doesn't interest me.

MSJ: In or out: Capitalism?

EV: In. Money is a megaphone. Money is credibility. Money turns rich people with opinions into change-makers with gravitas. I mean, that's why you're talking to me, right? I know as much about programming apps as Bill Gates probably knows about international development, but people ask him about humanitari-an aid. They shouldn't. We're not the experts, we hire the experts, but it's our names that get clicks, right?

And let's be honest, this country is too racist to em-brace socialism, anyway.

MSJ: Care to say more about that?

EV: Remember how the early pandemic was like "We're all in this together" until the news said that Black and Brown people were the most likely to die? Then suddenly masking up is political. Getting vaccinated is political. You can't force socialism on a country where a lot of folks still aren't comfortable with equality.

MSJ: Damn, shots fired.

EV: I'm just being honest. That's the real reason you can't compare the US to socialist utopias people like to bring up: Denmark, Norway—they're like 98% white. And even they get uncomfortable when they see like five African migrants outside their door.

MSJ: Billionaires—in or out?

EV: OUT absolutely. Like my dad says, "if you ever have so much money you don't know what to do with it, you owe someone a raise." If you have "going to space money," you owe a lot of folks raises.

MSJ: Careful, Emme—I'd hate to get you uninvited from Elon's Christmas party.

EV: [loud honk of laughter] Honey, I am a mere millionaire and a woman of color over 30. Elon Musk wouldn't let me near him without a catering tray.

MSJ: Emme Vivant, coming in hot.

EV: I'm just being honest!

MSJ: Let's go to the next one. Books—in or out?

EV: In! Especially audiobooks. I've been loving Rev. Gina Elton's *You Are Light*. It's one of the few things that gave me hope in the last year. And I tell people that you need the audiobook, because you need to hear Rev. Gina herself read her own words.

Oh yeah, and my book is out next week! Oh my God, I'm so bad at promo. Yes, please check out *(Ad)venture Capital: Girlbossing for Good.*

MSJ: Based on that title, I think I can guess your answer, but the "girlboss": In or out?

EV: I know this is unpopular, but in. As long as she's girlbossing for good.

Texts from Maya to Ant, April 25, 2021

Maya:

I swear the Girlboss is stalking me, Ant!
I was just trying to do this week's big
crossword and there she was! In the Post
Magazine.

Ant:

Your first mistake was doing the
crossword in the newspaper when
there's a perfectly good app somewhere

Hot cocoa and the Sunday newspaper is
a sacred Davis family tradition

Speaking of news I have news!
(See what I did there)

😑

I have my start date! Next Tuesday

May the fourth be with you

Ant:

And also with you

Maya:

Ha! He says he's not religious but the Episcopal jumped out

More like years of chapel and St Andrews academy. It was a reflex

Okay, okay, back to the topic at hand.

I'm so excited for you
You're out here making things happen with your awesome paid internship and we haven't even graduated yet

I'm just glad everything worked out

TBH I had only made it through the first round of interviews and came out here out kinda manifesting the rest

Wow! That's so unlike you, but way to take a risk!

It felt good to bet on myself

Maya:

Betting on yourself is better than betting on failure, which is what you do when you don't try

Ant:

I like that

It's from Rev Gina from the girlboss's Ted Talk
I didn't finish it, but she turned me on to Rev. Gina, so Emme Vivant can't be all bad

Maybe I'll watch that Ted Talk? Or read the article. I feel like if I don't, she'll turn up at the house

I'm just glad you didn't come all the way out here for nothing. I would have felt so guilty because of how much I've enjoyed spending spring with you.

It would have been worth it for that alone

5/1/21

Hey Ma,
Just when I thought all the flowering trees were done,
fluffy cherry blossoms started blooming EVERYWHERE.
It's like I remembered as a kid. I walk around the
neighborhood every day and there's always a new tree
in bloom. You were right about coming out in spring;
I would have been sad if I'd missed all this. Speaking
of fluffy blossoms, how is Keke doing? How are the
rest of my girls? Has Pua been around to help you
rig up the irrigation yet? I know it's part of her final
project, so she HAS to get to it. I can text her if you
want me to. Not much else to report here. It's wash
day so literally nothing else is getting done besides
a deep condition. They got Shea Moisture and Cantu
in every drugstore out here, though. No special trips!
Okay, running out of space. XOXO

        Your favorite Virgo, *
        Ant

        *Better than "Your loving son"? Hope this
doesn't make you feel 90.

Ant

Ant affixed the postcard to the metal mailbox at the end of the short but very steep driveway next to his new home. It was early (for him) on a Saturday morning, but he'd been awake for a couple of hours. Ant and the God of Jet Lag had come to a truce after wrestling for a solid month: he could sleep through the night if he got to bed by eleven, but no matter what he did, he'd wake up by seven.

Once he accepted this, Ant found he could always fill the time—mostly with Netflix. Recently, he'd started taking long mid-morning walks with the goal that, eventually, the walks would turn into more athletic jogging. Not today, though. This was a lovely morning for a stroll, and Ant didn't take the fact that he could do so comfortably for granted.

Once it was clear that he and Ma would be living in the US for a bit after his dad died, his mother had decided he urgently needed a crash course in American-style racism. Before they left Japan, Ma had asked a couple of her friends (Black servicemen, obviously) to take him out for ramen and give him a version of "the talk" that all Black American boys receive at some point in their lives. Ant was bewildered. It wasn't like he hadn't experienced being the odd one out as a chubby Blackish kid with curly hair and the decent beginnings of a mustache for a twelve-year-old. But this wasn't just about feeling lonely or isolated: this was life and death. Now that he was older, he knew there was no perfect place, but

Auntie Kay's neighborhood had good vibes and plenty of Black families. Seeing them let the worry slide off his shoulders.

Left first, today, he thought, walking north up the sidewalk on the hilly street. At least he thought it was north; he was still trying to figure out where the group house was positioned relative to the rest of Takoma Park. All in all, this seemed like a comfortable enough place to be a big, Black, asexual nerd. After a month of settling in and trying every restaurant that was open and within walking distance, Ant could sense that Takoma Park's vibe was more "bougie urban neighborhood" than "bland suburb."

It had a coffee shop, a vegetarian diner, and a yoga studio on its short main street. Notably missing were chains of any kind. The local Starbucks, CVS, and 7-Eleven were in easy walking distance, but on the DC side of the line, like lepers at the city gates.

The little city was welcoming to him, though. Good service in the restaurants and no one following him around stores, no stares when he went on his daily walks. The most important thing Ant had learned about his new home was that he could move about Takoma Park freely, so he did.

He turned the corner and saw his first cherry tree of the morning. It was in the yard of an aggressively modern house he'd nicknamed "the Tardis." The navy-blue structure rebelled against the surrounding craftsman bungalows with a tall, narrow frame and large windows. Ant didn't need to squint to read the labels on their cereal boxes from the sidewalk. But what's privacy when you're making an architectural point?

The tree was young, not even as tall as he was, but with thin limbs hanging with blossoms. The sight made his heart squeeze. Ant missed his girls. Nicole, his bold pink-and-yellow plumeria named for Nicole Scherzinger—every boy in Hawai'i was pretty much required to have a crush on her as a point of state pride. Emma—his adorable redhead—was a hibiscus bush named for Emma Stone (despite *Aloha*). Keke, for

Keke Palmer, was a fluffy cherry blossom tree. The first tree he'd cared for on his own.

When Ant told his mom about being "probably—definitely asexual" at twenty-three, she'd surprised him with her lack of surprise. Turned out his girls had given him away years ago.

"The only time you almost got in a fight was when your cousin Nelson kept making sex jokes about 'getting into Emma's bush.' I literally had to turn the hose on you and ruin his Jordans a little to save their vacation. You weren't embarrassed by the jokes—you were for real offended. Back then I thought it was because Nelson was an annoying little prick. But now"—she made a quick gesture with her fingers—"the math is math-ing."

Crushes that were very real at the time, which was probably why it took him extra long to figure out his orientation. He did feel butterflies when a woman took his breath away. He caught the spark of attraction in the middle of a conversation—the kind you move from the couch to the back porch at a party. He could distinguish between a pretty he admired and a pretty he desired. It was just that his desire didn't involve sex. For the longest time he'd thought that meant he couldn't be asexual—turned out he just wasn't aromantic *and* asexual.

In fact, Ant was very romantic. He liked holding hands. He liked kissing. He liked buying flowers and writing little notes. He'd been a wonderful (and occasionally frustrating) boyfriend to several good Christian girls in college. The last one had led him to be open about his identity for the first time—with Maya, of course.

∽

It all started because Mallory, a particularly dissatisfied ex, was telling anyone who'd listen that she thought Ant was gay. She didn't just confide in her friends; she shared her theory with pretty much everyone they knew, to the point where he'd enter their community college's anime club meetings or choir rehearsals and conversation would cease. This stopped only when Maya walked over to Mallory, sitting among her friends at the student union, and said, "He's not gay. He just doesn't want to fuck you."

Ant gaped at her through the entirety of this exchange. "I already dumped her, Mai," he chastised when she returned to their table. "That was bad enough."

Maya shrugged in response as she sat down. "That wasn't only for you. She said 'gay' like it's a disease. As a queer woman, I had to shut her up for all the rainbow-fam people." She returned to her spam musubi lunch.

"Besides," she began after a few bites, "there probably is some poor person in her youth group or whatever who crawls further back into the closet every time she talks about you."

They ate in silence for a little while. Ant took a long slug of his Dr Pepper before he spoke again, more quietly. "It wasn't that I didn't want to bang her, specifically. I think I don't want to . . . with anyone—ever." He took a breath, and waited. He'd grazed a pebble on the surface of this pond only once before, with his first and only white girlfriend, a fellow military brat. She'd asked if "it" was because he grew up mostly in Japan. Later, over several emails, she sent Ant several articles about "herbivore men" in Japan to show that she wasn't racist. He hoped that Maya wouldn't say anything as disappointing as that.

Maya looked at him and sighed. "I hope you're telling me because you want to tell me and not because you feel like you owe me—or anyone—an explanation for your sexual choices. You shouldn't come out for anyone but yourself."

Ant sat up a bit straighter. *Not the direction I thought that would go.*

"No, I wanted to say it out loud," he replied, mostly casually. "People look at me and see this big Black guy who, biologically, must be a sexual dynamo."

Maya tossed her locs. "A nice way of saying you're constantly fetishized, but keep going."

He rolled his eyes but continued. "I feel like I could avoid situations like"—he tilted his chin toward where Mallory had been sitting—"if I get the no-sex thing out, earlier on."

That made Maya smile. The kind of smile that warmed him all over. "Antonio, seriously, thank you for sharing your truth. I'm glad you feel that comfortable with me." She dabbed her mouth with her napkin, then reached over to squeeze Ant's hand. Maya seemed to know just what to say in this situation—probably because she'd been a peer counselor at the campus's LGBTQ+ center. Or maybe just because she was wonderful.

He squeezed it back and gave his own half smile in return.

∝

The memory was interrupted by another chime of his phone. He slipped it from his pocket and looked at the screen.

"Ma?!" he cried in surprise, answering the FaceChat.

"Hi, baby boy!" she said with a bright smile. She was in her car, with her white coat on and a bright, tired smile. He looked at his watch and mentally converted to Honolulu time: it was 6:00 a.m., which meant she had hospital duty today.

"How's the baby business?" He slowed his walk, stopping under a fluffy cherry at the nearest corner. Hopefully, the scenery was a relaxing backdrop before Ma's day of screaming infants and occasional screaming parents.

Ma let her face fall. "It's unrelenting. I left the hospital at midnight last night, but Dr. Cho tested positive for COVID, so they called me in. And we're down two nurses: one refused to get vaccinated, and the other called out because she got threatened by a family who didn't want to hear that horse medicine failed to prevent their elderly dad from dying from COVID—because it's *horse medicine!*" She slumped. Ant could see her heavy sigh clearly, thanks to the glow of a red stoplight. "I don't think I've ever hated being a doctor more."

The light changed and Ma drove on in silence. He coughed, wholly unsure of what to say. Ma never let anyone see her stress—even him. They sat in a beat of tense silence before Ant finally thought of some way to respond.

"I'm sorry things are so bad, Ma."

She gave the smallest shrug, "Anyway, I called to check on you, *mijo*. Now tell me all the new and exciting things you've been doing. Your postcards have been such a bright light through all this."

"The most exciting news is that I got vaccinated! Maya texted me the other day and was like, 'Let's go to Six Flags, they've got the Johnson & Johnson.' Next thing we're in her car eating Utz Cheese Balls with chopsticks while we waited. It was probably the most fun I've had stuck in line."

Ant began walking again, trying to think of other anecdotes to distract/amuse his mother. He told about rescuing Maya from her parents' backyard spades tournament for their church. "She said, 'Antonio, you gotta save me from all this sanctified aggression.'" He laughed. "We'll be doing a combo Eurovision / graduation party in their backyard, too. Maya said she'd teach me how to pick crabs. Which . . . don't I just point, like 'that one'?"

Ma chuckled. "It's a little more complicated than that. You should ask Kay—she's so Maryland she's got Old Bay in her veins."

Ant snorted. "I know if I want to get her something for Christmas, all I have to do is find the nearest object with a Maryland flag on it."

Auntie Kay seemed to be mildly obsessed with being from Maryland—particularly with rocking the Maryland flag. She had Maryland flag mugs, shot glasses, slippers, socks, face masks, oven mitts, an apron, and a cozy Maryland flag blanket in the living room. Once you noticed that bonkers-looking flag, you started seeing it everywhere. "No offense, but I didn't know anyone could care so much about Maryland."

He looked at the screen and saw his mother looking back at him with raised eyebrows. She was parked, so she presented the full force of her sardonic expression. "Excuse me, Antonio—I know you're *not* talking about obsession. We've been talking for twenty minutes about you moving five thousand miles away, and this is the first time you've managed not to mention Maya."

Ant's face fell. He knew what was coming.

"Are you sure things are completely platonic over there?"

His sigh was as predictable as her question. "Yes, everything is platonic, Mother. As it has been every time you've asked the question. I think this makes twelve," he responded flatly.

Maya may have inspired his move out here, but Ant wasn't dumb. It would be ridiculous to hope for anything besides friendship. He wasn't even sure that Maya was still dating cis men. Her last serious relationship had been with a nonbinary person, and the last two relationships he could remember before that were with women. There was no reason to—

"On both sides, Ant?" His mother interrupted his thoughts again. "Are things platonic on *both* sides? She's in pretty much every picture you take, and every story you tell."

"She's my only real friend out here, Ma. It's hard to meet people in the middle of a plague."

"And you haven't talked to me about needing friends. You talk about Maya like she's all you need."

But she is, his mind protested. *That doesn't mean I'm in love with her.*

Ant watched her look away and sigh before picking up her phone and holding it so that her face filled most of the screen.

"Look, maybe I don't know what I'm talking about," she began. "There you are on the mainland, with a fancy internship like you planned. Honestly, I didn't think you had a plan after graduation. I was preparing to have a serious talk with you about your goals and . . . moving out. I'm so glad I didn't have to."

He swallowed, not sure how to respond. As far as Ma—and Maya—knew, he'd been applying exclusively for internships in DC because it was the only other place in the US where he'd lived. She couldn't know that his great act of personal initiative and responsibility had been sparked by the prospect of missing Maya too much.

Ma was still talking. "Now that you've launched, thank God, I should step back and let you be grown. But as someone who knows you, I think the best thing you can do for yourself is turn one of your housemates into an actual friend. Stop being polite, start being real. If I know you at all, you need to hear that."

Ant had to admit Ma knew him too well. He'd spent the last month mostly trying to be out of the way and not put too much strain on the Wi-Fi. But this was his home, even if Auntie Kay was giving him a great discount on rent.

She smiled a little sharkily. "Do it for Maya. You need another friend before you can give that potential romance a little runway." She looked off-screen and then back. "Okay, baby boy, I gotta run! Love you most."

"Love you best," he responded. It was the way they always ended phone calls. He slid his phone into his pocket and headed back to Auntie Kay's.

He wasn't going to listen to his ma about pursuing something romantic with Maya, though. It didn't happen often, but occasionally his mom had no idea what she was talking about.

Texts from Ant to Maya, May 7, 2021

Ant:

I downloaded your girl's app

Maya:

Who's my girl?

Emme Vivant! Sorry, I should have said "your girlboss's app"

Anyway, all my housemates are on the Spark

It's a weird but good combo of Hinge, Reddit, and the groups part of Facebook

I'll have to check it out, too I need to start rebuilding my social life

Aww, I was hoping to meet some of young Maya's old high school friends

Maya:

Sorry, pal
The few friends I've kept in touch
with managed to leave and not fail
so hard they came back home
One girl is a tattoo artist in Iceland
She recently got engaged to her partner

Another friend, last I checked works
for a game designer in Seattle

And Byron does HR for Cartoon Network
He always wanted to work for them so
he's living his dream. He's also doing
drag story times on TikTok exclusively
with books about Black kids

Ant:

Of course you knew the coolest kids

We were the weirdos

We're still the weirdos
It's only being basic now is less cool

On the flip side, being queer, liking
anime, horror movies, goth music,
none of that makes you distinctive

Maya:

Jocks know how to code, pretty popular girls who watch The Bachelorette also do cosplay.

MANY racists love Drake and Drag Race. EVERYBODY watches Marvel movies and Star Wars.

Your pop culture choices don't define you anymore.

Ant:

So true! What's left for the self-identified nerds?

Star Trek?!

Hey! Have you SEEN Sonequa Martin-Green in Discovery? And I've heard good things about Picard. It might even be prestige-y. You should plant your flag in D&D. The nerds will always have D&D.

I'm not sure if I'm that level of nerd

Texts from Maya to Ant, May 23, 2021

Maya:

It only took two months, but I finally have good news!
You are talking to the brand-new bookseller for Velma's On H Street

It's 4 days a week, and pays enough to be worth the metro trip downtown
Plus it will be a way to FINALLY start connecting with the queer community in DC. It's been hard living without it.

A feminist bookstore with a "sapphic romance" wall is bound to give me some shiny new queer lady friends

Plus, I'll get to keep up my sign language since the store is so close to Gallaudet

Ant:

That's awesome all-around!

Maya:

And the dog-walking agency finally called You know how I love other people's dogs

So, I'm gonna have 1-2 jobs very soon

Ant:

We should make the most of your last free weekends

Lord knows those will be gone with my retail schedule!

Ooh! Wanna go to Ocean City this weekend?

On Memorial Day Weekend?!

I think things won't be so bad if we go on Sunday

It was the inspiration for Beach City . . . I know how you love Steven Universe

I'm sold. Overnight or a day trip?

Maya:

It's a two-hour drive away
We can do a day trip

Ant:

Sounds perfect!
You know, I don't think I've
ever seen the Atlantic before

SUMMER 2021

5/30/21

Dear God,

Thank you for the ocean and my best friend. This has been the best day since I came home.

Yours,
Maya

Maya

The sand in Ocean City was pretty much the opposite of Hawai'i sand. It wasn't soft, and thanks to the weather deciding to do its best impression of March until yesterday, it wasn't that warm. None of that mattered at the moment. When Maya heard the ocean, she felt something inside her release. She felt better when she was near the ocean.

Even though she'd been talking up "the boardwalk experience" for much of the ride over, she suddenly wished she'd taken Ant someplace quieter, like Dewey Beach—where the focus was a little bit more on the beach itself and not the ability to buy T-shirts or calzones twenty feet from the sand. But there'd be time—even when they both had jobs. There was no reason *not* to go to the beach as much as their gas money would allow.

"Hey, bestie!" Maya unselfconsciously gave a goofy wave to the ocean. She tossed a slight glance over her shoulder to where Ant was shaking his head at her with a laugh.

"Even if you're doing this to make nineteen-year-old me feel better, it is very silly."

So he remembered.

Back when they were both community college students, Maya and Ant had made the transition from friendly to close friends through a series of deep conversations. During a walk on the beach, Ant had revealed that he'd never had a real best friend before. "I was always a third member of a trio, or a fourth in a quartet. The closest thing I've had to a best friend: always there, always, is the Pacific Ocean.

"In Okinawa, I remember riding my bike to the beach when I couldn't be in the house anymore. I sat there for hours—can't quite remember what I did. The beach wasn't just somewhere I was out of the way—it was the only place I didn't feel that lonely."

When Ant stopped speaking, it was clear he wished he hadn't said so much. Maya wanted more than anything to put him at ease. "I think it's awesome that you've had the same best friend since elementary school and that she followed you all the way to Hawai'i." Her heart swelled when Ant smiled in spite of himself. "Next time I'm back in Maryland, I'm going to make the Atlantic my best friend. She's more temperamental than yours, but she's more fun."

Ant snorted but Maya could see her words had the desired effect. She could see the tension leave Ant's shoulders. It was the beginning of a beautiful friendship.

∾

"We should do this all the time!" Maya shouted, half in glee and half to make sure Ant could hear her over the ocean. She turned to face him and caught his bemused smile. Then she noticed that she was holding his hand—tightly. Maya realized that she must have dragged the poor boy from the parking lot, across the boardwalk, to the middle of the sand. She shot Ant an apologetic smile and dropped his hand.

He returned her smile warmly. "Let's find a place to settle in." He gestured down the beach with his chin before walking toward the water.

Maya took a moment to slip off her sandals so she could enjoy the sand, then caught up with Ant in a few sprinting steps. The hem of her teal maxi dress bounced as she went. They found a spot closer to the water than the boardwalk, set down their burdens, and spread out their blanket.

Maya dug her towel and floppy hat from her tote bag, then involuntarily gave a little squeal. "Guess I'm excited to be here," she said with a small laugh. Ant laughed, too. Which was a relief. She was starting to think she'd freaked him out a bit with her beach-focused intensity.

"There's nothing like it," he agreed, kneeling at the edge of the blanket. He was trying to find the perfect angle for the solar-powered backpack he'd brought for charging his Switch. Once he'd laid it against the cooler, just so, Ant settled in on the blanket with a smile. He looked like sunshine with his peach swim shorts and Creamsicle-colored aloha shirt. "Being in Maryland makes me realize how spoiled I was. For most of my life I've lived on islands, so the beach was never more than an hour away—even with Honolulu traffic."

"They would be Japan, Guam, and then Hawai'i, right?" Maya asked as, for no particular reason, she began scooping sand in both hands and letting it fall slowly onto her feet.

Ant pointed a congratulatory finger at her. "Got it in one."

"Lucky you." Maya tugged on her sun hat and groaned with envy, before flopping back on the blanket. This was much less comfortable than she'd hoped, so she made a pillow with her beach towel and tried again.

Much better.

"Ever since I had a say in the matter, I've tried to put myself close to water of some kind: Oakland, Seattle, Hawai'i of course. But in only one of those places did I have regular access to the beach, and that's the place I spent seven years—even though it took two jobs and some parental support to stay there."

After trying three big cities, Maya could confidently say that they were fine, but her perfect place would have been a quirky beach town. *It is a pity that most beach towns are either expensive, racist, or both,* Maya thought. *Even Ocean City.*

The first time Maya had visited the Eastern Shore was with her friend's family in high school. Her parents, Daddy especially, had strong memories of the days when the city was pretty unwelcoming to Black folks who weren't washing the dishes. And that was in the late eighties. Virginia Beach was "where Black folks go." And so it was the place Maya's family had spent the rare summer vacation that didn't involve visiting relatives. But she'd bet good money that if you googled "racism Virginia Beach" you'd still find something alarming at the very least.

Truth was, there's no perfect place for a Black queer woman, especially one without a small fortune. She'd been trying to think of one as it became clearer that she couldn't live with her parents forever. Even though they were getting along well, a nameless dissatisfaction had settled in her stomach, one that she couldn't ignore. One that caught her in the middle of loading the dishwasher or watching *The Voice* with her dad that said, "Your move. You're standing still too long."

Though she wasn't really one for vision boards or manifesting, Maya had a strong idea of the kind of life she wanted to live. She'd made a list at the age of nineteen, during her first few months in Oakland, after she got real with herself and admitted the starving-artist life wasn't for her:

1. A stable day job with health insurance
2. A nice-ish apartment in a place where she wanted to live
3. A cat
4. A loving, committed relationship
5. To have all these by the age of thirty-five

This didn't seem like much to ask for. In fact, according the girl-boss's TED Talk (yes, she'd actually watched it), Maya was probably dreaming too small, shrinking her goals to fit her circumstances. (You know, that thing all non-rich people did to survive?) But it had been twelve years since she'd made that simple list, and even with her shiny new degree, everything still felt out of reach.

Aside from the obvious job stuff, DC was almost as stupid expensive as Honolulu, so she couldn't afford her own place. She couldn't get a cat because her mom was allergic, and she couldn't get a significant other because the only person she knew besides her parents was sitting right beside her and she couldn't mess that up. Now that thirty-five was a mere forty-eight months away, Maya felt the sand rushing out of her hourglass.

Or was that the sand between her toes?

No spiraling! she said to herself.

Maya sat up and dug into her tote bag for the romance/mystery novel her sister had been raving about. It was about rival jewelry designers in 1960s India.

"It's like *She Loves Me* but gay, and there's a murder," Ella had written in the letter that accompanied the book. She'd sent Maya a massive graduation care package, which included several fluffy novels to enjoy, along with the hat she was currently wearing.

This is the perfect thing to get me out of my head, Maya thought as she cracked the book open. She refused to spend any more of her first day at the beach this year spiraling.

Slipping on her oversize sunglasses, Maya reclined on her side this time, propped up by her elbow. She was learning about the glory days of her heroine's family business when she felt Ant's eyes on her. She looked up to see that he'd taken her picture with his phone.

"Hey, give a girl some warning." She laughed.

"You know I like candid," he replied unrepentantly. "Plus you looked really lovely." He showed her the photo.

"Oh hello, Rihanna." She giggled. Skin tone and a love of dark eyeliner were the only things Maya had in common with the superstar, but she ran with them. She gave her septum ring a light, satisfying squeeze. She hadn't liked a picture of herself so much in months.

"Let's take a selfie," she proposed, sitting up and scooting closer to him.

Ant quickly obliged, moving closer to her and throwing a coconut-scented arm over her shoulder. Maya had two thoughts in quick succession:

He smells really nice.

And *when did he put on sunblock? I forgot to bring some.*

"Can I borrow your sunblock?" she asked.

"Of course! I didn't realize you weren't wearing any." Mildly horrified, Ant handed her the bottle of SPF 50. Ever since his dad passed away from skin cancer, Ant had become a human PSA, reminding his friends / family / nearby strangers that "Yes, you need sunblock!" And where applicable: "Skin cancer isn't a 'white-people thing'!"

Maya felt slightly chastened as she vigorously rubbed the cream into her skin. Ant had suddenly turned quiet and thoughtful.

"It's wild," he began. "You, me, chilling on the beach. Me reminding you about your sunblock—it all feels so familiar, but last time we did it, we were five thousand miles away from here."

"I'm glad you're not sick of me yet." Maya chuckled. "Or busy with your new friends."

"Never," he said with a surprising fierceness. "After my mother, you're the most important person in the world to me. That won't change because of location."

Maya responded by hugging him tight. She couldn't help her sigh into his shoulder and her struggle to believe him. Her location had changed a lot about her life when she first left home at eighteen. She'd gone west thinking she'd rarely, if ever, be back home. Though her high school friends had reached out, they'd been outshone by the possibilities of her brand-new life. Eventually they let her fade, too.

But then, Ant didn't have the younger Maya's strained relationship with her parents. Ant didn't seem to feel a little trapped and very bored in Honolulu, the way she once felt in Green Park, Maryland. (It was hard to be surrounded by aspiring Huxtables when she wanted to be like Basquiat.) Ant wasn't fleeing; he was running *to* something. Besides, he'd always seemed steadier and more content than her—even at nineteen.

Maybe Ant could say never *and mean it?* Maya decided to believe him.

Ant released the hug, but neither of them moved away. Instead, they found each other's hands and let their fingers tangle. They found each other's eyes and silently allowed the moment to shimmer between them. It felt too important to be rushed and was impossible to ignore. They sat holding hands and feeling the ocean breeze until Maya let go and stood up suddenly.

"We need to get a picture of you with your feet in the Atlantic!" she declared. She offered her hand to help him up. "Come on, I'll introduce you. We're old friends."

Laughing, Ant took her hand and followed, not releasing it until they were at the shoreline. They ran into the shallows until the water covered their ankles. Then, startled by the cold, they ran back out again.

6/16/21

Hey Mom,

Greetings from the 70! I'm riding the bus and listening to "The Bus Song." Listening to Jay Som when I'm out and about makes me feel like the protagonist of something. My internship is going pretty well. It feels good to actually use some of the stuff I spent four years learning. Plus, I'm starting to think/hope there may be a place for me on the team in the fall. I just hope they don't post the position until after June 22nd! I need Mercury to be out of retrograde before I submit my application for the Smithsonian job.

Love,
Ant

Ant

Ant couldn't say when he went from quietly mocking his friends' belief in astrology to crediting a good stroke of luck to his moon being in Jupiter. But astrology was to Gen-Z kids what Christianity was to, like, Texans—even if you don't fully buy into it, you pick up the lingo. Then one day you're going to Bible study of your own volition.

That's why Ant was spending the day catching up on emails, returning calls, and finally sending the postcard to his mom that had been crinkling in his backpack for more than a week. Now, many people would say that an optical illusion that made it look like Mercury was moving backward meant nothing to our little blue planet—but Mercury was the planet that ruled communication, and bad communication could wreak all sorts of havoc. Especially in the last hundred pages of romance novels.

For most of the month, he'd taken precautions, leaving extra time for bus delays and avoiding trash-talking in text messages (after he almost told Maya that Rev. Gina sounded like she was trying to start a Christian version of that NXIVM cult). Besides that near miss, it looked like Ant was going to make it out of Mercury retrograde unscathed: no fights with roommates, no missent emails. He had forgotten his phone at home today, but that wasn't a big deal. He wasn't expecting any important texts or phone calls, and he was able to slip into one of the museum's libraries and check his email.

He looked out the window with a soft sigh, watching the rowhouses merge into storefronts that occasionally sprouted condo buildings. Golden hour gave everything a warm glow. He had to admit it; he liked it here—a lot. And he really hadn't expected to. From what Maya had said, he'd thought he'd be surrounded by uptight, bougie people who only spoke in résumés. It wasn't that those people didn't exist, but you didn't really run into them if your working life didn't involve an office. Auntie Kay worked in a public library, his housemates were a nanny and a future firefighter, and of course, Maya was still figuring stuff out.

Maybe this meant he still needed to meet some new people. Maybe some of those people would be insufferable. He'd leave that for the future. Right now he was happy with his big impulsive decision. Ant pulled the cord for his bus stop, which was conveniently next to a postbox: the perfect place to deposit his latest postcard.

He happily dropped the stamped postcard to his mom in with a wave and continued down Blair. He smiled at everything he recognized. The combination KFC and Taco Bell, the house with the three-foot statue of Buddha in the yard. The older brick apartments directly across the street from new pricey ones, a fountain in the driveway. Every landmark he recognized, every turn he anticipated, reassured him that he was learning this place. Making it his home. Every day he liked the idea of settling in this area. Silver Spring was only twenty minutes on foot, with a comic book shop and a list of international restaurants he'd stumbled upon during one of his long walks. He wanted to spend the summer trying them out—and he wanted to see what DC was like when it wasn't so COVID outside.

If things went the way he hoped after his internship, it could be more than an idea soon. He thrilled at the idea of being so close to his dream work. Ant had fallen in love with plants while gardening with his abuela. It was how she'd made their house in Hawai'i a home, first with an herb garden, then with ever more new plants (including his girls).

When he started community college, he knew that he wanted to work with plants—but didn't know what kind of career he wanted.

There were only two things Ant was certain of: he didn't want to spend forty hours a week in an office until he could afford not to do so at seventy, and *no golf courses*. Ant hated those big green sponges with the fire of a thousand suns. They seemed actively harmful, especially in Hawai'i, where land was scarce, housing was expensive, and most of the people who played on O'ahu's premium golf courses couldn't have cared less about the people who actually lived there.

Ant believed that plants were good for people. He knew the physical sense of calm that came over his body when he had his hands in wet earth. He didn't know how to make that a career, but helping maintain the public green space for the Smithsonian Gardens was a hell of a way to start.

Public green space was almost sacred to Ant. Everyone deserved a place with trees or soft grass that they didn't have to own or rent to enjoy. He and Maya had spent a lot of time in parks—both of their neighborhoods were covered with them, making it easy to turn take-out meals into picnics. She warned that Ant should soak up as much outside as he could, because mosquitoes and humidity usually pushed most people back inside by July.

For now, it was a lovely evening. He tangled a warm breeze in his fingers and walked on. He was halfway home. It felt too good to stay inside; he'd drop his bag, grab his phone, and see if anyone wanted to get dinner. The restaurants on Carroll Ave had all turned their street parking into outdoor seating, and it was a perfect night to eat out. Ant turned onto his block humming something sweet.

The humming came to an abrupt stop when he stepped into the foyer of his shared house. That was because Ant heard his phone chime, right where he'd left it, on the mail table. He picked it up and saw that he had a new email from his boss at the Smithsonian, with the subject heading: "Bad News about the Fall." He took a deep breath and opened the email quickly, like he was ripping off a Band-Aid.

Hi Ant,

I'll come straight to it: the position I was hoping to offer you on my team no longer exists. It was partially grant-funded by an organization that ceased operations during the pandemic. I'm so sorry for getting your hopes up. I'll keep my eye out for any opportunities that could use your talents.

Best,
Rhonda

And just like that, Ant's vision for his horticulture career path blew away, like dandelion seeds on a puff of air. He was still trying to figure out if he wanted to be a park ranger in the mountains or a gardener working his way up at the Central Park Conservancy. He just knew that he wanted to work with plants and be outside more than inside if he could.

As dreams go, his were pretty simple. Unfortunately for Ant, these days the simple ones were expensive, too. The starting salaries for these jobs were often hardly anything to live on; he knew that from working part-time landscaping jobs after high school. It had always bothered him how little people seemed to value those who worked outside.

Since he wanted to live someplace where he could grow in his field, as a Black man, Ant knew he needed to live in or near a city and hope for a decent salary. That was why he'd latched on to the Smithsonian job as a remarkable stroke of good luck, a fast track to interesting work for good pay.

Now that it was gone, Ant wanted to drown his sorrows in something fried. He tossed his backpack on a hook in the foyer and turned right back out the door, heading for Carroll Ave. The street was humming with that particular energy only summer nights have. He dug out his phone and was about to text Maya when he remembered: she was walking dogs until almost ten tonight.

With a sigh, he trudged up the hill to the main street, hoping one of the restaurants would sell him onion rings. Strangely, it felt more humid than it had when he got off the bus—or maybe it was just his change in mood. There was a prickle at his elbow. Ant slapped it, and frowned as his palm revealed the squished corpse of a large mosquito.

"Okay, universe, what else you got," he grumbled, wiping away the sweat at his brow. As if in response, his phone started chirping with text messages, one after another, like he was getting all the day's text messages at once. There were at least five from his mom: four variations on "call me when you see this," and a last one that had a bit more information.

> It's about the house, technically you're an investor since your trust money helped buy it

> I said yes because I hated living on base, not as an investor

> Phase one of my 5-year-plan seems to be working out so I think I'll stay here for the foreseeable

> I'm fine leaving the rest up to you

The truth was that Ant just wasn't in the mood to have this conversation. And he didn't feel like letting his mom know the day's setback. She'd have some constructive criticism that he wouldn't want to hear.

∽

Later, after dinner and some *Breath of the Wild* with his housemate Rio, Ant looked at the messages from his mom and frowned. Something was up. It had to be if his mom had spent every moment between patients trying to reach him today. Suddenly Ant felt like he wasn't coming out of retrograde unscathed, after all.

7/12/21

Dear God,

Soooo... what's next? I'm open to suggestions. The sooner, the better.

    Your Pal
    Expectantly,
    Maya

Maya

She smiled at *expectantly*, darkening the line she'd scratched through *your pal*. It was the only way she could think of to emphasize the sense of urgency she felt. With a sigh she slumped back in her plastic lounge chair and let the journal fall next to her tote bag. She'd pick them up later. There were probably another ten minutes until the lifeguards blew the whistle and she could go back into the pool.

Ever since she'd worked out the reservation system, Mondays had become her favorite day of the week because that was when she'd forget her troubles in five feet of cool, chlorinated water. She avoided the lanes; she didn't even want to pretend to be exercising. Instead she floated on her back from one end of the pool to the other and watched the sky. There was something astonishing about the feeling of floating—how if you kicked up your legs the right way, the water would carry you. She didn't worry much in the water. Worrying was for every second she spent outside the pool.

Now that she was air-drying poolside, all her worries came back in a flood. She'd been enduring a lot of clarity lately, and unpleasant things had become apparent:

(1) She'd run out of time to heal.

The school year was approaching quickly, and both of her parents were being asked to return to their buildings earlier than usual. Breakfast smoothies with her mom and late-night *Dr. Mario* battles with her dad would soon be things of the past. So would free access to her dad's car—he was going to need it more. That meant it was going to take a *lot* more effort to spend time with Ant. Which brought her to her next point of clarity:

(2) She should move out of her parents' place by the end of the year.

It was going to take scrimping, saving, and probably more babysitting than she really enjoyed doing, but to have any kind of life of her own, she needed to move. She couldn't deal with how the pandemic had made her parents almost unrecognizable to her. Her dad smoked weed now. Her mom was no longer a diligent washer of dishes. They both watched trashy reality TV like *Married at First Sight* or *Love Island*— the kind of stuff they would have forbidden when she and Ella were growing up. Back then her parents had a "garbage in, garbage out" philosophy across the entertainment spectrum, which they'd clearly abandoned. Mom even watched YouTube recaps about said trash reality TV. It was too weird.

Combine that with the fact that everyone else on her block was either a parent or a grandparent. Maya knew that socially she wasn't going to be able to launch herself into her new life from her parents' guest room, just like she knew she couldn't afford to move anywhere on a bookseller's salary. It was becoming apparent that she needed suck it up and find a boring-ass office job—the choice 90 percent of former artists usually made by the time they hit thirty.

Finally, there was another big point of clarity:

(3) Her situation wasn't unique.

Many people had been forced to move in with their parents in the last year or so, and many more folks had been forced to let go of their carefully made plans. Something kept happening when she told an old family friend, or church member, or longtime neighbor why she was home: the other person inevitably had their own story of loss.

Some had lost loved ones in the past year—not only to COVID but to new addictions or despair. Her aunt was getting a divorce. A high school acquaintance she'd run into had lost a job she loved after her day care center closed. A friend of Ella's had moved home to help a parent with long COVID. Cousin Gigi had thought she had a minor case of COVID until she lost her sense of taste for six months (and counting). Lots of people were swimming in the same sea of confusion and pain. Even more were trying to help their loved ones in that sea get to shore. Maya had to reckon with the notion that her struggles didn't make her special, which meant that—

(3b) Time was of the essence.

A little while back she had streamed *Uncle Vanya* on PBS because Ella would not shut up about the production. (It had been the last thing her theater-loving sister saw onstage before the *panorama* and had clearly struck a nerve.) Once she got over seeing the guy from *The Hobbit* at his full height, Maya was struck, too. The whole play is about a guy realizing he wasted his life at forty-seven. Forty-seven! Now, late forties was much closer to death in the olden days of Russia than it was in 2021, but something about the number forty-seven still clicked in her head.

If there was ever a point in life that felt like there was no return, Maya would have guessed age forty-seven. Married or single, social worker or office manager, it was hard to imagine making a new start at forty-seven. She didn't like starting over again at thirty-one. Forty-seven, the number, the concept, shot an existential panic through Maya that she had never felt before. Never in her life had it seemed more urgent to have a plan. She needed to grab the next opportunity—whatever it was—and start trying to build a life she could call her own. It was impossible to know which step was the right one.

Without thinking, Maya traced the tattoo on her wrist with her index finger. It was a matchstick with a flame and a spark, designed so it looked like it had been struck where her wrist met her hand. The tattoo artist had written *It's just a spark . . .* on the small stick in tiny letters—the start of a line from Maya's favorite Paramore song, "Last

Hope." The song was her musical serotonin; she listened to it when she needed things to be a little less daunting. After tracing her tattoo for the fifth or fifteenth time, Maya gave herself another coat of bug repellent, fished her phone out of her bag, and popped in her earbuds.

Why have the quote when I can have the whole thing?

Maya closed her eyes and took a deep breath. The acoustic guitar kicked in—and then Hayley's voice. All at once, Maya could feel herself lifted from her overheated plastic chair. The same song had lifted her out of ten-hour days and her truly god-awful shared studio apartment in Seattle. The song made her believe, even more than prayer, that there was something beyond her present circumstances. She needed to have hope to pray. The song gave her enough to keep going.

Or it would have—if the second chorus (the really good part) hadn't been interrupted by an actual phone call. Maya sucked her teeth, looked at her phone's screen, and groaned. It was her work, the bookstore. Nothing good ever came of your job calling on your day off. Reluctantly, she answered the call, trying to sound unhappy without being rude.

"Hello—"

"Oh, Maya, thank God!" It was Sarah, one half of the married couple who owned Velma's Books. And she sounded panicked. "Can you come in—like now? Alayah's son is having a mental health crisis and we need someone at the store."

Maya didn't know what was more confusing: hearing that the store was going to be open on Monday (it usually wasn't) or hearing her typically unflappable boss so very . . . flapped.

Sarah rushed through her explanation: "Emme Vivant is coming to sign a bunch of her books and put us all over her social."

Maya frowned at the phone. "Wait, the girlboss?"

"You can't call her that." Sarah sighed. "But can you come? If things go well, she might do an event with us—which would be huge. *Huge!* I'll give you the day off tomorrow—can you come?!"

To be honest, Maya had known she was going to say yes when Sarah said the words *mental health crisis*. It was the kind of emergency she couldn't treat lightly.

"I'm at the pool. I gotta shower and change, but I can be there within the hour. I'll be coming in one of my Hawaiʻi sundresses. I hope that's okay with the apparent empress of DC." She would have to save her floating for another day.

Sarah was audibly relieved. "You could wear pasties and a smile as long as Emme Vivant does not arrive to a locked door."

ᴄᴢᴏ

Maya had about an hour before she needed to open the store for Emme's visit. Since she had the place to herself, she hooked her phone up to the store's speakers and set a playlist on shuffle. The music filled the store, instantly improving her mood—which had darkened considerably since she forced herself from the pool and onto the metro and endured the sweaty, ninety-five-degree walk from Union Station to her store. The first song was from a singer-songwriter Ant loved—her bestie was the only reason she'd listened to any new music since 2019. The song had a bossa nova tinge that was a great soundtrack for moving furniture.

She gathered the store's stock of *(Ad)venture Capital* and arranged them on the table near the door. Emme Vivant had requested to sign books near the open front door for COVID safety's sake. Maya was quietly grateful to be dealing with a powerful person who believed in the disease rather than one who didn't.

Between Rev. Gina, her mom's praise, and the pretty decent TED Talk, Maya was slowly coming around to the idea of "the girlboss" as a useful rich person. After all, she didn't have to be doing any of this: starting businesses or signing books. Vivant was an heiress. She could be buying a third yacht or flying private jets around the world. Instead she'd stuck around DC and was choosing to put her money back into local businesses. There were probably better ways to make money. Emme Vivant's way felt . . . sweet.

Once the table was in place, Maya positioned the books in the best sort of attractive tableau she could manage so she could take some decent photos for the store's Instagram. She needed to check and see if the girlboss was allowing photos of the signing.

When everything was done, Maya was surprised to find that she was a little nervous. It wasn't just that Emme Vivant was rich and influential; she represented new DC in a way Maya didn't recognize. She suddenly felt compelled to study. There were twenty minutes left until Emme's arrival, which was just enough time for Maya to slide into her retail personality and gulp down a couple of interviews. Emme Vivant seemed like the kind of person who would expect to be known.

Leaning against the cash register's counter, Maya did a quick browse through the first page of search results. *Washingtonian* called Emme Vivant "handsome (WTF?), clever, and rich," before praising her investment in the Spark app. The *City Paper* took a different approach, interviewing people who'd met on the app. That was how Maya saw that the Spark fulfilled its promise: it really was for every kind of relationship. There were gay couples, straight couples, a pub quiz team, and a ladies' barbershop quartet that all connected on the Spark. Despite talking to Ant about it months ago, Maya hadn't gotten around to checking it out. Now she planned on downloading it after work. She needed more friends.

Her phone alarm went off, a five-minute warning before the big arrival. Just enough time to swipe on some last-minute eyeliner and head for the door. (She could do her trademark razor-sharp cat eye without a mirror. It was her party trick.)

Maya unlocked the door and opened it to let fresh air in. She peered down the sidewalk to her left and saw no sign of the VIP—only to have the woman on the back cover of her book materialize to her right.

"Oh!" Maya moved to let her in. The tall woman stepped inside, her smile evident despite her KN95. "Hello, and welcome to Velma's on H."

The heiress didn't return the greeting. Instead she looked at Maya with a surprising intensity. "Has anyone ever told you, you have astounding eyes?"

Maya blinked, the unfamiliar feeling of a blush flooding her cheeks. She hadn't thought there was anything special about her eyes since her grandma used to call her "sparkly-eyed Maya."

Emme continued. "You use navy liner, don't you? Not black. It's dramatic, but still warm."

All she could do was nod. No one had ever picked up on that particular detail before. She did use a particular dark-blue liquid with a metallic tint. It was cheap and sold exclusively at beauty supply stores. She suddenly felt shy. All this being noticed was unusual for someone working in retail. People often noticed how *you* treated *them*: if you were friendly, or brusque, or too slow for their taste. But people rarely noticed you, the human being behind the register. Emme, who could have easily gotten away with treating her like a helpful robot, really noticed her.

"Thank you," Maya said at last, leading Emme into the store. Between the taller woman's warmth and her attention, Maya was totally disarmed. If this was a tactic, it was brilliant.

As Maya got Emme settled, she complimented everything in the same specific way: the feminist slant store's book selection, the inclusivity of the slogan on the store's shirts ("We only make passes at those who wear glasses"), the quality of the store's audio as Maya's playlist continued on. Suddenly they were listening to "Ain't It Fun" by Paramore.

Emme Vivant was five books into her signing when she started to shimmy her shoulders. "You have excellent taste in music, too! I love Paramore. It's the only thing that keeps me from being a wholly disappointing Black girl."

Maya chuckled. "Looks like we're in the same fan club. I'm an unapologetic Paramore-stan. My favorite tattoo was inspired by 'Last Hope.'" She offered her arm to Emme for inspection—right before a wave of self-consciousness hit her. She must look like the biggest overgrown middle schooler, talking about the tattoo she got for her favorite band. She started to pull her arm back, not wanting to look at Emme and see that new admiration leave her eyes. Instead, Emme caught her wrist.

"Whoa." Emme's fingers seemed to unconsciously seek the ink on Maya's forearm. Then her hand paused in midair and pulled her blazer to the side, revealing a smaller tattooed spark at the edge of her collarbone. One that looked like the head of a sparkler or an illustrated North Star. "Most people think this tattoo is for my company, but the spark in 'Last Hope' is what our company is named after." She smiled at Maya again, brightly this time. "You don't have to explain. I get it completely. However, we're officially required to be friends now."

"Sounds good to me." Maya tried to quell the rush of feeling inside her. She couldn't nod, couldn't even laugh. This moment felt too significant. Not only was she finally making a new queer lady friend, but her potential pal also happened to be the unofficial queen of DC! She'd asked for a sign, and she had gotten one. Whatever happened next was going to happen with / for / because of Emme. And Maya wasn't the kind of person to let a message from the universe go to waste.

Emme Vivant slides into Maya's DMs, July 17, 2021

—EmmeVP: Eureka! It took two whole days of scouring Instagram but I found you. Hi Maya!

—Signs&1nders: Holy shit! Hi Emme, you've been looking for me?

—EmmeVP: I've dropped by the store a couple of times, but I didn't see you. So I had to stop relying on fate and seek you out. Or your DMs, rather.
—EmmeVP: BTW, you are so unbelievably talented! What is an artist/graphic designer/children's book author doing in retail?

—Signs&1nders: I'm not an artist anymore, but all creatives have day jobs. As for "what am I doing in retail?" I ask myself that, every day.

༄

EmmeVP has invited you to the Disappointing Black Girls group chat July 18, 2021

—Signs&1nders: I object to "disappointing"

—Signs&1nders: I make no secret about being a big weirdo. Other people's expectations are none of my business.

—EmmeVP: Good point, I can change it.

—Signs&1nders: Now, am I disappointing to my parents especially when compared to my genius sister? 🧑🏿

—EmmeVP: Your parents are proud, I'm pretty sure your dad comments some version of "that's my Maya" under everything you've ever posted

—Signs&1nders: Thanks for that. I'll return the favor with some wisdom From my mom.
—Signs&1nders: She said: At some point people told Jimi Hendrix he wasn't Black enough, Whitney Houston got told her music wasn't Black enough. And "River Deep, Mountain High" allegedly "flopped" because it wasn't "Black enough."
—Signs&1nders If you've gotta a choose between being "Black enough" and being yourself, baby be yourself.

—EmmeVP: Oh my God, that's so wise. Your mom is great.

—Signs&1nders: She is.

—EmmeVP: It's funny, I won't let anyone tell me how to wear my hair, how to dress, that I'm not queer enough, that I'm not "a real business woman"—I've even accepted that I will never be smaller than a size 12
—EmmeVP: But if someone called me an Oreo, today at 35, I would still cry in the bathroom like I'm back in middle school again

—Signs&1nders: Full disclosure, it took living thousands of miles away from home for over a decade for me to truly not care what other people think
—Signs&1nders: Since I moved back home I'm trying not to feel overwhelmed by the things that I think I should be
—Signs&1nders: God, sorry for vomiting my feelings all over you, like 48 hours after meeting

—EmmeVP: No please, vomit away
I feel like COVID has made us all cut the BS and get real
—EmmeVP I'd like to get real with you, Maya

—Signs&1nders: I'd like that, too

Black Girls Love Paramore Chat, July 20, 2021

—EmmeVP: How disappointing is it that I
can't give up John Mayer

> —Signs&1nders: I mean, I think it's
> disappointing for anyone to support John
> Mayer because he seems intensely wack
> —Signs&1nders: Daughters alone is a war
> crime

—EmmeVP: And the "David Duke dick"
comment

> —Signs&1nders: What does that even mean

—EmmeVP: Back when you were probably
in middle school he talked about having a
racist penis

> —Signs&1nders:I call that a win
> for Black women

—EmmeVP: 😂 😂 😂
Does it help that it's only that one song?
(3x5)
—EmmeVP: It sounds like late nights in
college and I love it so much

—Signs&1nders: Only the one? You're fine
That's your broken clock
—Signs&1nders: Like a broken clock is
right twice a day, you're allowed to like UP
TO 2 john mayer songs
—Signs&1nders: But that's the limit

❦

Black Girls Love Paramore Chat, July 24, 2021

—EmmeVP: I remembered you talking
about how much you like the National
Gallery of Art. It's reopening next week.
Would you like to go with me?

—Signs&1nders I'd love to, but why me?
I'm sure you have 1000 friends who'd love
to go with you

—EmmeVP: I actually have
a pretty small circle
And my bestie found out
She's pregnant, so she's waiting until
she has the all clear to get the vaccine
—EmmeVP: So what do you say to me
sending you an uber, some quiet morning
next week

—Signs&1nders: I'd say the store is closed
Mondays and I'm off Tuesdays ☺

—EmmeVP: Let's say Tuesday! I'm excited

—Signs&1nders: Me too, see you then

∽

Black Girls Love Paramore Chat, August 2, 2021

—EmmeVP: Hiya, I'm coming to your store day to sign some more stock. Want to get some coffee after

—Signs&1nders: I'd love to, if you're not sick of me yet.

—EmmeVP: You're really great to be around.
—EmmeVP: BTW, I saw some of your old projects. The craftbombing house in Oakland. The murals in Seattle. I even found your old insta with your arty nails. You're even more talented than I thought!

—Signs&1nders: 😲

—EmmeVP: Oh stop you know you're great

—Signs 1nders: Talent isn't everything in the art world though, that's why I switched gears. I knew I couldn't handle that intense level of competition

—EmmeVP: To that youth center?

—Signs&1nders Yeah, I got my BA in social work to become the second in command there
But unfortunately, it burned down

—EmmeVP: OH MY GOD
I'm so sorry

—Signs&1nders : Thanks.
—Signs&1nders My problem is that I don't KNOW what to do with my degree my resume just means less here
—Signs&1nders: I had very different plans for my life in Honolulu, but they literally went up in smoke.
Now I'm starting over, again.
—Signs&1nders: At this point I'm interested in almost anything as long as it is stable and has a decent salary.

—EmmeVP: My poor career orphan! You have to tell me the whole story when we see each other
. . .
—EmmeVP: I've been thinking and thinking since our last conversation and the more I think the more I believe that my next project could be your next project

—Signs&1nders: Like an internship or a job?

—EmmeVP: Not quite a job, but more than an internship. Much more! I'd like to make you my protege
—EmmeVP: I want your help to find a tremendous outlet for all your talent and ability, that pays what you deserve

[after a lengthy pause]

—EmmeVP: Would you perhaps be interested in letting me change your life?

[after a shorter pause]

—Signs&1nders: Do proteges get health insurance? I'm in my 30s so I can't pretend that doesn't matter anymore

—EmmeVP: It can. I'll send the details and a formal contract and you can think it over.

(Unsent)

8/5/21

WTF, MA?!?!?!

-Ant

Ant

He'd never send it, but it felt good to write it. Ant tossed the postcard in the direction of his small desk and flopped back on the bed. Really, he shouldn't have been surprised. Ma had been talking about leaving the navy since the summer. Ant could hear how deeply tired she was of being a doctor during the pandemic. She'd gone from gallows humor to complete silence on the subject. The only time he needed to worry about Ma was when she was quiet, so he should have known something was up when he barely heard from her after those weird text messages in June. She was good at staying in touch. It hadn't occurred to Ant until now that she might have been avoiding him.

Not until he spent the week flattened under a barrage of emails.

In the first, Ma let him know that she was retiring from the navy and would be leaving Oʻahu in the following year. It was leaving Hawaiʻi that really threw him for a loop. They'd moved to Hawaiʻi after his dad died. It was the place they'd healed together. Ant always thought of Hawaiʻi as his real home. Okinawa was a beautiful, hazy dream. Guam was where his dad got sick, and Hawaiʻi was where they healed. And when his grandmother came, his family had felt whole again. That's when they moved off the base. When Ma bought the house, she said it was so that Ant would always have his home and no one would be able to take it from him.

Ant had assumed Ma leaving the navy would mean her easing into some cushy private practice in Oʻahu. Instead she was moving to San Juan. This made Ant's jaw drop.

Yes, Ma was Puerto Rican—from Puerto Rico (not New York or Florida)—but from her stories, she had been a restless soul since she was a child. From those same stories Ant had learned that she hadn't had it the easiest being chubby and dark, with a grandmother who wouldn't let her play in the sun. That's why she'd joined the US Navy despite its name being mud in PR for everything that happened with the cancer clusters and whatnot.

His mother didn't seem to long for Puerto Rico the way, like, Lin-Manuel Miranda did. Ma was a zephyr, a swashbuckling adventurer. In all his years at home, he couldn't recall one instant of homesickness. Ant was the one begging his grandmother for *asopao de pollo* on cool nights or *plátanos maduros* with ice cream for his birthday. But something about Hawaiʻi had curdled for Ma. She was itching to leave, and she'd set her sights on Puerto Rico because it had the highest vaccination rate in the country. He could practically see her frustration on the screen when she wrote, "The vaccine is just the vaccine there—I can do my job without people trying to fight me for it. I don't think I could be a doctor anywhere else, right now."

Before Ant could fully recover or respond with something appropriately supportive, a second email came two days later. Since he was probably getting his first real job pretty soon, Ma was going to rent their house to one of her clients: a lesbian couple expecting triplets in February of next year. Did Ant want to come home to pack, or should Ma have the movers do his room? That was the email that left him gasping. Particularly the postscript: Don't worry, one of the moms is a big gardener. The girls will be taken care of.

Ant couldn't trust himself, so he didn't write back at all. Instead he spent his days doing mindless data entry for his new temp job and his nights stress-cleaning the bathrooms. Every day, multiple times a day, he tried to remind himself that he was a grown man and his mother was not required to consider him when making radical changes to her life. Also, as a lifelong military brat, he should be used to rolling with the punches.

Two days after that, Ant lit up at an email with the subject heading "JOB OFFER." He opened it too quickly, too hopefully. He badly needed some good news. It was an offer from his temp agency. The association he was doing the data entry for wanted to offer him a six-week contract with a bump in salary—all he had to do was come into the office every day with a blazer and tie.

An office job, with a suit and tie—Ant's literal nightmare.

That was when he called Maya. She felt like the only person he could depend on right now. Maya let him attempt small talk for ten uninterrupted minutes before she said, "You sound upset. Would it help to scream in a field?"

Ant sat up; how did Maya always know exactly what he needed? "Yes, very much."

"I got you, be there in an hour."

∾

His phone buzzed. Maya was downstairs.

Before he knew it Ant was resting his face against the cool glass of her mother's Honda while Maya took the side streets to . . . somewhere. The highway went from a busy eight lanes flanked by large strip malls to a four-lane road bordered by sprawling low-rise apartment complexes.

The sun was setting as they turned onto a windy lane that passed some old cottages and newish developments with huge homes.

"Another one? At least they're not fake brownstones, I guess." Maya was visibly relieved as they rounded another few bends in the road to see a large crumbling brick structure surrounded by a couple of acres of tall grass. The large building looked like a cross between a fancy British boarding school and a castle. All red brick and dozens of broken windows, and a height that dwarfed everything in the surrounding area.

"Oh, thank Christ," Maya muttered, turning the car onto a short gravel road—or a long driveway. Either way it ended with a chain hung to stop people driving in the grass. She cut the engine and slid the mask from her wrist to the change tray in the car.

"We're here," she said, nodding toward the field with the decrepit building. She tilted her head and faced him. The reddish ends of her locs drifted over the right shoulder of her hoodie. "You wanna talk now, or you wanna scream?"

Ant turned and looked out at the green grass, thinking of catharsis—but also of mosquitoes that weren't quite dead yet.

"Quick scream at the tree line. Then let's talk." He used the last of his will to get out of the car and make the short walk from the gravel to the copse of birches at the edge of the green field. Maya was behind him, crunching through the gravel in her Mary Jane–shaped Crocs. She didn't seem worried, but she was waiting for him to decide the next move. When he stopped and leaned back on a tree, she did the same, a few feet away.

He looked at her a moment, watching her watch the sunset. The golden light gave a spark to her eyes. For some reason "Wildest Dreams" started playing in his head—which was not the vibe of this current moment.

He was distracting himself. Ant closed his eyes and took a breath, determined to face what he was feeling. He was resolved to open his mouth and let whatever needed to come out.

"FUUUUUUUUUUUUUUUUUUUUUUUUUUCCCCKKK KK!" he cried into rapidly approaching darkness. He screamed again, no words this time, only sound. Something long and angry that hurt his throat.

It must have released something because Ant suddenly felt his face wet with tears. *It was my only real home, Ma! It was a big deal!*

Ant tried to dry his face with his own shirt, with futile catlike gestures, until Maya materialized next to him, wordlessly drying it with the sleeve of her zip-up hoodie. They leaned against the nearest tree and gazed into the distance.

After a few minutes Ant felt the warm pressure of Maya's hand on his back, reassuring. He looked across and watched the sun dip behind the trees. Once he allowed himself to sit in his sadness instead of poking around the edges, the ache wasn't so overwhelming. He could feel himself finding a way to live within it. He didn't need to scream anymore. Ant took a deep breath and turned to Maya. "Ready to get outta here?"

She nodded and led the way back to the car. "I've got two ears and a heart, if you want to tell me what this is all about," she called over her shoulder.

So he did. He told her about his mom's new job. He told her about Ma's big move to Puerto Rico and how after Christmas he couldn't call Hawai'i home anymore. Which meant he couldn't call anywhere home anymore.

"It's like the ground beneath my feet suddenly turned to Jell-O." Ant sighed and leaned back against the headrest. "And on top of all that, all the good parts of the summer are gone. Now the swampy weather sucks, mosquitoes suck, temping sucks, and trying to not hear Auntie Kay and her girlfriend have sex *really* sucks. I've been pretty much a sex-neutral ace person, but this might push me to sex-repulsed.

"When things felt like too much, I could tell myself, 'If it all goes to hell, I'll head home to O'ahu.' I don't even have that anymore. Everything feels like it's slipping out of my grasp."

He looked at Maya and watched her face twitch. She was probably discarding her first and second thoughts before responding. Early in their friendship Maya'd had a tendency toward giving advice—she was five years older, after all. Eventually, Ant told her that if he wanted solutions, he'd ask for them. What he really wanted was someone to listen. Over time he noticed (gratefully) that Maya tried to advise less and support first.

She released the wheel and slipped her hand into his. "There are so many sharp, unexpected pains of adulthood." Maya sighed as she eased the car to a stop. She turned to face him, a softness in her face that wasn't often there. "I'm so sorry you're hurting, friend." Her eyes held a depth of understanding that Ant knew he couldn't find anywhere else in the world.

A warmth spread inside him as Maya squeezed his hand. Then the light changed, and she shifted her focus back to the road.

"You wanna get some dinner and watch TV at my parents' place?" she offered. "They have HBO now. We can finally watch that show your friend Pua kept raving about in the before-times."

Ant gave a small smile. He couldn't think of anything that sounded better.

They ended up picking up Ledo and taking it back to her parents' house. Ant didn't think rectangular pizza was quite the regional delicacy people like Auntie Kay made it out to be, but it was tasty enough and Maya let him pick the toppings. She was happy as long as she got the spicy-ravioli things.

At Maya's house, they settled next to each other on the ancient basement couch, where they watched the entire first season of *Los Espookys* in one go. He was able to think about eating spam musubi with Pua while she ordered him and Maya to watch the show. It was the first time since he got his mother's email that he thought about Hawai'i without immediately feeling sad. It made him realize that ache would go away eventually. He could bear it, in time. He could learn how. Until he did, there was pizza, and TV, and Maya.

⤟

As the night drew on, Maya let the algorithm lead them from *Los Espookys* to an offbeat comedy special, to an over-the-top craft competition that was almost insulting in the way it pandered to younger millennials / Gen Z. Maya had been trying to make her DVR cough up

Spider-Man: Into the Spider-Verse when he apparently drifted off. Now, as he woke in the chilly basement, Ant realized he wasn't the only one who'd zonked.

Maya had snuggled against him at some point—probably the reason that his chest was warm even though the tips of his ears were cold. Maya's head was on his chest, just over his heart. She was breathing evenly and not giving any sign of waking. This was surprising but not unwelcome. Looking down, he could tell that Maya had retightened her locs. The combination of shea butter and whatever was in her blue spray bottle made Maya's hair smell like cookies for days.

Don't sniff your friend! Ant's good sense shouted at him—even as his nose seemed to drift to the crown of her head. Thankfully, before Ant could truly embarrass himself, Maya began to stir, lifting her head with a sleepy sideways yawn.

"Hi, friend." She gave a small wave and shifted until she was leaning against the opposite arm of the couch. "Hope I didn't drool on you."

Ant touched the space on his chest where Maya's head had been, already missing her warmth. "Dry as a bone," he replied with a half wave of his own. He wasn't wearing his glasses, but somehow, in the dim light of the basement, Ant saw her clearly. She was all autumnal tones: red-brown locs, copper shoulders. She'd even unzipped her hoodie, revealing a loose yellow sundress that seemed to swim around her.

"You can sleep on me anytime," he said, yawning.

Maya tapped her chin, her warm eyes seemed to shimmer with mischief. "Is that wise, dear Antonio? All that proximity, combined with your tendency to reflexively flirt—if I didn't know you so well, you could be in grave danger of getting kissed."

Wait, what? Was Maya drunk? She wasn't making sense. "That would only be a danger if someone wanted to kiss me, and not a lot of folks are out here thirsting over chunky Black lumberjacks."

Maya poked him with her big toe and frowned as if pained. "Don't do that. Don't sell yourself short. You are so desirable, outside and in. Also, as an experienced pansexual, I can tell you that many, many people would kill to be cherished the way you cherish the people you choose. That's why I get so angry when you waste your time with unworthy women. You're a catch, Ant."

Suddenly she was close again, all warmth and sugar-cookie smell, her hoodie half-shrugged off her shoulders now. Someone would probably find all this overwhelmingly sexy, but that wasn't Ant's problem.

This was overwhelming but not with the prospect of sex lurking below the surface. It was overwhelming because something Ant hadn't known he craved was only a breath away. Ant wasn't wearing his glasses, so Maya should have been a little blurry—soft around the edges. But she was close and clear and looking at him expectantly. He could see the way her eyes darted to his mouth. He could feel the pull of her orbit; all he had to do was lean in.

But then what?

"Aren't you the one who doesn't date your friends?" Ant said weakly. One of them had to come to their senses. It was the reason he had never allowed himself to even imagine . . . this. He'd watched many a mutual friend gently but firmly shot down at the start of their pursuit.

"Everything else is different—why can't one thing change for the better?"

Now their knees were touching, and they were looking into each other's eyes—and Ant saw an understanding so deep that it almost hurt. "You know what this means, right?"

She nodded, fingers brushing his cheek, then his chin. "Quickly, before we get cold feet."

Ant blinked and looked down. His feet were encased in ice—actual rectangular blocks of ice! Before he could shriek, Ant's eyes snapped open.

He was alone, stretched out on the couch in Maya's basement. His feet peeked out from a thick comforter he had pulled to his chin. Ant shrank himself so his feet would again be covered by the blanket—then he sighed, willing himself to forget the dream with limited success. His subconscious had been remarkably clear on the issue. It was a problem he didn't need. Those feelings, whatever they were, needed to stay buried. Maya didn't date her friends. Maya didn't see him as anything more than the little brother she'd never had.

Those feelings his brain wouldn't shut up about were going to have to stay buried.

⁑

Texts from Cousin Gigi to Maya, August 17, 2021

Gigi:

Hey Cuzzo

Maya:

Hey Gigi, what's up?

So now that I looked over that proposal from Emme Vivant And provided you a couple negotiation points

Which Emme accepted, and thank you

Great! So I'm calling my favor.

Maya:

Ahh, and what will your freelance legal services cost?

Gigi:

A week of housesitting Beach housesitting actually I'm helping my dad and Gary with their place in Sag Harbor

Long story but we need to make it an Airbnb

We have a bunch of repair/ contractor people coming and we need someone to let them in
You up for it?

Is that it? Absolutely, if it's between now and Labor Day

Thank you, you are saving my life right now

You're not a very good negotiator, though

I'm sorry, WHAT? Explain

You could've held on to the favor I owe you

Maya:

You know I'd do anything for your daddy

Uncle Stephen was the first out queer person in our family he made a lot of things easier for me when I came along

Gigi:

TBF it doesn't get much harder than Black and gay in the 80s!

ikr

Since my dad saw everything he went through I didn't come out so much as tell momma and daddy to "expect girls, too"

Well . . . My dad is kind of opposed to this whole thing

Huh
Is he gonna be mad at me, though?

Probably not
😅😬

I take it back, you are a fantastic negotiator

Maya:

And possibly a demon

Gigi:

Thank you

Can I bring a friend?

Sure! Who you bringing?
Someone special?

Hopefully my best friend
emphasis on FRIEND

You know, my dad would
Probably be cooler with you taking
Gary's side if you pretend you're
taking a new love to the bungalow
He's romantic that way

Eww, no!
Why?

Is he creepy?
Like, an acceptable range of
creepy, but still . . .

I wouldn't be best friends with any kind
of creep

Gigi:

Smelly?

Maya:

He smells really good
Sandalwood soap I think

Engaged to someone else?

No

Then what's the problem?

Nobody willingly signs up for a broke,
unemployed girlfriend who has no other
friends I mean, pick a struggle

Oh calm down, you're still Maya

. . .
Am I?

I am a bad negotiator
You need this weekend at the beach
more than I need the help

You may be right there

Texts from Maya to Ant, August 19, 2021

Maya:

Antonio, I have two words that are going to make your day

ROAD TRIP!

Ant:

Ooh! Those are two very good words When? Where?

how would you like to spend the last of summer in the Hamptons In a beachfront bungalow? (meaning small) I was thinking your birthday week

That sounds amazing!

Gigi says the wi-fi is good so you can work during the day if you need to work

My contract will be up the week before. I didn't want to be temping on my birthday

Maya:

BTW, Rental Car, gas, food

All on my cousin Gigi

Ant:

Okay now this is all a bit too good I'm sensing a catch

TBH, there are a couple

We're the ones letting the repair people in
So we can't wander too far

Except for Friday when the painters come and we have to be out all day

Also we won't have a stove/oven for most of the week. Just a fridge, a microwave and maybe a toaster oven

That all sounds . . . fine

Is there anything else?

Maya:

Not really
There's only one bedroom but my cousin
said it sleeps 3 adults or 5 models
So I'm thinking there's a daybed and a
real bed in the bedroom

We can take turns using it

Oh! There's a classy futon
in the living room

Ant:

Is there such a thing as a classy futon?

That's the only kind they
allow in the Hamptons

💀

Ant

Help Me Spacey Aces, You're My Only Hope

Hello my internet friends. I need you to help me survive a week at the beach (I know, the hardship) with my allo, pan, cis-lady best friend. (I'm ace cis-heteromantic)

Soooo, right before my friend invited me to house-sit with her for a week at the beach, I was whining to said best friend about feeling trapped in my group house for a month, so this sounds like a lovely gesture. The problem is, a couple weeks before she invited me, I had a rather intense dream that made me realize I might be developing more than platonic feelings for my friend.

Like I said, I'm a romantic ace, so this is not a crisis of identity! . . . but of everything else. Not only is my best friend too wonderful to lose, at present she's my only friend. I moved across the country last spring, to a place where I have older family but no friends besides bestie. She's been my rock through a lot of stuff in the last 6 months—and that's in addition to 7 years of friendship. She was the first person I told I was ace.

Anyway, I'm not asking how to get over my friend, there's plenty of good advice in the forums for that. Help me get through this week. Thanks!

COMMENTS: HELP ME SPACEY ACES, YOU'RE MY ONLY HOPE

—u/nFLoridaMan1979 Times like this I'm glad I'm a run-of-the-mill aroace. Life isn't easy, but it's simple

> u/nColorMeSurprised So helpful, and yet so considerate

>> u/nfieldsofgold I guess someone's got to fit the smug ace stereotype

—u/nCinnamonTwist You sure it's platonic both ways? This beach trip sounds like the start of a romance novel or a cozy K-drama. The whole thing is too cute.

—u/nRihannaIsGod My first tip: Stay busy
Second: Don't get drunk with her
Third: Make new friends THIS WEEK. Try meet ups, hang out in bookstores, take up birdwatching, whatev, get out there. You NEED other people, no matter what happens with your bestie.

> u/nFLoridaMan1979 Hard agree with you needing new people. If you squint this looks a little codependent. It's no good to make one person your everything, even if it's convenient.

>> u/nTheBotMod says DON'T diagnose strangers. It's not cool, and against our rules!

u/nFLoridaMan1979 Je ne regrette
rien, BotMod

—u/nfieldsofgold I feel the need to point out that your dream,
however intense, may not mean that you're interested in your
friend. It may not mean anything.

—u/nLilyfromtheValley OP, if you're still reading: STOP and go
make some plans

—u/nColorMeSurprised Hey, OP! I run the DCSpaceyAces
forums on here, and we've got some cool events happening
between now and Thanksgiving

Maya

Ant eagerly volunteered to take the first leg of the trip behind the wheel. Maya acquiesced just as easily. She was happy to DJ, especially since all that involved was pressing play on *Dirty Computer* (a favorite driving album) for the first hour. Usually the highway found a way to stay clogged, even on Sunday mornings, but today they were breezing along so fast there was actually a point to rolling down the window instead of just blasting the AC. Ant did the same and opened the sunroof with a hoot.

Seeing his happiness warmed her heart. Ever since he'd agreed to house-sit with her, Ant had seemed to come alive again. He'd apparently redirected the energy he'd been spending on worrying about his job search or trying not to resent his mom into planning their itinerary.

She knew he was excited at the prospect of a real road trip, though she didn't know how excited until he started sending texts like:

> Philadelphia is only 2 hours away!
> It's closer than Ocean City, Maya!
> How do we not go every weekend?!

It was just the kind of thing Maya took for granted that Ant would appreciate. When you grow up on the East Coast, you kinda forget that most places don't have a new major city strung like pearls every two hours. If her new job with Emme didn't take up all her time, maybe she'd surprise Ant with bus tickets to New York. They could do a pilgrimage to Central Park in October. New York was made for fall the way DC was made for spring. She turned to share this thought with Ant . . . but her thoughts skidded to a stop when she looked at his face lit by the early-morning sunshine. He positively glowed. With his well-trimmed facial hair and new nape-length hair, Ant had shifted from cute to approachably hot—like a Daveed Diggs crossed with Bryan Tyree Henry. Add in his amazing personality, and Maya would bet money some cool girl would scoop him up in the next three months. He was just too much of a catch.

Her heart sank a little at the thought of having to share him, but that was a problem for future Maya. Instead she turned up the music and let the wind blow her locs around. Eventually, they'd have to yield to summer heat and turn on the air-conditioning. Best to enjoy this while they could.

❧

As it turned out, Ant's enthusiasm for the City of Brotherly Love was actually about satisfying his inner foodie. The sole purpose of their stop was to get tacos from a lady who had been featured on an episode of *Chef's Table*. After waiting in a line that stretched down the better part of a block, Maya and Ant were able to snag a table outdoors, where they could be comfortably unmasked.

Ant set down a tray and tied his curls up in a quick bun. Maya couldn't help admiring his outfit. He was determined to make the most of the last of summer and had put away everything but a week's worth of aloha shirts and matching shorts in a literal rainbow of colors. Today's set was cornflower blue with white printed flowers. Ant topped the whole thing off with white sneakers with blue piping and periwinkle laces. She remembered how long Ant had searched for those laces in just that shade of blue. He had style and commitment to an aesthetic—something Maya had never quite managed.

She was wearing bike shorts and a cheetah-print swing dress from Old Navy because it fit and didn't show stains. Her look was topped off with red Crocs because they were comfortable, with unicorn-printed socks to keep her feet from being sweaty. The most thought she'd put into her outfit was choosing her rainbow septum ring to make sure her facial jewelry didn't clash with the rainbow pom-pom earrings she was wearing.

"Let's eat!" Ant declared once he'd plopped into the shady seat across from hers. August in Philly wasn't much less oppressive than August in DC, but they'd found a breeze and open restaurants. After being forced inside not that long ago, summer sweat didn't seem worth complaining about.

Maya made short work of her nopales tacos and whipped out her phone to review the details for the week.

"There will be three repair people coming this week: an electrician, a repairman for the garbage disposal, a plumber for the water pressure in the shower—so we should know there are problems with the electricity, the garbage disposal, and the shower. Also the sunroom is off limits until someone fixes the floor."

She gave a one-shouldered shrug and looked at Ant, who seemed to take these developments with aplomb.

"All I'm learning is that there may be a sunroom down the line. You told me you could not guarantee a fully functional kitchen. I figured we were indoor camping and hoped the toilet worked. The toilet works, right?"

Maya scrolled for a second before responding. "It's supposed to. Gigi would like us to report back on that—she'd like us to make a fire in the fireplace, too. Apparently, the flue was recently repaired." She took a long sip of her horchata and looked across the small table. "And she'd like your feedback on the futon in the living room. Gigi said it 'should be fine but bedroom sleeps three regular people or five models—worst-case scenario.'"

"Hmm?" Ant had stopped paying attention. He was lost in his own barbacoa paradise: eyes closed as he savored the last bite of his second taco. A sunbeam passed over his face, drawing her attention to Ant's thick fringe of curly eyelashes, which made him look like he was wearing eyeliner when he wasn't. Wait, was it weird that she'd started noticing Ant's eyelashes?

"That good?" she asked quickly, taking another sip of her horchata and hoping he didn't notice her staring.

Ant nodded and blinked his eyes open. "Better than good. I'd offer you a tiny taste but . . ."

"It's okay—I've been pescatarian for so long that I'm sure red meat doesn't do it for me anymore. Happy this was worth the detour, though."

He shot her a smile across the table. "Thanks for indulging me." Ant leaned back in his seat and sighed happily. "Why can't I live here?"

"Philly?"

"I mean at this table, forever, so I'm never more than ten feet from the most incredible tacos in the world." He stretched an arm toward the mosaic tile. "Oh, South Philly Barbacoa, I love you too much to be parted from you now."

Maya snorted and downed her drink so she couldn't risk choking again. "Well, I hate to be the villain of the piece, but I'm going to have to part you from your love in about an hour. The Hamptons await. And while the tacos there are probably made of brie and cocaine, we'll have the ocean."

Ant stroked his goatee, brushing away the notion of crumbs. He was fastidious about his new facial hair. "I thought you said we were going to the regular-degular part of the Hamptons, Sag Harbor Hills, right?"

Maya shifted in her seat and scrolled through Gigi's email. "We are indeed going to 'the historically Black neighborhood of Sag Harbor Hills.' Good on you for reading the whole email."

Ant made a courtly gesture with his hand. "I did some googling, too, and turns out Sag Harbor Hills is one of several Black beach communities in East Hampton—'Uncle Phil' Black, not 'Diddy White Party' Black. Yes, there's a podcast about it, and yes, I downloaded it. Maybe we can listen to it on the way up?"

"Sure. Since I'm driving the next leg, you can DJ."

"Nice." He rubbed his hands together and moved on to his penultimate taco. "I've also got the new Billie Eilish album. It's really good."

"I love how you still buy albums. I think you and my sister are the only people under thirty who do." She didn't mention that her sister had the taste, habits, and opinions of a forty-eight-year-old librarian—a cool librarian, though, the kind with pink hair and tattoos who quietly thwarts the NSA.

I really miss Ella. Sometimes she wondered if she should have taken her sister's offer to stay with her in London. But if she'd said yes to that one, she couldn't be here with Ant eating tacos. And definitely wouldn't have made a millionaire friend who gave her a job and maybe a book deal.

That's still too weird to process over a very full stomach. She pushed her tray away and dug through her tote bag for her Carmex and some gum. "I really like Billie Eilish's music," she began, pausing to moisturize her lips. "Even though the fact that she's nineteen makes me want to pack up everything and move to Crone Island."

Ant chuckled. "Is this a bad time to tell you that neither Chloe nor Halle Bailey is old enough to rent a car?"

Maya gave the only viable response: she threw her balled-up napkin at him.

"Hey!" Ant protested, dodging the paper nimbly for someone who'd grown up without siblings. "Didn't you always used to tell your Ohana kids that you're never too old to like cool music?"

She shrugged. "I say a lot of things. Finish your tacos."
At least SZA's my age . . . I think.

᪐

They arrived at Sag Harbor in the late afternoon. The sun was still bright and strong, and they could smell the ocean. "I can't wait to go to the beach!" Ant bounced in his seat, half leaning out the car window, the watery view almost pulling him out entirely.

"Gigi says we have access to a small private beach from the house— like a five-minute walk." Maya felt herself flush with excitement as she said the words. They were really spending a week at the beach! Nothing could be better.

Of course, there were groceries to buy and errands to run, so it was almost evening when Maya and Ant pulled into the gravel driveway of their temporary home. It was a small but welcoming cottage, white with cheerful blue trim and a big bay window. She cut the engine and said the thing her momma always said at the end of a long drive: "And brothers and sisters, we are here!"

Gigi had mentioned that her step-grandparents had put on pinions after Hurricane Sandy, raising it a good ten feet off the ground. The little cottage looked like it had sprouted legs and was liable to walk away. With its big windows and two chimneys, the house reminded Maya of her well-worn copy of *Howl's Moving Castle*.

This seems like a lovely place to spend a week.

They both took a moment for a couple of spine-cracking stretches. Then, since Ant insisted on carrying her suitcase, Maya climbed the creaky steps to the beach house's front door. Unlocking her phone again, she punched in the provided key code. Ant arrived with their bags just in time to witness her little victory dance.

Maya opened the door and grunted, walloped by a wall of warm humid air as she entered the bungalow, sweat immediately beading at her hairline. It was hotter inside the little house than outside in the eighty-degree air.

She held the door for Ant and rushed over to the large window over the sink. First thing they needed to do was get a cross breeze going.

Ant wiped his forehead and dropped both of his bags on the large leather recliner near the door, rolling Maya's suitcase next to the chair. "I'll get the windows over here," he offered. Almost immediately she could feel the air moving, and life felt bearable again.

"Thanks, hon." She turned her attention to determining which appliances were functioning. Most importantly: the fridge and freezer hummed along happily. The faucet ran *and* offered hot and cold water. She moved on to the oven (not working), dishwasher (not working, but they had dish soap—and paper plates for when they felt lazy). The stovetop was working, thank goodness. So was the toaster oven, and the microwave seemed to function, if slowly. "We have half a kitchen!" she declared, turning to Ant.

He was frowning at the living room ceiling. There was a modern ceiling fan / light that looked like the propellers on an old-timey plane. But this stylish fan did not move, and its light did not shine. "Uh-oh, no electricity in the living room means no fan and possibly no TV."

Maya gave a small hum. "I've been promised that the Wi-Fi is very good, so we can stream stuff on our laptops, at least." She leaned against the cool marble of the kitchen island. "I think the electricity is only out in that part of the living room, but the kitchen, bedroom, and bathroom are fine. Hopefully once we get a nice cross breeze in here, it'll cool down."

She checked the weather on her phone. "The days here are in the eighties, but the nights are in the fifties, so we'll be okay without AC until the electrician comes." Maya checked the details on her phone again. "Gigi says that the air-conditioning should be working in the bedroom, so worst-case scenario you can take the daybed until the electrician comes."

Ant scratched his chin. "Daybed? You only mentioned the classy futon."

Maya shrugged. "Gigi definitely said the bedroom sleeps 'three adults or five models.' And I think she mentioned a king bed. To my mind that means there is some sort of convertible furniture: a daybed, rollaway—maybe a little Murphy bed, that could be cool."

Her friend didn't seem particularly convinced, but he wasn't terribly invested, either. Ant responded with his own small shrug before moving his bags and plopping backward into the nearby leather recliner.

"I'll let you settle 'the great daybed question.'" He reclined with a smile and reached for his phone. "I'm going to familiarize myself with the restaurants who deliver to our neighborhood, then I'll claim a closet and unpack."

Maya gave Ant an amused look before taking her roller suitcase down the hallway. If she knew him at all, he'd read a dozen restaurant reviews before he unzipped a single bag.

She bumped her suitcase along the little house's surprisingly long hallway, noting the location of the linen closet and the bathroom. The bedroom was at the rear of the little house. She opened the door and gasped. The room was about 80 percent bed, specifically a California king. But more surprising than the size was the fact that there was only one bed. Of all the scenarios she'd imagined, somehow her mind had never conjured up five models sharing the same bed—she wasn't Hugh Hefner!

She parked her suitcase and explored the rest of the room. Everything else seemed to do two jobs: the mirrored wall was in fact a pair of deep closets. The bookcase hid a small safe. A beachy mosaic on the wall across from the bed opened to reveal a good-size TV. No sign of a second bed, or a cot, or even a rollaway sleeping mat. The dark wood four-poster had some clever underbed storage, but that was all that could be said for it. In a pinch, the headboard looked like it could be used for light bondage.

Are they trying to appeal to the economic swinger market?

After a full minute of waffling between whether to put her clothes away or freshen up in the bathroom, Maya turned to face the elephant in the room. The elephant-size bed, anyway.

"This doesn't matter," she told herself. First, Ant had a perfectly good futon in the living room. Second, on the off chance they had to share this gigantic bed, Ant was ace. The only thing she had to worry about was not making *him* feel awkward. It was not a problem. It was a non-problem. So it did not matter that Maya felt a sudden fizzy something in the heart/sternum region at the thought of sharing a bed with her best friend. That was probably indigestion. Wholly inappropriate indigestion. Now was the time for unpacking, figuring out dinner, and not thinking about this. Because this wasn't a problem. Really.

Ant

They did all the settling-in things: putting away groceries, unpacking clothes, locating the sponges and the towels. They explored the outside, finding a woodpile under the house and a stone firepit in the backyard that was covered in soft dirt and sparse grass. He left Maya hunting for the outdoor shower her cousin had promised was there to rinse her feet. She'd ditched her Crocs as soon as they got in the house and probably wouldn't put them on for the rest of week. There was a time in their friendship when he *might* have called her "Maya the Hobbit" because she was short and refused to wear shoes unless she absolutely had to.

Somehow it was almost sunset. Evening had thankfully brought cooler air, and Ant found himself splayed on the classy futon—which was remarkably comfortable—grimacing at his phone. (Specifically, the responses to his Ace Space post, which had turned into "What to do when they don't love you back.")

"Thanks for the vote of confidence, folks," he grumbled. He had followed one of the more useful bits of advice someone offered: Ant had scheduled himself silly this week. If there was a trail, he'd be hiking it. If there was a museum, Ant was visiting. If there was a boat tour, he'd be on it, smiling at the elderly tourists and joking with the wine moms. He was doing everything he could to make sure his thoughts stayed platonic and he did not make things weird for Maya.

As if his thoughts had called her, Ant heard Maya's door open with a squeak. He hastily closed the Spark app window and returned to the many tabs of pizza reviews.

Be cool. Act normal.

"Have you ever had clam pizza? There's place here that's known for its clam pizza, and I've gotta admit, I'm curious." Was he shouting? He felt like he was auditioning for the role of mayor in some community theater production.

"Sure, I trust your judgment," Maya said absently. She went to the kitchen and opened the cabinet doors until she found the glasses. She filled her glass from the faucet, gulped it down, then looked at her glass for a long moment and filled it again.

"Something you should know," she began after another gulp of water. "The bedroom actually only has one bed—it's probably the biggest bed I've ever seen, but it's only one." She bit her lip and frowned, looking strangely unsure of herself. "I'm sorry I didn't check, but it looks like the classy futon is our only alternative."

Sleeping next to Maya for the next five days would definitely poke a big ol' hole in his plan to give her space this week. But as his mind spun, looking for a joke or some kind of witty comeback, it landed on a question.

"Why would it be a problem either way? You're not making me watch porn or read any of your weird space erotica . . . right?"

She sniffed. "It's a spicy sci-fi romance, and no, I'm not sharing." She gave Ant a half glare.

He snorted in response. "In that case sharing a bed should be no problem," he lied. If Ant hadn't had that weird dream—okay, a couple of weird dreams now—that involved kissing his friend, or sharing a gondola, or waltzing across a candlelit ballroom, there would have been no problem. But the most important rule about both weird dreams and possible romantic feelings was that Maya must not know. She must not even suspect.

That's why Ant stifled a sigh of relief as Maya set her glass down in a fit of giggles. "All right, I was being extra."

Ant smiled at her; he'd gotten away with it! "You were doing your part to keep the ace/pan alliance strong."

She laughed and sat next to him on the futon. Briefly, he wondered if she might fall asleep on his chest again tonight.

Wait, that didn't happen.

He looked into his friend's face so he could concentrate on the words she was actually saying, right now.

"Let me try this again," Maya began, still on the edge of laughter. "Ant, if it gets too cold, too hot, too whatever out here, please sleep in the giant bed with me."

He responded with a gallant nod. "Thank you for the kind offer. As we spoke, I took the liberty of ordering the clam pizza—and their margherita, in case the clam is weird."

Maya smiled. "You know it's fancy when they say 'margherita' and not 'cheese.'" She elbowed Ant lightly and rose. "Come on, let's explore."

Ant stood and followed Maya. As a strategy, it had been working pretty well so far.

∽

Later, after the pizza was eaten and the room had cooled to an enjoyable temperature, Maya and Ant were peacefully coexisting on their respective phones. Ant lounged on the futon watching Tiny Desk Concerts while Maya scrolled through TikTok, thankfully not offering to play him any wisdom from Rev. Gina.

Ant looked over and saw Maya recording herself—which was weird, because she refused to put her face on TikTok. She was admiring herself in a filter that gave her red hair. It was a pretty cool look, to be honest.

"What made you change your mind?" he asked after she stopped recording.

Maya set her phone down and turned around sheepishly. "I didn't," she began. "I am just preparing myself for Montage Week."

Ant tilted his head in a way that asked the question for him.

"So as part of my new thing with Emme—assuming everything goes well with the final interview—I'm letting her give me a makeover, head to toe. The full *Princess Diaries*." She picked up her phone again. "I'm just using the filters to imagine possibilities. Not posting."

Ant tried to sound casual as he probed. "So she's not telling you what she's going to do."

Maya shook her head. "She asked for a list of things I would quit over—like no shaving my head, no tattooed makeup, no khakis—but aside from that, I have no clue. I'm considering it a trust exercise."

Huh. Ant didn't trust himself to say more, but what kind of job insisted on giving you a makeover? And why was Maya so comfortable with it? Three months ago, they were snarking on "the girlboss" together. Now Maya was turning her whole life over to Emme for this mysterious opportunity that still didn't quite make sense to him. Everything about this said *scam*, at best. But Maya didn't seem to care. She'd just brush away the possibility of concern with "what's the worst that could happen—everything falls apart and I end up in my parents' guest room? Oh wait, that's my actual life now."

There was a sadness, a bitterness, in that sentence that scared him. Which was why whenever she began talking enthusiastically about Emme changing her life, Ant just smiled and nodded. Broaching the subject almost felt scarier than his current romantic feelings for Maya. Ant looked at her again and saw she was back to scrolling. She yawned in a kittenish way that made her look ever more adorable, then released another that made her eyes crinkle, followed by a giant yawn that was not cute at all but made Ant snicker.

Maya shot him a look, then shrugged and rose to go to bed. "Good night, Antonio," she tossed over her shoulder with a friendly wave. Ant waved back and started his nightly routine, brushing, putting on his pajamas, and sliding a satin pillowcase over the pillow to protect his hair. He was tired in a way that ensured he would sleep through anything— the classy futon could have been made of cement and he'd still be more comfortable here than he'd be lying next to Maya in the dark, trying not to reach for her.

He shook his head at his own weakness and then flopped back on the futon. It creaked loudly in response. Then it whined. After a few beats of silence, Ant heard the distinct *twing* of a spring snapping, followed by a metallic crunch—and suddenly the classy futon was collapsing beneath him.

Ant was still splayed on the ground when he heard Maya's door open. She rushed out from her room. "Oh my God!" He felt, more than heard, her hurry to the fallen couch. He sat up slowly, not hurt but stunned. Maya looked down at him with concerned amber-brown eyes behind her glasses—wait, glasses?!

Since when does Maya wear glasses?

I only make passes at girls who wear glasses. The thought popped in his head, making him giggle.

That made Maya hum in concern. "Come close, hon." She beckoned, reaching for him.

All capacity for thought exited Ant's head when Maya started touching him gently but emphatically. She ran her hands over his arms, then laid her palm against his cheek. Ant couldn't help but lean in to it. Beyond giving the best hugs, exactly when you needed one, Maya had never been hugely touchy-feely—even before the pandemic. Her current attentions were mildly startling . . . but nice.

"Are you dizzy, hon? Did you hit your head on the way down?"

Ant shook his head slowly. "I don't think so—my head doesn't hurt. I'm . . . surprised." Maya was looking at him intently as he blinked his eyes open.

I didn't realize my eyes had closed.

She hummed a sharp note of concern and ran her fingers through his hair tenderly. It took a second to realize she was feeling for bumps or bruises. After a moment she stood and offered her hand.

Ant took it and stood before he thought to ask: "Where are we going?"

Maya stopped and turned in the narrow hallway. "The big bed. You shouldn't go to sleep yet. You might have a concussion. You probably don't—but you might."

Ant stopped their progress and frowned. "But if I'm not going to sleep, why are you taking me to bed?"

Maya turned back and looked at him with a small, sympathetic smile. "Because if I don't bring you back now, I'll find you sleeping in that recliner tomorrow morning because you were afraid to wake me. You stay up and read or watch TV; I'm gonna put on a podcast to sleep to." She turned back toward the bedroom and lightly tugged Ant along. "I shouldn't have said anything about the one bed. I feel like I spoke this into being."

One part of Ant wanted to tell Maya not to be so superstitious. The other part wanted to check and see if Mercury was in retrograde, again.

She looked past Ant, back at the mangled pile in the living room. "What a mess." She sighed and shook her head at the futon. "I'll have to tell Gigi tomorrow. I'm not breaking this to the uncles myself."

Then she turned and walked in her swaying way down the hallway, seemingly unperturbed by anything but Ant's health. And why not? He had spent a good twenty minutes telling her she was making something out of nothing by even worrying about them sharing a bed.

He wondered what CinnamonTwist from the Ace Space forums would say. She already thought he was living a romance novel. How would she respond to them being forced to share the same bed?

Texts from Cousin Gigi to Maya, August 24, 2021

Gigi:

Hey Cuzzo, Good news and bad news about the futon

Good news is that it's still under warranty
Bad news: we won't be able to get you anything this week

Maya:

We've shared the big bed okay
We can make do

Oh that's great!

Silver lining for me, BTW
This minor disaster has surprisingly cooled hostilities between
Dad and Gary. So thanks!

Ooh, does that mean I can get another round of free legal services?

You can keep my card in your wallet to threaten people

Maya:

Deal! Y'all should think about targeting
this place to Black people who want the
historic Hamptons experience

Put Uno decks out get some Toni
Morrison on the bookshelf

Make a list of the Black Owned shops,
and the ones WE should know to avoid

Gigi:

Like a little Green Book for Sag Harbor.
We could get some brochures about
the Black history of Sag Harbor from the
historical society too

Exactly!

Dad and Gary will both be really into this

If you made an Instagram for it,
the house guests could share their
experiences and tag the account

It would be a way to sell your cottage
and Sag Harbor Hills

Maya:

My friend Ant has done a bunch of
tours and stuff since we've been here

Gigi:

You have so many ideas

What can I say? They just come to me

Maya

Maya stepped into the repaired sunroom and turned on the brand-new underfloor heating, the first completed project of the week. Her toes were already grateful; until now, the surprising chill from the floor had made her skip across the tile like a stone on a pond. Today, since her feet weren't shrieking at the contact with the ground, she walked, like a person, to the center of the room.

She'd become addicted to the view. Thin but sturdy trees lined the path to the beach. The sun was rising, fire and gold spreading across the sky, warming the clouds and brightening all over. She wanted to rush back to the giant bed and wake Ant so they could enjoy this moment together—but then, she would have murdered someone for waking her at six thirty in the morning when there was no salary-mandated reason for it. Maya was surprised by how much she missed Ant when he wasn't there—even when he was snoozing just down the hall—the same way she was surprised to find herself curled around him in the early hours of the morning, like he was her teddy bear, or her boyfriend.

It would be nice to be Ant's little spoon; he's probably a great cuddler.

Maya frowned. These were very inconvenient thoughts to have about her platonic friend. She really didn't need those complications now that she was finally getting some stability in her life.

"I know what I'll do," Maya whispered to herself. "I'll put the last touches on Ant's present."

Tomorrow would be Ant's birthday. He insisted that she didn't need to do anything since she'd already arranged this beach week, but the cottage wasn't from her heart. Her gift was. She'd been working on and off for a month. Now it was finished, she was sure of it. She only had to sign it and put it in a pretty envelope.

Okay, time for yoga. She'd gotten into it back in her Oakland days, when she was living in a fifteen-person artists' house and literally only slept at home. Her yoga teacher, Big Brenda Russell, led three sessions a week in the park for anyone who turned up, passing a coffee can around at the end for payment. Big Brenda was an older Black lady with a bald head, Buddha belly, and personal mission to take yoga back from rich white women.

At the beginning of every class, Brenda would tell everyone to stand still and breathe deep. "This is not about staying thin. This is not about getting flexible. This is about finding peace." She believed you needed only a yoga mat and knowledge of the poses to do yoga right. She wanted the folks who learned under her to be able to take their practice anywhere—and Maya had.

Yoga had turned the tiny concrete backyard of her group house into an oasis of calm. When she lost herself in Seattle trying to be who or what her ex needed, yoga was an anchor that kept her from slipping away entirely. It was probably the most consistent thing in her life besides her sister and Ant . . . and there he was again.

Maya rolled her eyes at herself. It was time to stand still and breathe. She closed her eyes and silently strained to hear the sound of the ocean. The velvet-soft crash of the distant waves calmed her, slowing the rabbit run of her heart and helping her deepen her breaths. Slowly Maya brought her hands in prayer position over her heart, then raised them above her head to go into her sun salutation.

∽

After yoga, Maya made a beeline for the french press. She squeaked with surprise when she came into the kitchen and found Ant already awake and crouched over the kitchen counter, examining the toaster oven. "Morning, almost birthday boy!"

"Morning!" He offered a cheery smile. Too cheery, more *coaxing*. "So I know my birthday is tomorrow, but I woke with a sudden and undeniable craving for cinnamon rolls, your cinnamon rolls specifically. The ones you made for Heather's breakfast birthday party . . ." Maya let Ant ramble persuasively as she made coffee in the french press. He moved to stand next to her with his back against the sink and batted his eyelashes. "So whaddya say? Feel like baking?"

She sighed theatrically. "Well, I suppose I could . . . I did get a bunch of baking stuff in our grocery delivery because I'm finally in a house where no one is dieting . . ."

She tilted her head to the side. "Since I know you've already checked, how is this toaster oven for baking? The real one isn't getting fixed until Thursday and cinnamon rolls won't keep—okay, they'll keep, but they won't be great by Thursday." Maya knew Ant had an answer; she liked to watch him go when he got a sudden burst of enthusiasm.

"I did a quick scan online. It looks like this brand of toaster, according to both *Tiny House Living* blog and *La Vida de Van*, is 'the only oven you need' for very small spaces." Ant paused and briefly derailed his own train of thought. "You know, the whole van-life thing . . . I can't tell if they're all rich kids cosplaying poverty or what, but no one has ever been *that* excited composting. Like it's so fun to park at Walmart." He rolled his eyes and tucked a stray hair behind his ear.

Maya felt a slight twinge of disappointment. *She* wanted to tuck that hair behind his ear.

Again with the loopy thoughts.

"Coffee's ready." She handed him a mug and shoved sugar in his general direction. He sipped indulgently, then remembered his pitch.

She added cream to her coffee and listened. Then she delivered her verdict.

"All right, Antonio, cinnamon rolls will be made, and *we* will make them." This time she waggled her eyebrows. "You did some great research on the toaster oven, but we only have a hand mixer here. The last time I made cinnamon rolls, I had access to my roommate's fancy-ass stand mixer with bread hook." She took a long sip of her coffee and pressed her arm against his. "I'm gonna need you for kneading." She laughed. "Your upper-body strength, that is."

Before long, Maya had prepared the dough while Ant followed her instructions: gathering and measuring out the cinnamon and sugar for the filling and double-checking that they did, in fact, have enough cream cheese to make the frosting. Then Maya met him at the marble kitchen island and eased the dough from the bowl to the countertop. "I need you to knead for five minutes. Can you do that?"

Ant nodded, reaching for the dough in a way that told her he didn't have a clue. He took off his class ring from high school and made a fist before Maya gently placed a hand over his. "This isn't bread dough, hon. It's soft dough: tuck and fold—no punching."

Maya demonstrated from her side of the counter, petting, then nudging the dough with her open hands like a stubborn cat. Ant still looked hesitant, so without much thought, Maya went around to his side of the counter and put her hands over his. "There's really nothing to it," she said, trying not to stutter as another bright spark of something shot through her body. There was no denying that she felt . . . something when their hands touched. Something that had nothing to do with the warmth of rising dough—or friendship.

Intellectually, she knew her friend's hands were big. He played a concert ukulele, and when she complained about learning the piano with stubby pinkies, he wiggled his fingers and said, "Can't relate," with a laugh. But she hadn't been aware of his hands until now. Quickly she helped him develop a rhythm with the dough and then rushed back to her phone. "I'll put on my timer for five minutes."

Ant was hard at work, folding and tucking the dough with those large hands, scooping it up and thwacking on the counter with extra relish. "I remember you said you do that when dough is too sticky." He gave her one of his easy smiles.

Maya felt like she watched his hands for a length of time that bordered on inappropriate.

I'd really like to hold Ant's hand.

She frowned at herself. They'd known each other for seven years. She must have held Ant's hand a hundred times—not for much longer than it took to offer a reassuring squeeze or a pull in the right direction, but she'd definitely done it. What was she wanting now? What was different?

"Earth to Maya!" Ant called from across the kitchen island. He had apparently been talking to her.

"I'm sorry." Maya looked down and saw that she'd really, really over-buttered the bowl in her hands. Quickly she put it down and started washing her hands in the sink.

"Am I done?" Ant pointed to the dough and shrugged. "I don't really know what I'm looking for here, but your alarm went off."

How on earth had she missed the sound of that chime?

"You should be good," she replied, not particularly caring. She was thoroughly distracted by the flour on Ant's face. He'd gotten a little on his hands and left parentheses on either side of his mouth when he called to her. It made Ant look like he had deeper smile lines than usual. It was adorable.

Maya crossed the short distance and scraped the dough into the buttery bowl. "Sorry, daydreaming, I guess."

He chuckled. "You sure were." He reached over and tapped (booped?) her nose. "Got a little buttery nose."

The contact was more than a little surprising. Maya stepped back and wriggled her nose like a cartoon hedgehog.

"Well, you've got flour in your goatee." She put the bowl down and reached across the counter to brush it away. She could detect the warmth of Ant's skin just beneath his neatly trimmed facial hair. It felt good. They gazed at each other for a long moment, waiting for a question to be asked or answered.

Finally Ant said, "What happens now?" His voice hummed low. He lifted his hand to Maya's and took it away from his face. "To the dough, I mean. How far away are we from cinnamon rolls?"

He stepped back and wiped at his goatee to get the rest of the flour. The moment—Maya was pretty sure there had been a moment—was gone.

"About two hours. You should have enough time to have one without singeing your tongue before you run off. What's happening today?"

"I'm taking a tour of this historic farm. It's got a windmill and a cutting garden—"

"You can't resist a garden," she chimed in.

He shrugged with a smile. "It's true. It'll be me and like five elderly white women, but I was becoming kind of an accidental hermit at my auntie Kay's, so I'm trying to make sure I go somewhere every day." He paused. "You can come if you want."

Maya shook her head. "Dishwasher guy should be here about an hour after the cinnamon rolls are done. Let's just go down to the beach when you get back, like we did yesterday."

Ant nodded. "I'll bring my uke. I feel like your personal pied piper: the only way to make sure you go outside is to play music."

Maya rolled her eyes and gave a salty Girl Scout salute. "On my honor . . . I will leave the house before you come back." She stuck her tongue out.

"That's all I need," Ant said, passing her as he headed to the bathroom.

"Wait!" Maya called out. She wanted to ask him to stay—but it felt selfish. It wasn't his fault all the repair visits were in the middle of the day. She felt herself about to say something stupid like "I'll miss you," but quickly course-corrected. "I forgot what I was going to say. Enjoy your tour, I guess."

Ant gave a final wave, then disappeared up the hallway. Maya covered the dough bowl and set a new alarm; it needed an hour and change to rise.

What now? The kitchen was quiet, colder. Maya dug out her phone and popped on Rev. Gina's latest: a poem called "God Is Outside." She looked out the kitchen window at the sun-kissed water. What was wrong with her? The electrician wasn't due for more than an hour. There was no reason for her to be inside. Yet here she was, still in the kitchen.

The poem ended and Maya frowned. She was worried that at some point in the last few years, her default setting had flipped to "in the house." Leaving felt like a huge hassle.

You never waste an afternoon reading. The thought popped into her head, light and cheery as a soap bubble. There was no better escape from your own head than someone else's story, and she desperately needed an escape from her mind. Thus resolved, Maya grabbed her Kindle and went back to the sunroom. Between her endless supply of monster romance and her cinnamon rolls, she probably wouldn't even think about Ant (much) until he returned.

Texts from Ella to Maya, August 25, 2021

Ella:

Hey Lady, How's tricks?

Maya:

Hello, my little chimney sweep
I'm just sitting quietly while
other people fix things

You sound a little lonely

You got that from a sentence?

Well . . . Yeah
You never do anything quietly
And you rarely "just sit"

You're a weirdo

Of course I am!
I'm your baby sister.
I was taught by the best

Fair

Ella:

Is Ant with you?

Maya:

No, he's touring a historic windmill

Ooh, which one?
The one with the museum?

No, it's a farm with a windmill

Only you would know about more than
one historic windmill in the Hamptons

Ant

Ant's birthday started with leftover cinnamon rolls and ended with an excursion to a nearby lighthouse—that accidentally turned into a hike. It was evening when he returned, happy but exhausted. Back when Ant was turning his anxiety about the trip into research (which was also how he got through college), he made a special point to find out which Long Island lighthouses would be open and allowing visitors inside despite the current plague.

As the Lyft drove away, Ant took off his mask and climbed the creaky steps, careful to move his shopping bag behind his back as he entered the house. On a whim he'd gotten Maya a glittery snow globe from the lighthouse's gift shop. It was easier than pretending he hadn't been thinking about her the whole time. Ant had enjoyed himself, even though he definitely overdid it climbing the stone steps to the top to take in the view.

He tried the door and smiled when the knob turned easily. Maya left it open for him; she knew he'd never remember the code. She was so thoughtful in little ways. As the door opened, Ant caught the smells of garlic and olive oil. Maya was dancing around the kitchen to a jazzy song blaring from her phone about . . . tomatoes. He listened quietly as he stashed the snow globe in his book bag. *That's some solid innuendo,* he thought as the singer outlined which fruit could and could not be squeezed.

Ant looked at Maya and thought about how he'd like to squeeze her. People thought asexuality was about lacking all desire, like you were born to be a monk wearing scratchy robes and delighting in lumpy oatmeal. But being ace only meant being free from sexual desire. Ant still longed for physical intimacy. He wanted to cross the room, take Maya in his arms, and dance with her. He wanted to settle his palm into the small of her back, his thumb and index finger grazing the skin just above the waistband of her leggings, and feel the warmth there and catch the sugar-cookie smell of her hair when he drew her in close.

Dammit, I'm already pining.

Of course, this *would* be the moment that Maya turned around with a smile. Her smiles had the unique ability to blaze right through him, but also make him feel like all was right in the world.

Maya beamed. "I made mai tais! And your birthday dinner is arriving in ten minutes. Five-star *sushi*! According to DoorDash, anyway."

How is she this good? "Thanks for a perfect birthday, Mai." He stepped toward, but Maya stepped back, putting up one finger. Then she got an A4-size envelope and put it in his hand. "Here is my gift, made with my own broke hands."

She stepped back with a shy smile as Ant carefully unsealed the envelope. It was a line drawing of a cherry blossom branch, a plumeria blossom, and a hibiscus bloom all sprouting from an accurate, but not graphic, human heart. Maya had given him back his girls.

"You can frame it or use it as a design for your first tattoo. That way you'll always have Hawai'i with you, no matter what."

Ant felt his eyes fill. He swallowed hard and took Maya into his arms until he could trust his voice—until he trusted himself to say anything but "I love you."

"Thank you," he managed with a roughened voice. "You gave me home."

Maya squeezed him back. They held each other tightly until the moment was gone. "C'mon, big fella. The electrician came back today, so we can finally watch something on the giant TV."

She led the way to the love seat, and Ant followed. After all, following Maya had been working out so far.

⌒⌯⌒

That evening, after dinner and a couple of episodes of *Drag Race All Stars*, Ant and Maya turned the lights down (there was a dimmer!) and Maya put on a record. She, who had been learning the secrets of the house while he was on his excursions, had discovered one cabinet that turned out to be a record player and a small collection of albums. A woman with a clear, warm voice was singing about a naughty flea— more innuendo. Or was it? The lyrics were about a literal flea. Ant mentally shrugged. It was nice to listen, in any case.

"Hey, DJ," Ant called to Maya. "Who are we listening to?"

She was sprawled on the rug reading or writing. Ant wasn't quite sure; he could see only the event horizon of her knotted head wrap.

"Miriam Makeba," she replied without looking up. "My uncles believe the best music ever produced in the world came out between 1965 and 1975. Their record collections basically exist to prove their point. They tend to lecture at family reunions, but you can't knock their album collection. I need to text Gigi and make sure they know these are here."

She sat up and Ant blinked at her. Maya was wearing glasses again. This time they were oversize cat-eye frames.

Maya in rectangular frames was cute. Maya tonight, with her auburn locs twisted up on her head and her big, adorable glasses—this Maya was heart-stoppingly gorgeous. Even the tiny tattoos behind her ears were somehow more adorable.

Thankfully she was unaware of his gaze. Maya was writing intently in the Spark-branded "manifestation journal." It was surprising that she was still using the journal from her sister, but her manifesting because Emme said so—that was plain disturbing.

Ant shifted in the armchair and discreetly watched her write. Maya's eyes seemed sad, but also determined. After a long stretch of writing, Ant looked down and watched the singer-songwriter on his screen. When he looked up again, Maya'd closed the red book with a small smile.

"I still can't believe it: in two weeks I will finally be turning things around. I've tried dreaming big. I'm pursuing work I love, so I'll never work a day in my life . . ." She rolled her eyes at this sentiment. "Now I'm finally being smart. Even if it means putting my faith in a random millionaire." She picked up the journal and stuck out her tongue.

"I don't get why you need Emme." Ant sat up, shaking his head. "You're fluent in sign language, you have years of experience with youth, you had a 3.6 GPA—and you type insanely fast. I've seen you. If you're looking for stability, you should be able to get some kind of office job that pays decently and won't lay you off. I know I'm not from here and I don't get the allure of the Vivants, but to me, you're the one doing Emme a big favor—not the other way around."

Maya bit her lip for a couple of beats of silence. It was clear that she knew what she wanted to say but wasn't sure how to say it.

"I've temped a lot, Ant. I've interned. I've been at many an office. At every place I've worked, there's a woman who is everything and nothing at the same time. She's Black, Brown—either Filipina or Native Hawaiian in Honolulu. She does her job plus half of everyone else's. People always ask her to bring the birthday cake, or organize the Christmas party, or take the meeting notes; even if there are interns or assistants, she's always asked because she's so nice. She's always passed up for promotions because she's needed where she is. The office can't function without her, but no one really notices her until she retires—which is the happiest day of her life. It's honest, steady work, Ant, but it would crush me. And I know if I launch my career here without some kind of backing, that is who I'll be: the fat, Black lady everyone appreciates but nobody thanks. From the bottom of my heart: fuck that. No one can ignore Emme Vivant, and with a bit of her shine, no one will ignore me."

Maya held his gaze from across the coffee table for a long moment, and they both looked away when he had no response. He couldn't debate her. It didn't take much thinking to remember every Hawaiian auntie who fulfilled this role. He thought of the hard shell his mom seemed to have at work with everyone but her patients. Then he looked at Maya.

She'd reopened her journal, but her pen seemed frozen above the page. Ant eased himself out of the recliner and sat next to her. If he knew Maya at all, she was embarrassed by sharing so much. Ant hoped to spare her the need of any more words.

"Can I hug you, Mai?" Ant asked, opening his arms to receive her. Maya slid into the place Ant made for her, squeezing him back. They sat like that, enjoying the comfort of each other's warmth, and this quiet moment in a borrowed beach house they could never dream of affording. And even with his secret feelings that he found new ways to bury, there was no place in the Hamptons—no place in the world—he'd rather be.

God,

Quick favor: Would you erase my huge overshare with Ant from his memory? Both our memories would be great but his will do.

Please and thank you,
Maya

Maya

Maya woke on her last full day in Sag Harbor and reached for her phone, which was somewhere in the giant bed. She patted the sheets and rolled over twice when—aha! It was almost eleven. For the first time this week, Maya had been able to sleep in. Actually, it was the first time she'd been able to sleep in since her depressive episode. The bigger problem had been getting out of bed. She'd been miserable then, but she felt wonderful today.

What now? Maya had made a vague stab at her daily journaling, first in her usual line-a-day prayer thing. She couldn't quite believe how long she'd kept that going, honestly. Especially when deep, true feelings that you didn't expect started spilling out onto the page, or onto your best friend.

The silver lining to that embarrassing episode was when Ant took her in his arms and wouldn't let go. Maya had let him; she was that emotionally spent. His quiet warmth was everything she needed in that moment and nothing that she would let herself ask for. All her fears from earlier that week had been eased the moment she felt his arms wrap around her. He was still her Ant. Maya was grateful. She could have stayed in his arms forever.

That's a totally normal thought to have about a friend, right?

Thankfully, her phone chimed, interrupting any further progress down that train of thought. She picked up her phone to find that Ant was texting her from the living room.

> U up?
>
> j/k I mean, are you awake sleepyhead?

"I'm awake!" Maya shouted, trailing off into a giggle.

> Look under your door

Without another word, Maya launched herself off the bed and hurried to the door, where she found a folded piece of paper with her name on it. Ant apparently was going on whimsy and mystery at the same time. Both modes suited him well. She eagerly unfolded the paper and began to read.

Maya's Itinerary

In celebration of your first, and only, free day this week and recognition of your kindness, I humbly propose this itinerary of events for Maya Day in Sag Harbor Hills
- Noonish: Before Lunch/Lunch: Visit to Best Croissants in East Hampton*
- 3ish: Visit Sculpture Gardens and Pond for a good long wander*
- 7ish Dinner: Sushi or Seafood
(We can do takeout if it's too cool for eating outside)*
- Afterish: Beach Bonfire (Yes, I got a permit)*
Everything is my treat to thank you for this wonderful week! I didn't know how much I needed it.
*We don't have to do anything you don't want to do.
I'm down for pizza and Mario Kart too
Shout Yes or No if you want to go

Maya couldn't suppress her smile. It was the perfect day. It was all her favorite things: pastry, art, sushi, and a bonfire! She didn't know how Ant had managed that. All without the pressure of too much planning. And she wouldn't feel like she'd wasted the week. Ant knew how she was so much better at recriminating than she was at planning. Plus, nothing on this required a change of clothes or getting super dressed up. He truly had thought of everything. There was only one thing Maya could say. Well, shout.

"*Yes!*"

✑

Once Maya dressed herself in something she wouldn't be ashamed to see on Instagram, she and Ant hopped in the car and headed toward the croissant bakery in East Hampton. Since it was after one o'clock, they also tried the bakery's fancy lunch options, parking themselves in the new outdoor seating.

Ant bit into his *pain au chocolat* and closed his eyes. "I don't think there's anything better in this world." He sighed.

Maya took a bite of her butter croissant and nodded as the pastry crackled into fractals of deliciousness. It was the kind of pastry that made you want to bake. Like the joy of baking itself had been laminated in the dough along with the butter. She smiled at Ant. "If this was the only thing we did all day, it would be totally worth it."

She finished off her dessert and then got back to her salad—it was great to be an adult. Ant finished his sandwich but held his croissant until the end. Then they were back in the car and off to the sculpture garden, which felt made for both of them. Soon she was lying in grass below a massive Buckminster Fuller dome, taking photos of the perforated sky. Ant lay near her with his eyes closed, running his hands through the soft, sun-warmed grass.

"Let's get a pic?" Maya called to him. She saw him nod, eyes still closed.

"As long as I don't have to get up."

She chuckled. "All right, but I call upon the power of your long arms." She stood up and crossed the short bit of grass between them. She settled on him "*An Education*-style" so that their heads were on each other's shoulders while their bodies pointed in opposite directions. Maya opened her camera app and handed him her phone. "Look up but don't smile. I want us to give 'arty independent film.'"

Ant obliged before demanding, "One silly, so all demographics are represented under this dome."

"Okay." Maya laughed. She tilted her head until it bumped his lightly and tried to approximate the classic anime wink–peace sign pose. Then another with her tongue sticking out. She laughed as Ant took a couple more photos and then turned to say something to him—only to find Ant looking directly into her eyes. Suddenly she was aware, in a new way, of how close they'd been this entire time. At this distance she could see that the rims of his glasses were a speckled tortoiseshell, not simply black. The same way his eyes were a rich, fathomless dark brown but would probably be described as black from farther away. This close she noticed the uneven sprinkle of freckles under his eyes: flurries under the left and the beginning of a steady snowstorm under his right, but none on his nose.

Was it weird that neither of them had said anything yet?

"This has been a nice escape from the real world, hasn't it?" Maya said softly, finally looking away from his eyes. She sat up and resettled in a cross-legged position. Ant joined her, and they leaned against each other for a moment, listening to the sounds of the garden.

"Seriously, though, thank you for reminding me that life can be different. This trip got me energized again. I've been spending my bus rides to and from different places looking for jobs and internships. I've got a bunch of stuff I'm ready to apply for back home. This trip has

147

been less of an escape and more of a recharge." He turned and looked at her seriously. "And I owe it all to you."

They were caught in each other's eyes again, but before Maya could say anything, she felt a drop of water hit her right in the middle of her forehead. She looked up and, with a gasp, realized that sometime between their selfie and this conversation, some foreboding clouds had rolled in. More drops came. Maya and Ant got to their feet and exited the dome.

"We'd better get to the car before things get serious."

Ant snorted. "No way this could beat a sudden Honolulu downpour." He took a deep whiff of the verdant petrichor. "I love how it smells right before it rains."

Maya grabbed his hand. "And I love not having a head cold. All this time masking has kept me from getting sick—I don't feel like doing it now. Come on."

Maya yanked, and Ant ran with her. At some point he decided that what their run needed was a soundtrack and began belting out the chorus on "Unwritten"—she was feeling the rain on her skin, after all—an action that was equally confusing and amusing. Maya decided to stop pretending like she was ever too cool for that song (which she definitely was when it came out) and sing along. In the next weeks, next months, maybe even the whole next year, Maya would be letting Emme change her life. This—holding Ant's hand and scream singing some corny song in the rain—was the best way to close the door on everything that had been. Feeling lighter than she had in some time, Maya turned her face up to the rain and kept singing.

Everything else could change but not this, never this.

FALL 2021

9/3/21

Dear God,

I know other people will think it is super weird, but I trust you and truly believe. If you open this door for me, I will walk through.

Gratefully,
Maya

Maya

Maya was standing on the outdoor metro platform, trying not to pace. Early September was still summer in DC, which meant it hit eighty-eight degrees at nine in the morning, with humidity that made you feel as if you were walking through pea soup. She didn't need to be any sweatier, especially when wearing one of her mother's work dresses—a black one with strong shoulders and long sleeves that Momma wore for serious union meetings and hostile parent conferences. It was a dress that meant business, and Maya meant business today.

Her locs were in a low bun. Her feet were in a pair of her sister's black riding boots. She was wearing glasses. She'd even swapped her FUCK THE PATRIARCHY tote bag for one of her dad's sedate messenger bags and a small F%&# THE PATRIARCHY pin.

Today's "interview" seemed to be purely for the benefit of Emme's family friend Nico. He was a bigwig at Vivant and Associates and apparently the only person who could give Emme advice. "Even if I don't listen, I run things by him anyway," Emme had said.

So here Maya was, in her best impersonation of a serious business lady, hoping to hop the last hurdle to her career.

As the train pulled up, Ella's face appeared on Maya's phone screen. She popped in her AirPods and took the first seat inside the blessedly air-conditioned car. "Hey, Mai!" Ella chirped. "Momma told me your big interview is today. And I was like, 'What big interview?' Which is why I'm calling you."

"You would have heard if you weren't so busy working ten-hour days. This was too big to text."

"Fair, but Brexit has made building things really annoying. Enough about that, tell me about the job. And tell me fast. I know you only have like five stops until you're underground."

"I'll give you the short version. I met Emme Vivant at my bookstore this summer, and we became friends. Now she's offering to make me her protégé with a lot of training and job shadowing, ending with an internship at one of the V&A entities . . . which will hopefully end in a job. The position itself is twenty dollars an hour with health insurance on top."

"Emme Vivant of the gentrifying Vivants? Not a judgment, just a fact."

Maya rolled her eyes but nodded.

Ella added, "I'm living rent-free in Camden due to my boyfriend's inherited wealth, so it's not like I'm building barricades and hearing the people sing."

That made Maya chuckle. An electronic voice warned folks to stand clear of the doors, and the train was moving. She gulped. "I'm so nervous. I know she wants to give me the job and it's her decision, but still I have to interview with her family friend."

"Mai, rich people only fear two things: losing their wealth and looking dumb. Once the family friend sees you're not a swindler and not an idiot, you'll be fine."

That actually did make Maya feel better. "Thanks, sis! I love you."

"I love you, too! Good luck."

❧

When Maya arrived, Emme met her at the reception desk, tapping her fob on various security measures as they talked. "We're going up to Nico's office. I sent him a PowerPoint all about you, so he knows how cool you are." They stepped inside the elevator. It was old-fashioned in a way that felt intentional: wood panels, brass, and mirrors. The lobby had a decidedly art deco feel, too. Maya had entered through the side that used to be a Greyhound station in the 1930s.

Nico's office rebelled against the rest of the building's twentieth-century style. His space was all minimalism: concrete, glass, and chromophobia. The man himself was lean but attractive, somewhere in his late forties, with a full head of salt-and-pepper hair and—in Maya's humble opinion—a stick up his butt. Maya hadn't seen a soul since a security guard with cool nails at reception, yet here was Emme's Nico in a full three-piece suit on a ninety-degree day. Even though Maya had to admit he looked dang good in that suit, men like him were the reason office air-conditioning was set at fifty-two and all the women in the office wore cardigans all summer.

"Good morning, Nico. Have you had your coffee, or are you going to be too grumpy to bear?" Emme breezed up to him, and they exchanged cheek kisses in such a stereotypical fashion that Maya had to stifle a giggle.

"I got an iced Americano from Dolcezza and thankfully there was no line, so I drank it there, too." Nico had a European accent Maya couldn't place, staccato in some places and lilting in others. "It made me realize how much I miss Chinatown Tea and Coffee. We're losing so many good cafés." He drummed the table mournfully. "But that is a topic for another time. Maya, it's a pleasure to meet you."

He made a stiff bow before returning to his seat. "I'm afraid our meeting will have to be pretty short. I have a Zoom with the GM of the Chicago Blaze. We're thinking of bringing professional women's soccer to DC."

Maya's eyes widened. They were gonna have to change that name! She knew her dad was not the only one who believed the rumors about Emme's dad and the apartment fire. Emme charged in before she could say something. "You're here, we're here, let's get started."

Nico calmly proceeded to interrogate Maya about her résumé: Why did she start undergrad at twenty-five? What had she learned from her years in the art world? What skills could she bring to Vivant? Typical interview stuff. Maya gave her best responses, but both she and Emme noticed that nothing she said seemed to impress. Nico brought the same enthusiasm to meeting Maya that most tween boys brought to sipping tea with their sisters' stuffed animals. Emme started doing damage control. She gushed about Maya in a way that was almost embarrassing:

"Nicky, did you see the mural Maya did in Seattle?"

"Nicky, did you read that Hawaiian language children's book? Maya did the illustrations!"

"Nicky, did you know Maya is fluent in sign language?! I mean, how cool is that."

"It's clear she has many qualities," he replied with a politeness that told Maya how little those qualities meant to him. "I'm concerned about your lack of corporate experience, Maya."

"That's why she's here to learn, Nicky! You spent most of your twenties packing snacks for grumpy cyclists."

Nico sniffed. "I was a *soigneur* for one of the most important cycling teams in Europe."

"Is that French for *snack packer*? 'Cause all I remember you telling me about was a different way to stack protein bars."

Emme smiled and gave Maya a wink. She clearly valued Nico's opinion, but not enough to listen to whatever objections he'd probably already shared behind Maya's back. That meant the fellowship was truly hers. Emme was showing her that she was willing to stand up for her, too. That was crucial.

At the close of the interview, Nico shook Maya's hand as Emme welcomed her to Vivant and Associates.

"Thank you," Maya said brightly. "And now that I'm part of the team, I'm gonna tell you: if Vivant helps bring the Blaze to DC, you have to change the name."

Both Nico and Emme blinked in surprise. "Why?" Nico asked.

Emme's response was more telling. "But there was an official probe clearing my dad of any involvement."

Maya watched Nico blanch. He'd recovered his cool when Emme looked at him. "I'll have someone on the team look into it."

Maya gave a small shrug but did not back down. "I'm just saying, search 'Vivant+Blaze+DC,' and you'll see the ORM issues."

Nico raised his caterpillary eyebrows, more curious this time. "ORM?"

"Online reputation management. I did all the social media for the Ohana Center—when you're doing youth work, you have to be really careful about your org's online reputation. I took as many free webinars about it as I could find, which was a lot because I still had access to my college library."

Emme was still mildly indignant about anything being negatively associated with her dad. "Changing the name sounds like overkill to me."

Nico tilted his head. "Or simply an abundance of caution." He smiled at Maya for the first time. "And it would do you good to have that around." He elbowed Emme playfully. It was the first indication that he possessed a sense of humor. "Anyway, I have no objections to you, Maya, though I can't speak to the wisdom of this . . . project. Good luck to you."

She returned his smile, a little uneasily. It was good not to be objected to, at least. Emme seemed so pleased that he approved that she wasn't annoyed about Maya possibly speaking out of turn.

Outside Nico's office, Emme wrapped Maya in a big hug. They were doing this! Even if Nico was skeptical, he wasn't hostile. Maya was used to skeptical. That's why she knew what her mom's question would be after she shared the good news.

⚬⚬⚬

"Did you get everything in writing?"

They were in the living room. Maya had found her mom lying in the dark, listening to Nina Simone, when she came home. That meant it had been a particularly rough day in the life of her favorite guidance counselor. She was glad to lighten her mood with the good news.

"Of course, Momma!" That's what Maya had done for most of the last few weeks, over many virtual and in-person coffees with Emme. Every conversation had felt like she'd been offered a magic lamp to wish herself into a new bright future, but she was too old to just say *yes and thank you.* She needed a salary and a job title. They'd eventually landed on "Vivant Futures Fellow."

"I even got the all clear from Gigi." Maya's cousin (an entertainment lawyer, but still a lawyer) had said that things looked fair and flexible for Maya. "She put in a clause that says Emme has to pay me twenty-five thousand dollars if I'm still doing seventy-five percent admin stuff in six months."

Her mom beamed warmly at her. "This is the happiest I've seen you in months! I'm so glad to see your eyes bright again. Sit down here and tell me everything."

They'd work out of Emme's office in the Vivant on New York Avenue. "The building is right next to the National Museum of Women in the Arts—appropriate, right?!" Maya bounced a little as she spoke.

Her mom nodded with a small smile. "You okay working in person?"

"I'm vaxxed up, and I'll be around fewer people in Emme's office than I usually am at Velma's." Maya sat up straight and took a cleansing breath. "I think this will be the start of a new chapter," she said, squeezing her mother's hand.

She was quickly wrapped in a warm hug. "I hope you get everything your Emme is promising and then some!" Her mom gave her a second squeeze for emphasis, reached for her glasses on the coffee table, and put them on. "We need to celebrate! Something big. It feels like we haven't had anything to celebrate for far too long." She was practically vibrating now. "Let's go out to dinner this week! Invite your Hawai'i friend."

Maya blinked in surprise at herself. "I haven't even told him yet! I'm going to text him now." She stood and suddenly felt the oddness of still wearing her mother's clothes. "And change," she added.

She saw her mother reach for her phone and pause. "Would you like me to tell your dad?"

Maya felt her shoulders sag in relief at the offer. "Yes, please." She should have said no. Maya should have been past having her mother fight her battles. Then again, at her big age, she thought she was past the point where her dad should be expressing a hard opinion.

While her mom had generalized reservations about Maya's plan to trust her future to a wealthy stranger (it sounded really bad when you said it like that), her dad had specific grievances with the Vivants—beyond rumors of mysterious and convenient fires. According to her dad, every time a go-go club, a punk club, or a gay club got shut down, you'd see the same banner plastered over the empty windows—VIVANT AND ASSOCIATES—sometimes as early as the next day.

That was true. Well documented, even—Maya had done a little of her own research. But the Vivants had at least built apartments for normal people. They partnered with the city on affordable housing. They created neighborhood-specific scholarship funds. They hired a hundred kids from the DC Summer Youth Employment Program every year. They were nothing like the developers who came later and built four-hundred-square-foot "microunits" and charged two grand a month for the privilege of living in them.

Since new waves of gentrification just kept hitting DC, most of the people who hadn't moved on from hating the Vivants had either left the region altogether or lived in the suburbs. She wasn't going to be the one to point that out to him. On this side of thirty, she understood why people might get a little touchy when forced to acknowledge that the world had forgotten the things they held dear. She chose to not engage and do her own thing. That was growth.

Instead, Maya went to her room and flopped victoriously on her bed. "Yes!" she cried, looking up at her ceiling. "Things are finally changing for the better." She'd felt so stuck for so long, and now she was moving. It was a strange new direction, but she was moving. Progress was progress, right?

Texts from Ella to Maya, September 8, 2021

Ella:

Mai, I've been thinking about your whole work deal.

Let's recap
You: a friendless young woman has a random encounter with a member of the wealthiest family in 100 miles

Maya:

Not friendless, I have Ant

Mostly friendless then

Thank you

Said rich person says I can give you a life you never knew you wanted
And fulfill your wildest dreams
Just agree to dress like I tell you
And do what I ask

Maya:

Accurate, but much creepier
when you put it that way

Ella:

I think I've read this book before . . .

What are you referencing?

You sound like you're
referencing something

Taylor Swift!
And people say I live under a rock

Ella, I've been telling you the
same thing since you were 10.
You can't make me care about

Taylor Swift. You can't make
me care about Twilight
And you can't make me
care about Drake.
I. Just. Don't.

And you call yourself a millennial.

Do I?

Ella:

> Anyway, the song isn't important
> What's important is that
> you know what book
> You're living right now

Maya:

> The first part of 50 shades?

> NO! EMMA!
> You're living Jane Austen's Emma!

> You're Harriet
> The friendless, naive orphan

> How am I naive?

> All normal people are naive about really
> rich people. I'm lucky that Will hates all
> his super wealthy rich friends except Lee.

> These people have never met taxes

> Anyway, you should read Emma

> Absolutely not
> I swore off the 19th
> century books
> AND YOU KNOW WHY!

Ella:

You're never gonna forgive me
for Tess of the d'Urbervilles

Maya:

Never

You could watch the movie version
The most recent one was REALLY good

You know how I feel about period pieces

I can always see slavery in the corners

Can you tell me how things
shake out for Harriet

She comes out okay
But not Because of Emma

An email from Emme to Maya, September 10, 2021

Maya,

Glad to see you're boosted and ready. Since Delta is acting up, I have to be sensible about the wisdom of in-person shopping sprees and hair appointments. Don't worry, we are still doing Montage Week, we'll just be bringing it to my house. I've got air filters in every room and I'll bring everything to us.

My personal shopper has already filled the hallway with three racks of beautiful plus-size clothes, so we'll start there on Monday. Also, I found a highly recommended loctician who does house calls, and an equally fab nail tech who will take care of us on Wednesday. The rest of the week is choosing shoes, accessories, and skin care.

That leads me to another decision. With the current COVID situation, I think it would be best if we worked out of the carriage house on my property instead of Vivant Tower. It'll be ready in about a month. Hope this isn't too disappointing—a whole new wardrobe should make up for it, right?

Bisous,
Emme

Maya

Should you dress up for a makeover?

This was the question that plagued Maya for a full two days before Montage Week arrived. On the one hand, you want to dress to impress on your first day of work; on the other, it would be pretty demoralizing to turn up in her best only for Emme to say, "Yup, it's a teardown."

In the end, Maya decided that she'd bike to Emme's place from the metro in her paint clothes: gray/black overalls too faded to wear most places and a My Chemical Romance T-shirt that was still in the back of the guest room closet somehow. They were clothes that took Maya back to her high school emo phase—which she had (mostly) outgrown. And since she'd bought everything a size too big back in the day, they still fit comfortably for bike commuting.

She finished off her look by putting her locs in a halo braid. It was a style that would fit under her helmet and was kind of a tribute to Emme since she rocked the halo in her TED Talk. If her style wasn't impressive, then arriving via bike would be. Emme and her family lived in Rock Creek Park, a sizable urban forest that occupied a large slice of Northwest DC. The park had several trails, bike paths, and of course, the creek. In some places it was so wild you could almost forget you were in a city. It looked like Emme lived in one of those tucked-away corners, which meant biking or driving.

Biking would show that she was still taking Emme's advice; her new friend was the one who had encouraged her to take up bike commuting when the metro started getting uncomfortably crowded again. Once she looked into it, Maya found a series of trails that took her from Green Park all the way to Velma's in about an hour. When she had the strength for it, the time on her bike was the best part of her day. It was the only time she truly felt free and in control. Rev. Gina was right—God was outside. Occasionally Maya got to meet God there when she was riding.

And with that happy thought, Maya hopped on her bike and rode toward her new future.

∽

> Happy first day, remember:
> she's only rich!
> XOXOXO

Maya smiled at the message from her sister. It would have been more necessary if she were still going to work downtown in the gleaming Vivant Tower on New York Avenue, which towered as much as anything could tower in DC. But while Maya was nervous about starting this off with Emme, she wasn't intimidated.

Until she saw the house.

Maya had not spent much time around rich people, so she wasn't fully prepared when she arrived, by bike, at the Vivant family *mansion*. Her breath caught at the sight of it. The house looked like something out of a fairy tale: it was made of variegated stone with stained glass windows, and a wide curved stairway led to the front door like a red carpet. And there were turrets! Multiple turrets! The house in any other location would have looked ludicrous, but here among the hush of the trees and the crunch of fall leaves, it was glorious.

Suddenly the large front door opened, and Emme came down the curved stone staircase in a periwinkle sweater that was probably made of sustainable cashmere or something, gray slacks, and pristine white sneakers.

"You're here! I'm so excited. And did you bike all the way here? That's amazing!" She clasped her hands together and bounced on her toes in girlish excitement. Maya took off her helmet and was about talk about her experience on the Northwest Branch Trail, but Emme continued. "You and I are sticking to the west wing of the main house, because that has the kitchen and the deck and my suite, where all the montaging will be happening."

Emme placed her hands on the bike's handlebars. "My dad has the east side, which we're trying to keep COVID-free."

Maya let her take the bike and swallowed; she did not want to be the person who accidentally killed Emme's dad. But Emme smiled reassuringly.

"Today is gonna be great!" Emme declared. "Let's head to my room and get started."

⌒∽

It was clear that Emme had not been exaggerating about how much she'd have to choose from. Maya had never seen this many clothing options—in her size—in her life! Online shopping was too expensive in Hawai'i, so she wore what she could find in Honolulu. She'd pretty much lived in stretchy sundresses from the flea market and thrift stores and leggings from Old Navy. Occasionally, when she needed something special, Maya trekked over to Macy's or Torrid and hoped for a sale. She probably had less of her own style during her Hawai'i years than she had in high school; she mostly took what she could get.

Now she fingered the wheeled racks of clothes that lined the hallway from the kitchen to the bedroom. Just from touch, Maya could tell that there was no polyester or rayon to be found. This stuff was *nice*, and everything was in a 20W or a 2x. And there was variety! Sweaters, dresses . . . sweaterdresses! There were pleated skirts, and striped slacks, plus a few shiny jumpsuits. She wasn't going to allow herself to even try and guess the prices or she wouldn't be able to accept any of this.

All the clothes were in earth tones and neutrals, though—mustard yellows, olive greens. The most vibrant they got was a persimmon orange. That part would take some getting used to. Once she'd shaken off her extended goth phase between Oakland and Seattle, Maya had realized that she did like color.

Even if the colors weren't her favorite, the clothes felt incredible. Maya couldn't help but run her hand along the fabrics as she made her way to Emme's room: cool and silky, plush velvet, soft jersey, chunky-knit wool. It only dawned on her at the end of the racks that she'd probably have to try every single thing on. There was no fun way to try on clothes.

"Are you *so* excited?" Emme chirped, materializing in the doorway to her bedroom. Maya jumped but recovered quickly.

"I am excited, but I'm also pretty overwhelmed." She gestured to the racks of clothes behind her. "Emme, this is too much!"

The taller woman gave her a reassuring pat on the shoulder. "Don't worry, I'll only be giving you like half the clothes here, max. Just think of them like a work uniform for now."

Maya released a breath she hadn't known she was holding. She didn't want to admit how worried she'd been about not liking what Emme chose. Her mentor had lost her usual cool and was practically bouncing on her toes. You can't look that kind of enthusiasm in the face and say, "I don't really wear beige."

But if these were her new work uniforms, well, she had worn far worse. Like the polyester pirate-queen getup she'd donned as a sea shanty–singing "bARRtender" at the Rogues' Tavern back in Seattle. That costume had come straight from some Spirit Halloween and felt like it was made of tissue paper and spit. Even that was still better than when she worked at Target in high school. She actually burned her khakis once she was finally able to quit. Emme was not putting her body anywhere near khakis. That thought alone brought a smile to her face.

"What do you think, Maya?" Emme cried, leading her to a closet the size of a studio apartment, only with better lighting and a wall of mirrors. Maya scratched her nose just above her mask and was about to speak when Emme said, "Get down to your skivvies, and I'll get your first outfits," and dashed out of the room.

Maya looked after her mentor for a moment, then turned to her reflection, toed off her Mary Jane Crocs, and slipped off her overalls. It felt odd, taking her clothes off in a strange room that wasn't a doctor's office. Then again, there was no normal way to be in someone else's closet. In the highly illuminated space, Maya's forearms and legs gleamed due to a double layer of lotion and cocoa butter. (What she was *not* going to be today was ashy.) Her T-shirt was next. Maya folded both items and placed them on top of her nearby shoes and gazed frankly at her reflection in the wall of mirrors. Did she look like a project? Or just a jumble of ideas?

Her halo braid seemed oddly dainty in contrast with her tattoos and skull-print undies from the Torrid clearance bin. What would she look like when Emme was done? What parts of her would still make sense?

Maya looked away from her reflection and exhaled. "Whatever happens next," she said quietly, "it will be nice to let someone else make the decisions for a while. God, I'm so tired."

Pandemic life overflowed with decisions, and every one of them felt life or death: Is that cough allergies or COVID? If I test every cough, am I being wasteful or careful? What's safer: taking the subway with a dozen people and social distancing or a Lyft with only one person but he's been driving God knows how many people around in his car all day. Is it moral or immoral to go to restaurants? Concerts? To see a play? There was so much to think about, Maya hardly had room for figuring out her actual life. She didn't mind handing that bit over, just for a little while.

For now, she was determined to learn from all this. Even if the version of herself that came out of Montage Week felt a little more like a stranger than she thought, Maya would know something: a little of what money and time could (or couldn't) do. That itself would be worth learning, and it would help her figure out what to strive for. What beauty meant. What comfort meant. She'd been getting by for so long on the way to her big goal at the Ohana Center, Maya had kinda forgotten what it was like to want everyday things.

Emme returned with an armful of clothes. She handed Maya a caramel-colored jumpsuit.

"It can go with everything, even those rubber shoes—which have to go, sorry. But we can talk more about that later. Right now we've got to figure out your armor."

"Armor?" Maya echoed, stepping into the jumpsuit. She wasn't shy by any means, but it was strange having such a serious conversation in the midst of getting dressed. She slid the jumpsuit up over her torso and put her arms through the sleeves. The fabric felt incredible! She relished the softness as Emme spoke.

"Clothing has always been for protection. From the freezing cold, from the heat of the sun. It's what we use to put a layer between our vulnerable, soft selves and the world. Clothes are a necessity. Style is language. That language is what turns clothing into armor." Emme zipped up the jumpsuit. "And right now, all we want your clothes to say is 'I belong in any room.'"

Emme took a step back and looked Maya over. "To be clear, you'd still *belong* in a sundress and flip-flops, but people can be judgmental pricks. Your armor is so you don't have to waste time explaining." She positioned Maya just so in the wall of mirrors. "What do you think?"

Maya focused on her reflection. The jumpsuit fit well and felt *amazing*, but it seemed more like a canvas than a showstopping outfit. "It looks good, but I need, like a necklace or something."

"I chose a lot of neutrals so you could still accessorize with your style. Like your fun earrings or your head wraps. As an artist—"

"Former artist," Maya interjected. She'd stopped thinking of herself as an artist long ago. It was too stressful.

"Okay, former artist, you have an eye, a way of seeing, that's unmistakably you. These clothes are your armor but also your canvas. Please, keep wearing your awesome earrings and your head wraps. Wear the little things that make you feel good. I'm only trying to make sure everyone can see you."

Maya was still looking herself over as Emme spoke. She could see the vision. The woman in the mirror wasn't so consumed with fulfilling needs that she couldn't think what she wanted. The woman in the mirror lacked for nothing—especially confidence. She didn't need to explain gaps in her résumé; she looked like quality. This new Maya could belong in any room. After all, here she was, in a millionaire friend's home, chatting about clothes, natural as breathing. Maya peered at herself in the mirror, and she liked what she saw. She turned to Emme. "Thank you."

Emme gave her a smile. "It's my pleasure. Try the sweaterdress next."

Ant

Between temp jobs, Ant tried to make sure there was shape to his days. Mornings were for tending the herb garden he'd installed and taking care of Auntie Kay's backyard: trimming the bushes, refilling the bird feeders, turning the compost. Evenings were for walks, now that September had brought back tolerable weather.

The midday hours were for job hunting and laundry: wash, dry, and put away all in one afternoon. He was fastidious about doing everything at once because clothes were otherwise too easily forgotten in the dryer—or worse, the washer. Ant was folding his llama pajamas when his phone chimed with a welcome break from the monotony. He swiped to an email from Rhonda, his Smithsonian boss. The subject read like a fortune cookie or a horoscope: Answer calls from strange numbers: good things to follow.

More confused than anything, Ant opened the email.

Antonio,

I took the liberty of telling a couple of good friends in the plant business about you and handing them your résumé. You should be getting calls this week from Casey Trees about their upcoming internships and the Donwell Family Flowers shop for a full-time job. I know commercial florists aren't what you had in mind, but trust me about TFF, they are an African-American family business. They survived the riots. They pay their people salaries, not merely wages. Also, Toni Donwell has some very cool ideas for the future that I think you might enjoy being a part of.

Anyway, they both should be calling this week. Our loss is their gain.

Good luck to you,

Rhonda

Ant blinked away from the screen. The primary feeling was relief. Rhonda was really looking out for him. In those weeks of silence since his interview, Ant had started questioning everything about his internship experience, especially if Rhonda actually liked him. He *had* made a good impression in his first mainland job. He had mainland references now—well, Rhonda was a singular reference, but she was apparently worth her weight in gold.

☙

A week later Ant had to steady himself as he stood along with Big Tony, a tall stovepipe of a man in ironed khakis and a green polo embroidered with the Donwell Family Flowers logo. They were seated at neighboring park benches down the block from the store's bright-blue storefront. Big Tony didn't fool around with COVID.

"So does Wednesday sound good to you, or would Monday be better?"

Ant straightened and blinked. "Wednesday sounds great, sir."

Big Tony shook his head. "No sir, none of that hierarchical bull. I'm Big Tony or Tony. My daughter, Antoinette, is Toni or Little Toni. The only person with a title is Ms. Maddie, but that's because she's an elder—don't tell her that, though." He finished his thought with a raspy laugh. "Wednesday it is, young man. See you then." With that, Big Tony returned to the store.

Ant could only blink after him until he was alone on the street. He wasn't sure whether he wanted to stand up or sit down. The first thing he did was check his astrology app to see if his moon had suddenly hopped into Jupiter. Things were going too well. Not only was he the interim assistant manager while Little Toni was on maternity leave, but his new job was designed to roll into a new plant nursery manager position in the spring, when the Donwells opened their new location to meet increased demand for locally grown plants and grasses. There was even discussion of a pick-your-own plot and greenhouses in the back; they were still discussing the project, but he would be helping to build it from scratch.

He didn't know what was more invigorating: the creative possibilities of the Donwell Flowers project or how excited Big Tony was about him. And it felt weird to think—even to himself—but he was excited to have a Black boss. In Hawai'i, he'd barely had the opportunity to work with Black people. Let alone *for* Black people. For the first time in his life, he didn't have to worry about trying to appear less scary because he was tall or worry about being called lazy for standing still.

Ant continued down the city street, waiting until he had turned the corner to break out his happy dance. It may have lasted the rest of the block.

As the good news sank in, he could feel the tight coil of worry behind his rib cage finally release. Coming to the mainland was one of the first big decisions he'd made from instinct. Now, after recovering from the summer's setbacks, it felt like his mainland life was finally beginning—for real, this time. He could really start planning his life here.

Ant continued his easy stroll up Fourteenth, sliding off his blazer and draping it over his arm. It occurred to him that he'd barely spent any time in DC since his internship ended. He'd been learning Takoma Park / Silver Spring from the long walks around his aunt's house, but somehow, once he'd started temping, he stopped trying to learn the city. Well, that was changing now. He was going to find a place to celebrate his new job. With tacos, hopefully. Maybe Maya could join him.

He dashed off a quick text.

> Hey friendo, want to meet me for tacos?

He was surprised to get a message back faster than anyone could possibly type.

> Sorry, Ant I'm mid-montage, hair,
> Stuck where I am for the next few hours

Ant deflated slightly at the message and paused next to the empty storefront. He didn't know if it was because he couldn't share his good news with his best friend or because Maya was actually letting herself be changed by someone else. He shook those thoughts off. Ant wanted to keep his good mood going—and didn't want to be alone if he could help it. That's when he remembered the DC Aces chat on the Spark. Ant sent up a signal flare.

> On 14th street. Anyone want to grab lunch outside somewhere? I'm willing to come to you.

❦

Facebook Messenger chat from Maya to her mom, September 14, 2021

FB Messenger

321432.jpg

Maya: This is the new hair!

> **Mom:** Wow!
> **Mom:** It's so different.

Maya: I know, it's wild. I thought we'd go darker, but here we are
Maya: Do you like it? You're the only one in the family with any taste

> **Mom:** I do. I love how curly she got your locs.
> **Mom:** You're VERY blonde. I'm expecting you to start singing about your close personal relationship with diamonds.

Maya: 😄
Emme said I gave her Marilyn Monroe, too.

> **Mom:** Like I said, I like it. It's unexpected.

Maya: I would never have
chosen this for myself, but I'm
really happy with it.
Maya: That's the promise of
makeovers right? Hopefully Emme
can do the same for my career.

Mom: As long as you're happy.

Maya: I'll take being
out of crisis mode
Maya: I am, and you'll be happy
with no rips no tears and no more
crocs with socks

Mom: Wait she killed Crocs?
Hallelujah! Emme is now my
favorite person.

Maya: I barely remember how to
wear real shoes

Ant

He'd gotten only half a block when the moderator of the DC Aces forum wrote back.

Oh dear God, please save me from my apartment

❧

Before long, Ant was sitting cross-legged in the grass of Lincoln Park, waiting for ColorMeSurprised—or as she was known IRL, Mira.

I look like the girls from 'the record player song': blue-green hair, knee-length vintage dress, doc martens, she wrote. My knees are fine though.

It still took Ant longer than it should have to recognize her. "Why did I assume she'd be white?" he chided himself. Mira had deep-brown skin with a hint of copper that, combined with her thick hair and facial features, indicated that she was probably Indian or South Asian. He searched his memory and remembered her saying something about family in Guyana, then mentally kicked himself again for thinking she was white. He set down his grilled cheese and gave her a friendly wave.

"Blackiosaurus!" she cried, waving back. This was why you had to choose usernames carefully—you never knew when someone was going to shout it across a large public park. He stood and dusted the dry grass from his pants, walking to meet her halfway.

"ColorMeSurprised! It's so good to see you! What are you doing these days? Do you hug? Do you high-five? Elbows?" Ant tried to gesture with his take-out container.

"I bow, I've been bowing. I had to pick some way to greet all my clients without inviting touch. For some reason when you do people's hair, they assume you're a hugger."

"Oh wow, you've been able to stay in business? That's great."

ColorMeSurprised pointed to her own hair. "I'm a talented colorist. My clients would rather die than appear anything less than naturally beautiful. We've gotten creative. That's the least interesting thing about me, though. Let's sit."

She nodded to a park bench. Ant wanted to know the *most* interesting thing about her.

"So how did the job interview go?" she asked after a few bites of her salad.

Ant blinked in surprise. "I didn't realize I mentioned it."

"Two days ago you posted about good interview questions to ask. Between that and the fact that you're clearly gussied up, I was able to put two and two together."

Ant chuckled. "You are as smart as you are colorful. The interview went great! I am now the assistant manager for Donwell Family Flowers' garden center. I'm getting to use my horticulture degree and the painful two years I was assistant manager of the last GameStop in Honolulu." He sat up straight and puffed out his chest. "It's like my whole life has been leading up to this."

Mira raised her hand for an air five. "I've heard nothing but good things about them. I think they moved to an equal-salary model during the pandemic—every full-time person makes a minimum of fifty k with health care on top. It was in the *City Paper*."

Ant nodded thoughtfully. "I read that article, but I didn't quite believe it until I got my salary offer. Now I'm thinking of a career with them. Not just a job for a couple years."

Ant hadn't realized that he meant those words until he said them, but it was true. Even though it was early days, with the job in place, he was ready to try and make a home here. He liked DC, and he liked Maryland—heck, he might even like Virginia once he started hanging out with people who didn't grudgingly mumble about crossing the river when the commonwealth was mentioned. He may have followed Maya to come here, but every day he was finding reasons to stay for himself.

"What's that smile?" Mira asked before taking a long sip from the tumbler she brought with her beet salad. "And don't tell me it's about the new job. No one smiles like that about work. Who is that smile about?"

Ant said nothing, frankly shocked that he'd apparently gone so googly-eyed at the thought of Maya that somebody who'd just met him for the first time in real life had noticed.

"Why are you so interested? Aren't you and FLoridaMan1979 king and queen of the aro-aces?"

Mira gave a prolonged roll of her eyes at the mention of FLoridaMan1979. "The only reason I insisted on being the queen of aro-aces is so *he* wasn't the loudest aro-ace voice. I *love* love, even though it's not for me. There's something magical about that kind of human connection."

She took another long sip of her drink. "So I'm going to need you to tell me everything about whoever is making you smile like that."

He couldn't help another smile; he was a visual thinker, and he couldn't think of Maya without seeing her gorgeous face.

"I don't know how to put Maya into words," Ant began, haltingly. "We met in community college. I was nineteen, starting to figure out that I made it through high school by being this sort of vague crowd-pleasing version of myself. Then into my life walks Maya, who was instantly the most authentic person I'd ever met. I remember the front of her hair was in tiny locs like bangs, and the rest was in two afro puffs. She was installing her locs herself, and it was going to 'take as long as it takes.'" He laughed. "She was the first proud Black weirdo I'd ever met—and not just in an 'I like anime and video games' way. She's always just been herself in the most incredible way as long as I've known her. I feel like she was the first person in my life to truly let me be myself. I don't think I would have let myself *be* ace without her, like I'd still be treating it like a problem to solve."

Mira nodded. "That's awesome. She sounds like an amazing, inspiring friend. But that's not what's making you smile . . ."

"Oh, you want me to tell you the embarrassing shit, like how she has the most amazing eyes—they're dark brown but have this honey glow. And when she looks at me, it's all I can do not to melt," Ant finished with his face in his hands.

Mira let out a hoot. "That's the shit! Inject it into my veins!" She rocked back and clapped giddily. "So are you going to do anything about it?"

Ant shrugged. "It just doesn't seem smart. For one, we're both trying to build our new lives right now. For two, I've never had a relationship while being fully aware of my ace-ness. It feels like I shouldn't experiment with the most important relationship in my life until I know what I'm doing there. Right?"

He'd looked for advice on ace/allo relationships before. Most of what he'd found had been written for married cisgender couples and was focused on comforting the confused allo partner. Nothing to help him and Maya start something new together. So what would they do if they fell in love—but were sexually incompatible? Would that just be it? He suppressed a shudder at the thought. Better to wait until some nice ace/allo couple wrote a book or started a YouTube channel. He needed a role model.

Mira tilted her teal head one way, then the other. "Perhaps, but the most important thing is having a partner who understands you and respects you. That sounds like your Maya all over. It seems too perfect *not* to go for." Ant felt Mira's words reverberate. She was right. And he knew she was right. That meant, despite his worries, he needed to scrape together some bravery and act. There was only one response to this revelation: Ant let himself dramatically flop back on the bench with a small groan. Mira slipped her mask on and gave him a sympathetic pat. "Let me know what you decide."

Ant nodded wearily. "So, can we talk about anything else?"

She smiled hugely under her mask. "Absolutely. Now that we're deeply bonded, can I tell you about the D&D campaign I am currently on? Because I need to vent."

❧

Mira was officially a con artist or a hypnotist, or both. Even though Ant had been skeptical about being nerd enough for D&D, somehow he'd agreed—with very little prodding—to be the tavern keeper at their next . . . match? What were rounds of Dungeons and Dragons called, anyway?

There was a wizard, a data analyst by day, who had decided he was the main character despite everyone in the group stating that he very much was not. He was derailing the journey and being kind of a dick. Ant's role would be to ask questions of the game's—the quest's?—members, ask to hear of everyone's adventures, and remind this wizard that he was one of six. Ant was up for it. People thought that just because he had a sweet face, he was afraid of conflict, but he had a gift for murdering with words that he tapped only on special occasions.

Worse than agreeing to be Mira's insult assassin, Ant couldn't get her advice out of his mind. He needed to tell Maya his feelings before they become a weird point of dishonesty between them. If he waited, his crush (love) would turn into the dreadful pathetic pining that never gets resolved and overwhelms a relationship. He was going to do it; he was going to do it before he lost his nerve. He just had to figure out how.

Maya

On Wednesday Maya woke to the staccato drum of heavy fall rain. She sighed; she wasn't physically or emotionally prepared to cycle to Emme's in the rain. She stretched and sat up with a lion's yawn, which was interrupted by a knock at the door. She tried to say "come in" while wrapping up her yawn. The sound she made wasn't quite words but did the trick, as her dad came in bearing coffee.

"Good morning, Sprout. I thought you might need some help getting out of bed on your first real cool rainy day since being back." He dropped his voice. "You didn't really leave the house in April, so you might have forgotten that transitional period that comes with four seasons."

Maya took the proffered mug from her father and squeezed his hand. It obviously pained him to remember the time of the octopus. It hurt her, too—and scared her. Which was why she was very glad to have a job she was excited to go to every day. As much she'd liked Velma's Books, it was only four days a week, and no introvert thrived in a retail setting. She wasn't shy, but she found lots of people exhausting. Working for Emme was nice because she only had to care about one person. She could do one-on-one all day long.

"I got in after you went to bed last night," her dad continued. "Had *our show* all to myself."

"Not cool, Daddy." Maya chuckled. "That's what the DVR is for," she chastised. "So you can wait for me."

She'd gotten more used to this new version of her parents. She and her dad had started watching *The Bachelorette* together because it had a Black-lady lead and they wanted to support her. Maya couldn't say if it was good or bad, but it was compelling.

"So . . . can I see?" Her dad pointed to his own head and waggled his eyebrows.

Maya nodded and reached for her Loc Soc tentatively. She was sure that as soon as she touched her head, all her locs were going to fall off. No living thing should be able to survive being so thoroughly stripped of color. She slid her scarf off and ran her hands over her hair. It felt . . . okay. Good, actually. It was soft and not too dry. She risked a look at her dad. He'd lifted his glasses and was rubbing his eyes like an old-school cartoon character.

"*Whaaat?!*" He rocked back. Maya shook out her hair, giving the full effect of the shorter, much blonder look. "Let me stop playing. It looks good. It looks nice. I was afraid it would be Lil' Kim in the nineties, but it's more like Solange . . . recently."

That made them both laugh, but then her dad got serious again. "Maya, you should know I may not be a fan of the Vivants, but I'm a big fan of you. And I'm here to support you any way I can as you try this big new thing. I like seeing you happy, and this is making you happy, so that's it."

The words warmed Maya more than the coffee could dream of. "Thanks, Dad. It means a lot." She leaned over and gave him a big hug. "Would support by any chance include a ride into DC? I'm still avoiding the subway."

Always expressive with his glasses, Maya's dad moved them down his nose to give her a semi-stern look, which he turned into a smile. "We leave in forty-five minutes," he said, rising and walking to the door.

"Thanks, Dad," she called after him. Hopefully, that gave her enough time to take care of the delicate Fabergé egg she had placed on her head—bleached hair was so delicate! According to her stylist, Maya's new hue meant that she needed to triple down on moisture/maintenance. This felt a touch ironic since she'd installed locs all those years ago so she wouldn't have to think too hard about caring for her hair. But she had promised Emme she would put in the work if Emme provided the vision, and that work apparently included a regimented beauty routine.

⁊

When she arrived for the day's improvement, Emme shared the best news since she'd given Maya the job. The designer was almost finished, and they would be working out of the carriage house starting in a couple of weeks. Maya was elated (and relieved) about the change in location. While getting her hair done on the deck had been delightful, hanging out in Emme's bedroom was beyond stressful. Everything seemed to be either two hundred years old or $2,000. It was like being in a museum but with no labels or glass cases. Yesterday she had picked up what she *thought* was one of many souvenir replicas of a Jeff Koons balloon dog in the world and said, "Oof! That's heavier than it looks."

"Oh yeah. The real ones are coated in porcelain," Emme said, as if she were talking about the weather and not a $20,000 piece of art.

Maya swallowed and gently set the statuette back on the desk.

She couldn't sit anywhere, either. Emme's bed was out because of common decency—this wasn't a sleepover—and the only other seating in the bedroom she could see was a pair of beautifully hand-painted alpine twin beds that some designer had accentuated with fluffy pastel cushions.

Emme sat on the one closest to the french doors. She patted the space beside her.

Rationally, Maya knew that the antique beds were much stronger than the best stuff on the market today, but she could take in only half of what Emme said as she talked about their plans for the day. Maya was too busy listening for creaks from the bed beneath her. It was too easy to imagine the beautiful antique cracking beneath her weight.

Thankfully, today Maya noticed the sturdy, stylish, wide-bottomed chair in front of Emme's makeup table.

Today was Nail Day. She was getting a "boring gel manicure" so her hands would be their most "presentable." Apparently, trimmed and unpainted wasn't enough. Maya didn't even bite her nails.

"When you're trying to move up in the world, you should never look like you need money," Emme explained, shifting on her giant bed. "Clean, unvarnished nails look like you're economizing. Same with cheap shoes. People with money like to give money to people who don't need it."

Maya looked at her hands, perplexed. "That's wacky." *And kind of messed-up,* she thought.

Emme shrugged and gave a half smile. "That's the nice thing about being rich—you're not obligated to make sense."

Thing was, it made perfect sense to Maya. She'd worked for enough crappy chain restaurants and aggressively awful bars to know that some small-business folks thought they were God on Earth for their ability to make money and hang on to it—as though it came from ancient and deep wisdom instead of luck and complete disregard for their employees. Maya would bet good money that people like that viewed having money as a virtue, and trusted people with it—or the appearance of it—without thinking.

And that's how rich people got taken in by big stupid scams like Fyre Festival.

And yet, despite knowing all this, Maya couldn't help feeling newly self-conscious about her hands.

Emme sat down on her bed, sipping her breakfast through a metal straw and tapping an odd staccato beat with her foot. She blinked at her phone, then frowned.

"What is it?" Maya tried to look sympathetic while holding herself very still. She tended to talk with her hands, but that seemed dangerous with thousands of dollars in skin care products and custom-made cosmetics behind her.

Emme sighed with deep irritation. "It's the lady coming to do your nails, Angie Bates. I. Can't. Stand. Her."

"Old nemesis?" Maya offered.

Emme shook her head. "Her niece is, though," she said with a tart little laugh.

"But back to the nail lady, what's wrong? Queerphobic? Fatphobic? Mean?"

Emme shook her head again and drummed her fingers on her comforter. "She's simply exhausting. But she's an old friend of the family. Her dad was the Rev. Dr. Theodore Bates." There was a brief pause for recognition before Emme went on. Maya made a note to herself to look up any famous DC Bateses when she had a moment alone. Maybe she'd ask her dad about them on the ride home.

"Rev. Bates married my parents. First Lady Bates was basically like my surrogate grandma since my dad's mom was racist and my gran Magi was still in Sweden. Nana Bates was a combo of Aunt Viv mixed with . . . the grandma from *Gilmore Girls*, but with Jesus." Emme looked out the window again and began texting and talking simultaneously. "The rain's stopped; we'll get everything set up outside. Ms. Angie will be here to do our nails."

She pinched the bridge of her nose. "If you can help it, please don't bring up the Peace Corps, Portugal, or anything about living abroad. Stick to that and you may get your nails done without us getting our ears talked off."

❧

Turned out, all it took to get Angie Bates talking at length was having an Uber driver who briefly refused to turn up the Vivants' long driveway. Maya couldn't help but giggle as she heard the older lady bulldoze over any attempts Emme made to keep her from talking as they approached the deck from outside.

"I'm so sorry I'm late, Emme," she began, her wooden bangles clacking fretfully.

"You're not late—" Emme began.

"Would you believe that man wanted me to walk up that hill at my big age?" Angie continued. "He said that the house wasn't on his GPS. *I* said, 'They like it that way, but there's a house up there.' He said he didn't want to get stuck. *I* said, 'I've been visiting this house for over twenty-five years. They have a turnaround and a garage.' Then he said the exercise would be good for me. I said, 'Sir, I know I look young but not that young.'"

"No need to explain," Emme cut in. "You're here. And you're doing me a favor."

Angie waved away the compliment. "As much as your family has done for the community, of course I'm saying yes—whoa there." Angie's high wedge boots wobbled a little in the gravel.

Emme offered her arm. Maya could see she was wheeling Angie's bright-pink hard-shell suitcase behind her.

"Thank you, Emme. I know you have that core strength from that ballerina exercise you like. Did you know that they don't call Vivant Tower *Vivant Tower* anymore? They call it *V Tower*. I mean, yes, the *V* is big, but *Vivant* is on the sign. People don't pay attention; everything has to be obvious. Oh, hello!"

The lady was *auntie* personified. She had a sizable auburn Afro wig that was halfway between Kelis and Chaka Khan. She wore a ruffled jumpsuit with a wide black belt, and her wedge heels and chunky statement necklace sparkled in the intermittent sunshine. There was something so sweetly familiar about her that Maya had to smile.

She came down the deck stairs and took the handle of the suitcase from Emme. "Hi, I'm Maya. Emme's protégé."

Angie gave the briefest of nods before shifting her attention back to Emme. "Look at you, growing talent like you talked about in your book. You don't talk about it, you be about it, like our Jazzy." The older lady stopped short. "You know she's back home with us for a bit."

Maya saw Emme's eye twitch distinctly. Angie didn't seem to notice, though, and Emme recovered quickly, pretending to be fascinated with the upper branches of a distant tree.

"Is she?" Emme inquired. She was clearly shooting for uninterested without being palpably rude. "I thought she was out in California working in TV."

Angie, clearly too thrilled with her subject, carried on as if Emme were fascinated.

"Apparently COVID has slowed things down a bit, so she's staying with us while she's between projects. Babygirl is already brightening up the place. Unfortunately, she can only stay for six months because she's under fifty-five."

Emme frowned again. "I thought you were still at the darling little house behind the Gideon AME?"

A small sad smile crept over Angie's face. "I wish, but after Daddy died, Momma agreed to sell the house to the church for a rectory. They'd been letting us stay in it until they called a pastor who wanted to live there. Momma had a little apartment not too far from the church, and the older members were looking out for her. And thank God, because someone was around to notice her getting confused and forgetting things and told me that I needed to come home—anyway, we got a nice two-bedroom in the Fairfax senior community. It took every penny we had left to get in there, but they've got great memory-care specialists, so totally worth it. You know how hard that can be."

Emme coughed and turned away. "Why don't you get set up? We're a little behind. I have to go make a phone call." And with nothing more than that obvious lie, she strode into the house.

Angie, who didn't seem to notice Emme's change in mood, opened her bag with a series of clicks. The suitcase transformed into an elegant nail stand. "All right, Miss Maya. Sit down, I'm ready to work."

By the time Emme returned, Angie had shaped Maya's nails and trimmed her cuticles.

Emme smiled at her, then glanced at Maya's phone. "Oh! Someone sent you a video."

Maya smiled. "That's probably Ant. He's always sending me something funny or wholesome. You can push play."

Emme obliged. "I hope it's a kitten befriending a seal or something adorable like that." She shoved a lock of bright-red hair behind her ears and sat in the neighboring chair, turning the phone and her body toward Maya, and pressed play.

Suddenly her screen was full of Ant from the waist up. Before he even spoke, Maya had the sense something was off.

"Hiya, Maya." She could hear his voice was tight. "I have something I'd like to say, so I ask for your patience."

Then he reached off-screen and grabbed a stack of poster board. That was the last moment in 2021 that anything in Maya's life made sense.

Ant

I SHOULD START WITH A CONFESSION

I DIDN'T COME TO THE MAINLAND FOR A BIG FANCY
INTERNSHIP

I CAME BECAUSE I COULDN'T IMAGINE BEING BACK
HOME WITHOUT YOU

AND I COULDN'T STAND SEEING YOU CRY

WHEN I COULD DO SOMETHING

SO 5,000 MILES AND 6 MONTHS LATER

I HAVE TO ACKNOWLEDGE THE TRUTH

YOU ARE THE MOST WONDERFUL WOMAN IN THE
WORLD

AND I LOVE YOU

I JUST THOUGHT YOU SHOULD KNOW

AND I'M HERE IF YOU WANT TO TALK ABOUT IT

YOURS (IF YOU'D LIKE), ANTONIO

Maya

During Maya's sophomore year of high school, her English teacher assigned a public speaking project. The piece had to be at least three minutes long and not a song. Always one to slightly bend the rules, Maya focused on recitation. She decided to memorize the "Wear Sunscreen" speech by Mary Schmich.

Half the fun was telling the turtleneck-wearing faux intellectual two desks over that Kurt Vonnegut had nothing to do with the essay. Turned out, all that advice came to Maya at exactly the right time. When the economy tanked in the fall of her senior year, it became clear that Mary Schmich was right: the only thing you could count on in this world was sunscreen.

She was also right that the things that rock your world don't come with bells and whistles; they come with a phone some quiet afternoon. For a moment Maya couldn't hear anything. There was a thundering in her ears that she soon realized was her own heartbeat. Or perhaps that was the blood rushing to her ears.

"Is that 'The Only Exception'?" Emme asked.

Maya hadn't even clocked that Ant had chosen Paramore's most romantic song for his background music. As it played softly, Ant revealed his feelings. Maya could only read the cards and watch in silence.

Emme sighed at the end of the video. "That was so sweet. Even though Hayley wrote that song for her ex, the song is still nice."

Maya couldn't process anything—because Ant was in love with her. She repeated the words slowly in her mind: *Ant* loved her, was in love with *her*.

Simply thinking those words felt like lying in the grass in early summer before mosquitoes and humidity chased most folks inside. His words were sunlight and warmth; they made Maya want to find Ant wherever he was and kiss him until neither of them could breathe.

But what did it mean? What did any of this mean? This wasn't something she'd hoped for, but now fully facing it, it . . . wasn't unwelcome. She hadn't been in a relationship with a cis man since, what, Seattle? But honestly that was more a reflection on the other men in her life. Some women held their dads up as the ruler to measure all other men, but Maya's standard was Ant.

This meant that anyone wanting to date her had to be curious, kind, funny, smart, antiracist, feminist, comfortable in queer spaces, comfortable in Black spaces, considerate, and a little bit of a weirdo. Most dudes fell down at the most obvious hurdles. Not that there was a stampede of men thundering after her all the time, but there had been interest from uninteresting quarters. Could she honestly say that she wasn't into him, at least a little? Not when so much of her soul seemed to be shouting yes.

Yes, at the words *I love you*, Maya's eyes did fill with happy tears. Yes, there was a sudden burst of warmth that radiated out from her chest to her toes and her newly manicured fingers. Did a voice in her head immediately shout the last line of *Ulysses*, a book she did not enjoy but somehow ended up quoting? Well, yes.

In the midst of this churn, it took Maya a moment to register that Emme was still talking. "I know people say to respond in the same medium you receive something, but I think you have to send an email. He is your best friend?"

"What?" Maya replied faintly. She felt dizzy, like she'd hopped off an old-fashioned merry-go-round and the world was coming back into focus.

"Turning him down by text is going to sound so cold, no matter what you actually say. Email is kinder—and there'll be no back-and-forth."

Maya blinked. "You think I should turn him down?"

Emme sat up and recrossed her legs. "Of course! That wasn't your first thought?"

This seemed to be too much for Angie, who'd finished coating Maya's pinkie nail with a final layer of topcoat. "Why would she turn him down?" She transferred Maya's hand to the little tanning bed thing to dry her nails. "That is the cutest thing I've ever seen."

Angie turned to Maya with serious eyes. "He is one of the good ones. If you find a guy like that, you hang on, no matter what. That's what my momma would say. She and Daddy were married for fifty years, and she loved him till his very last day."

Maya was watching Emme closely. Her mentor's eyes flicked from her hand to Angie with the tiniest glint of annoyance. "Angie, would you check Maya's thumb? I think there's a little ripple."

Emme tapped the questionable place on her own nail. Angie lifted Maya's and gasped. "This is what happens when you multitask," she chided herself, wetting a cotton pad with remover.

Maya felt like she was underwater. Her face mask suddenly felt tight, like it was pulling at her ears. It felt wrong to take it off since Angie was required to be so close to her—a little gross and Karenish— but suddenly the mask was suffocating. She turned away from watching Angie repair her thumb to Emme, who sat cross-legged in the matching chair that had been pulled six and a half feet away. Her mentor had stopped typing and was scrolling through Maya's phone with a fiercely focused expression. Maya couldn't quite bring herself to interrupt her— even though it was very much her phone.

"How . . ." Maya swallowed, trying to keep the tremor she felt out of her voice. "Why turn him down?" Her mind was still spinning, but her heart was pulling her toward him. How was Emme so certain that this was—that she and Ant were—a definite no?

"It's just . . . I think you're on opposite escalators." Emme bit her lip, unsatisfied.

Since they'd begun working together, Maya had noticed that when Emme gave advice, she talked like she'd inevitably be quoted. She was silent for a moment, likely choosing the best words in her head. "You're on an elevator, but he's on a moving walkway. That's gonna cause friction. When you date, you need to choose someone who is headed in your direction." Emme gestured upward at a sharp angle, blue cashmere shifting on her arm.

She returned to the phone. Maya noticed that she'd found Ant's TikTok and was clicking through his videos with an alarming speed. Maya couldn't help but watch her to ensure Emme's head didn't suddenly pop off. It was quiet on the deck, just the breeze through the trees and Angie's low humming of some distracted tune. Emme's voice somehow sounded very loud when she spoke again, cool but firm. "Looking at his socials and he seems more excited about getting this job at Donwell Family Flowers than he was getting the Smithsonian."

Maya shrugged as Angie moved her hand with the repainted thumb to the portable tanning bed thing to dry (she guessed) her nails. "I mean, accurate. He's happy to have this job and happy to not be temping. He *was* probably twice as glad to land this gig."

Ant had radiated joy when he FaceChatted Maya to tell her about the job. He was visibly lighter, with a relief that Emme could never understand. But Maya knew there was nothing to be gained by reminding Emme that she never had to worry about whether she'd get paid from week to week. She had enough trouble getting Emme to understand why she had no intention of going for an MFA, regardless of her "potential."

Angie made a small, distressed noise, then patted the top of the nail dryer and said, "You're all done, hon." She stood, with a noisy stretch that made her wooden bangles clatter. Turning her back to Emme, she packed away her tools of the trade slowly. The older lady may have been chastised by Emme, but Auntie Angie had no problems disagreeing—or obviously eavesdropping.

"The Smithsonian is a DC institution," Emme continued.

So is Donwell Family Flowers. Maya shook her head. Sometimes it was hard to believe that Emme was a true DC native. For all of Maya's childhood, she'd seen the store's round paper fans in every Black church she'd visited south of Baltimore and north of Richmond. Maya had probably fanned herself with dozens of them when she took gospel choir in high school for the "easy A." She'd ended up spending more weekends on the road than her school's marching band, singing in random churches. But there were few things she liked more than singing gospel in a choir. That and her deep love of Paramore were probably the Blackest things about her.

Emme was still talking, this time with a softer tone. "Don't get me wrong, your guy seems very sweet. I'm scrolling his TikTok feed. I see he plays ukulele. And trombone. And accordion—very impressive. He appears to be a real feminist—I mean, he's not posing as one to get laid, right?" She laughed, pointing to a video labeled "Ant Gets an Ace Ring."

Then Emme frowned. She twisted that same rogue curl around her index finger. "So he's asexual . . ."

Maya nodded.

"And you're not?" Emme asked, pitching up her voice delicately.

"Very not," Maya agreed.

"Look, it's a beautiful thing that we as queer people get to make our own rules, but . . . do you want to?" Emme went still and thoughtful again. "Do you think you have the bandwidth for a complicated relationship right now? Whatever relationship you two could have is gonna be super complex, more than either of you are anticipating. Isn't your life hard enough? We're trying to figure out the third act of your career right now. Heck, we're only on day three of Montage Week."

And just like that, the voice in Maya's heart that had been singing *yes* over all Emme's objections went silent. She suddenly realized there was a lot she didn't know about her best friend. Was Ant sex-repulsed? Was he open to non-monogamy? There was so much to figure out. Even if they did—and if they both wanted this—wouldn't she just screw things up? What if she ended up being too clingy? What if she drove him away? Could she handle somehow losing Ant the way she'd just lost the job and the home that she loved?

Emme sensed a shift and pressed. "Look, you have to be the best judge of your own happiness, so just sit still for a moment and ask the little voice inside: Do you have space in your life, right now, to make this relationship work?"

The *no* in her head was instantaneous. Maya knew she was not emotionally prepared for a relationship after she had only just started feeling like . . . well, not quite *herself*, but more than the hollowed-out husk she'd become after the twin disasters of eviction and fire.

"I can't say yes." Maya sighed, wringing her freshly manicured hands. There was too much to risk, not just screwing up her only friendship, but possibly messing up this astounding opportunity with Emme if she got distracted. "But I don't know how to say no."

Emme stood in stoic compassion. "Let me draft something for you. You can save your courage for emailing it later."

Maya felt frozen as she watched Emme begin typing—on her phone. She couldn't will her to stop, but did she actually want Emme responding for her?

Angie cleared her throat, shaking Maya out of her thoughts. "My Uber's arriving in five. Would you help me get this big block of bubblegum down the steps?" She gave her hard-shell suitcase a friendly rap.

"Of course!" Maya chirped, hopping up quickly, like she'd been caught napping. She didn't want to think about what Emme was writing. Instead, happy to have something to do, she grabbed the suitcase by the handle and headed to the stairs.

Angie was close behind, holding on to the banister as she descended. "These are supposed to be my comfortable shoes." She sucked her teeth and stepped carefully. "I would say that the *pandemmy* made me forget how to walk in heels, but I've been doing house calls since June 2020."

They crunched in the gravel at the bottom of the steps. Maya moved to offer her arm, but Angie waved it away. "Honey, I may be your elder, but I'm not actually elderly. Social Security ain't even kicked in yet—but you can still wheel my bag over to the driveway as a sign of respect." Angie elbowed Maya lightly, a wink in her whole being. Once they reached the flagstones, Angie's gait turned into a Naomi Campbell strut that carried her to the driveway. It was all Maya could do not to wolf whistle.

Angie was taking a call from her driver when Maya and her suitcase pulled alongside her. "No. I reject that. I rebuke—no. I will not. Sir—sir—you must drive up the hill. Sir—sir—I put it in the notes field as requested by my—yes. Up the hill. I will be waiting. Thank you." Angie disconnected with a small smile. "That was easier than I thought."

Maya couldn't help a giggle. "It was lovely meeting you. I really like my nails."

Angie beamed. "Wonderful! Let Emme know. Hopefully I'll see you again in two weeks."

"Two weeks?" Maya echoed. "That seems soon."

Angie shrugged. "Your average lady might stretch to three weeks between appointments, but Emme"—Angie's eyes drifted over the massive house—"has no reason to economize."

"Huh. I don't know how *not* to economize." Was she responsible for paying for her nails every other week? She was making more money than she had in her life, but how much was she expected to spend? Maya had to make sure she rejected any clothes that were dry-clean only, but she hadn't asked Emme about how much the rest of her new life would cost to keep up. "I don't think I signed up for all this," she grumbled. Then she shot a quick glance at Angie, hoping that she hadn't heard. Fortunately for her, the manicurist was fully occupied waving at the car coming up the drive.

As the car pulled to a stop, the older woman turned toward her with a surprisingly serious expression. "Have something on my spirit, so I'm gonna say it: you can close a door without slamming it, and you never go wrong with a handwritten note." With that, Angie and her pink suitcase were in the car, then gone.

Ant

The letter came the day after Ant's big declaration. He'd been pretty well distracted by his first day of work—he hadn't met so many people at once since the summer: the older ladies, who took phone orders and worked with the funeral homes; the flower artists who did all the arrangements; the delivery guys who drove the van. Ant had been pleasantly overwhelmed until Big Tony came to him at the end of the day to make him plain-old discombobulated.

"During our interview, I remember you saying that were gonna buy a car this month. I also know you have a good strong back, so I have a proposal: How would you feel about working out on our Christmas tree farm in Centerville? I know it's a lot to ask, but it would be a great opportunity for someone with your interest in North American trees. We'd house you, and of course we'd boost your salary for those preparation months. And you'd only have to be out there until mid-November. Our clients are going to be setting up their tree lots after Thanksgiving."

Ant looked at Big Tony in open-mouthed shock.

The older gentleman held up his finger. "Don't answer yet. Let me send you all the details, and you can let me know how you feel this time tomorrow." With that, Big Tony walked away, leaving a seriously perplexed Ant behind him.

∽

He'd been the first one home, so he was able to snatch the pale-blue envelope from that day's mail before anyone asked any questions. The letter had obviously been dropped off by hand since the envelope only read *Antonio* in beautiful calligraphic script.

Ant sat on the edge of his twin bed, holding Maya's letter and twisting the corner of the comforter in his hand. His finger traced over the elegant lilting *A*, one he knew she'd practiced over and over when she decided to make certificates for her students who passed their GEDs, one of her little gestures to show she cared. He knew Maya's answer before he read whatever was in the envelope. He was getting gently, lovingly turned down.

He swallowed hard and swayed with a sudden heaviness in his body. It felt foolish, but he'd hoped . . . he'd really hoped. The idea of them together had been this beautifully shining thing right before his eyes. Deep down, he'd thought, if he just got the courage to say how he felt . . . well, if anyone could figure out the rest, it was him and Maya. Now that dream was gone. The only question left was whether it was ever more than a dream in the first place.

"Might as well get this over with," he said aloud, unsealing the envelope with his thumb. Now it was just a matter of finding out whether his declaration had done any damage to their friendship.

My Dear Antonio,

I don't think I've ever received a more romantic gesture than the one you just gave. Your care and thoughtfulness were evident in everything from the song you chose to the words on the posters. Truthfully, my heart soared when you told me you loved me. I wanted to say fuck everything else, run to you, and figure everything else out later.

But a bigger part—a sadder but wiser part of me— knows that I'm not whole now. And I know you, Ant. If we got together, you would devote yourself to fixing all my broken pieces, whatever the cost, and that's not the kind of relationship I want. A friend recently told me that I have to be the best judge of my own happiness. Right now, I know that while I can easily see getting together and making things work, I can just as easily see everything crumbling under the weight of our present circumstances, so I can't return your feelings now.

I'm so sorry to disappoint you and I hope I haven't lost my best friend in all this. You are the dearest person in the world to me. Please do whatever you need to do in response to this. I understand if you need time and/ or space.

Sincerely,
Maya

Even though he'd known what was coming, Ant couldn't help but feel the sting of Maya's thoughtful rejection. It was both better and worse than he'd thought. She didn't say his asexuality was a stumbling block (good), she wanted to run to him (great), but she felt too broken for a relationship (bad, like years of therapy bad).

Ant put the letter on his bed and ran down the steps.

∽

Later that night, Ant sat on the front porch of the house and made a phone call—he didn't think he could look Maya in the face right now. She answered at the first ring.

"Hey." She sounded warm but hesitant. "I take it you read the letter—it's that or you're literally on fire right now, because you hate the phone."

They both gave little obligatory laughs. For a brief second, Ant thought he could pretend that he'd never sent that video. That things didn't have to change. That she didn't say no. He bit his lip. "I did. Thank you for taking everything so seriously." Ant's face suddenly felt warm, and before he knew what his legs were doing, he began to pace the length of the creaky front porch. Apparently he was going to try and channel all his nervousness into his feet instead of his voice. "I'm glad I didn't ruin everything between us."

Ant heard Maya exhale. "Of course not. You are still the best man I know. I would never throw away our friendship—even if things are a little awkward for a while. And if you need to hang out less or you want me to text less, I understand."

He swallowed hard. "I think I will need that."

"Okay."

There was a long pause. Neither of them seemed to know what more to say. Part of Ant wanted to ask what "friend" gave her the advice in her letter—but if he knew for sure, he might have to respect Maya a little less.

Ant coughed. Maya waited. Every second on the call grated like sandpaper. Never, not since the day they met, had conversation been this awkward between them. "I'm glad we had a chance to talk, Maya. Thank you, again, for the letter. I gotta run."

"Wait! Do you want to make plans for later in the fall? We could do some corny stuff like go apple picking in October."

Ant could hear the hopeful note in her voice. He wanted to say yes, but the thought of seeing her made him want to cry. Ironic, since only a few months ago, he'd followed her five thousand miles because the thought of *not* seeing her made him want to cry. Suddenly, another choice he had to make became a lot easier.

"My new job needs me to help with the Christmas tree farm in Virginia . . . so we won't be able to see each other for a while. And I think my signal down there might be spotty."

"Oh." There was a long silence. "Well, you're gonna miss the big conclusion of Montage Week. Emme's really pulling out all the stops."

Ant tried to swallow his irritation at the mention of Emme flippin' Vivant. Wanting to ask if all these makeovers came with a brainwashing, he instead said the sincerest thing he could think of.

"It sounds like she wants to change a lot. I hope I recognize you when I get back. Aloha, Maya." Ant disconnected before an apology could slip out. That wasn't the nicest thing to say, but he didn't feel like being nice—at least not on the subject of Emme. Then he sent a text to Big Tony.

> Sign me up for Centerville
> Looking forward to trying
> something new

He marched himself to his room. Maybe if he started packing he could get his mind off Maya for a while. Probably not, but it was worth a try.

Maya

The morning began with face masks in Emme's bedroom, which was helpful because Maya had cried a lot more than she'd expected to in the last twelve hours. Emme either didn't notice or was trying to save her the embarrassment of explaining why she looked so tired and drawn. Instead she said, "Today we shall focus on the foundation of beauty, which really starts mattering once you're out of your twenties."

Maya had never done a face mask—or any skin care more complicated than Noxzema in the morning and Pond's at night. Everything felt new and mildly ridiculous. Or maybe that was just her bad mood. They were sitting in Emme's bedroom, each seated on one of those alpine beds turned benches. They were unmasked and six feet apart, with the air filter on high—arranged so they could still catch both of their reflections in the wings of the large trifold mirror on the vanity. Emme was demonstrating how to apply these gold, sticky things under her eyes that promised to "brighten and reduce fine lines."

"Going through the Trump years and a global plague, we should all look like those dust bowl migrants from Dorothea Lange photos. But we don't have to . . . thanks to the multistep skin care routine."

Maya had gotten her under-eye masks out of the package, wondering at how unnaturally cool they felt, when Emme asked how things had gone with Ant. So she had to stick these things on her face, somehow maintain a conversation, and not cry—again. Cool. Cool, cool, cool.

"How did he take it?" Emme asked gently, while somehow effortlessly applying the gold commas in under a minute.

Maya watched her in the mirror and applied her masks while tilting her face up to keep them from slipping. "He took it well, I think. We were able to talk on the phone not long after he got my message, and I think we left things in a good place. He needs some space, but we're not losing each other." That was the most important thing: Ant was still her friend. "Needing space" was not only understandable but healthy. It was the only way she might get her best friend back someday. They just had to endure a little awkwardness and some distance.

Everything was fine. The ache she felt, the one that seemed to start in her chest and radiate out—that would go away once they saw each other again. Once they could be comfortable together again.

"Wow, my email really did the trick!" Emme gave a little, self-satisfied shimmy. Maya was going to tell her about the letter, but Emme was already moving on. "He's smart, though. Time and space will be good for both of you. Prevents wallowing. Wallowing leads to pining, and pining is pathetic—no one wants that. It's why I can't stand *Fleabag*: season one is all wallowing, and season two is pining. Exhausting."

Maya nodded. She hadn't seen *Fleabag*, but she'd heckled enough K-dramas with "Just tell her!" to know she found pining frustrating to watch. That's why her favorite romance trope was enemies to lovers. "I honestly haven't sat down to invest in a TV show since, like, 2012. Between the Ohana Center and school, I didn't have a solid hour to give anything. I think that's how I got so attached to reading romance novels on my Kindle; you can give a novel fifteen minutes here, twenty there, and still enjoy it."

Emme shook her head. "Clearly, you need some guilty-pleasure shows. The *Real Housewives* shows are perfect to watch on your phone in little bites."

That made Maya snap her head up in surprise so hard that her face masks almost flew off. "You watch those?"

Emme sat up straight. "Are you kidding? I love every kind of reality TV! *The Real World: Boston* was the first time I saw a young Black woman and a lesbian on TV. I realized then how little of the world you see in regular TV—reality gives you more slices of life. My favorite shows are *Big Brother* and *Housewives*. It's a miracle I get anything else done."

"Huh." Maya had never thought of it that way, but she had to concede the point: you could see more different kinds of people on reality TV than scripted ever showed. The first time she saw a Black same-sex couple, it was on *House Hunters*. And they didn't even have to suffer. They got to be loving and affectionate—even when they had a small argument about bathroom tile. "Why *Housewives*, though? You know how rich people live." Maya cast a pointed look around the room.

Emme shrugged. "I know how rich people in DC live, and we're not that entertaining," she corrected. "Papa got diagnosed with dementia a year after I graduated from college. Once the doctors broke down the disease, I knew I couldn't leave. There was only so much time before my dad wouldn't know who I was. I needed to stay close so I could have as many good years as possible." She stopped herself.

Whoa. Maya turned and saw Emme blinking away tears.

"I'm sorry, it's just so surreal. A year ago I was worried about how I'd survive his condition getting worse. Now I'm doing everything I can to make sure he can survive this stupid plague." She sniffed. "Not on my 2021 bingo card."

Maya couldn't find the words to respond. So instead she made sure her face mask was secure and moved over to Emme's bench, where she wrapped her arms around her usually self-assured mentor, pulling her close. Emme let herself be held. She'd never been this vulnerable with Maya.

Ever since Emme had showered Maya with compliments at Velma's Books, she'd been the one listening to all Maya's unfiltered trauma and self-doubt. Maya had tried to reciprocate, but Emme brushed off these attempts so strongly that Maya felt she must have been prying—or that Emme just had a pretty charmed life.

Up until this moment, she'd thought that Emme had moved home to be with a parent the way many people had in March 2020. Instead, she'd been her father's caretaker since she was twenty-three. It put her accomplishments with the Spark and her venture capital fund in a new light. Even the *Housewives* thing made more sense. Like Maya's mom said about *90 Day Fiancé*, "when life is hard, I need TV to be easy."

After a moment, Emme collected herself. "Sorry, you didn't ask for all that."

Maya released her from the hug and offered a reassuring pat. "Vulnerability is a beautiful thing."

Emme shifted thoughtfully. "Yes, to a point, but it feels like violating my dad's privacy when I talk about it. He's still a very proud man and—" She broke off, obviously regretting speaking at all.

"I think these are done." Emme shifted away from Maya and took off the eye masks. "Now, what do you say to watching your very first episode of *Housewives* while we do steps two through ten of this skin care routine?"

Two through ten?! was what Maya thought, but she said, "That sounds like fun."

Honestly it didn't, but Emme was sharing a part of herself, and Maya really wanted to deepen that connection. *Besides, who else gets to have a daytime sleepover and call it work?*

The Real Housewives couldn't be more painful than tending a hotel bar during wedding season in Honolulu. And it had the nice side effect of keeping her from wondering what Ant was up to.

✍

Once their faces were soft and plump as ripe plums, Maya and Emme ate some particularly tasty salads for lunch on the deck. Emme scrolled through her phone while Maya poked at her cheeks in idle wonder. Her skin felt really good.

"So I've been texting with my cofounder bestie, Taylor. And she is free this evening if you are."

That stopped Maya midbite. "Even though I'm not fully 'montaged'?" She looked down at herself. She was wearing black jersey overalls and a Rocket Raccoon T-shirt she'd won at a comic convention . . . probably a decade ago.

Emme looked her over. "You're golden. Taylor was somewhere on the goth/punk spectrum all through college. She'll appreciate the look."

❦

They spent the next couple of hours watching "classic" episodes of *The Real Housewives of Beverly Hills*. Maya struggled to see the appeal—and to adjust herself to the uncanniness of everyone's faces.

"We are all set. Diane has our itinerary for the night. The Edmondses have generously agreed to sleep over, too—my dad is still getting used to Diane. Loretta left us plenty of meals in the fridge, and Bryson is on standby if we need him. I know it's overkill, but you learn the hard way you don't play around with a parent with dementia."

Maya nodded despite understanding nothing and, after a short debate with herself, asked the most pressing question: "Who are *any* of those people?"

Emme shifted her weight to her hip and answered matter-of-factly. "Our household staff, silly. The Edmondses are Cynthia, our household manager, and James, our groundskeeper and backup chauffeur. Diane is my dad's home health aide; she lives here. Bryson is our chauffeur; he drives my dad and looks after the cars. Loretta is our private chef, but since the pandemic, we mostly ask her to stock the fridge with our main meals once a week and I warm them up. I make my own coffee, though."

"I see." Maya nodded again. She'd never considered what it would take to manage a place this big. "It makes sense—you're probably not scrubbing down the bathrooms yourself after a full day of venturing with capital."

That made Emme chuckle. "Exactly. I don't talk about our staff here because it can sound so la-di-da, lady of the manor, but I don't hide the fact that what I do isn't possible without someone else doing the domestic labor. I am a firm believer in hiring experts for the job, paying them well, and leaving them to it." She briefly checked the time on her Apple Watch. "Speaking of experts, let's go bring some delicious Indian food to Taylor and talk shop. She's much better than I am about talking up the vision of the Spark and its origin story."

⌇

"Get over here and hug me, bitches! I'm vaxxed!" Taylor Weston cried across the roof of her condo building. She was standing near a table, underneath a couple of those tall heaters that looked like a cross between a tiki torch and a sinister robot. Emme quickly handed Maya the thermal bags of Rasika takeout they'd picked up for dinner. Slightly overburdened, Maya made her way over to the hugging, bouncing friends. Like Maya, Taylor was shorter and rounder than Emme—which was a relief. Maya had imagined all Emme's friends to be skinny Europeans like Nico who'd probably judge her for eating more than one samosa. The self-consciousness that she'd been willfully ignoring on the trip over melted away.

Maya set the food down on the large table while Taylor and Emme settled into seats next to each other, now holding hands. To Maya, Taylor was either biracial or multiracial with her J.Lo complexion, fluffy dark hair, small features, and startling gray-green eyes.

"So I'm pregnant," Taylor began. "And ever since the little space invader made themselves known, my doctor husband basically begged me to cut down my human contact to nil until I got boosted yesterday, because Delta is real fucking scary. I have seen no human soul IRL but my husband, my sister who moved in, and our housekeeper." She squeezed Emme's hand and looked seriously at Maya. "You have no idea how happy I am to see and touch y'all."

Taylor's effusive joy was infectious. Maya couldn't help smiling as she gave a wave from the table. "Such a pleasure to meet you."

Ever the mistress of ceremonies, Emme started opening dishes and laying out the night's agenda to Taylor. "I was thinking we could eat, hang out, and tell Maya the whole story of the Spark together."

"Hold on, let me take in some of these aromas." Taylor waved the air in her direction, luxuriating in the delicious scents. Then she dished up some crispy spinach and took one very satisfied bite. "Let me take you back to the day we met. Picture it: George Washington University, 2006. I am TA-ing the undergrad business statistics course. The class has at least twelve guys named Kyle, five Matts, two Olufemis, and one Emme, who looked like she walked out of that Cake song 'Short Skirt / Long Jacket'—nothing but style and ruthless efficiency. I give her a wink of solidarity since we are the only women in the room—women of color, at that. And she says, 'Those are cool fucking boots' when I start handing out the syllabus. It feels like a blessing, I like her immediately. She must like me, too, because after she's out of stats, I'm her tutor for accounting. Then I'm teaching her how to code until I graduate. Along the way she becomes the baby sister I always wanted."

Emme reached over and squeezed Taylor's hand again. "Of course, the coding never quite stuck."

Taylor laughed. "Yes it did. You're fine—I'm better. But I'm the computer science major."

Maya took another bite of her fish dish and soaked in their easy banter. There was something so lovely about being around a pair of old friends. Suddenly, like a stiff breeze cutting across the roof, Maya found herself missing Ant. How often had they shared their own origin story, just like this? But . . . he'd asked for space, and she needed to respect that. Besides, she was making new friends; that's why she was here. Maya forced herself to tune back in to the story.

"So I'm in Chicago, which is the first thing—dating in Chicago is hell. I'm on dating apps and I'm chubby, bisexual, ethnically confusing because I'm Piscataway, so I kept getting fetishized incorrectly. Most of the lesbians I'm messaging are giving fatphobia or biphobia. On the other side of the apps, dudes are worse. After the fifth 'Hola, Mami!' from the whitest white man who ever whited, I tell this one, 'I don't care about love, I want someone to write something nice to me.'"

Emme picked up the story. "So I dig up the only app I'd successfully programmed, called Love Letter. It was a text app that had one prompt: 'Say something nice.' I designed it for people in long-distance relationships to help them remember to write to their partners. I share it with Taylor and say, 'At least we can remember to say nice things to each other.'"

Taylor hopped back in. "That's when I get this idea: What if you could connect with people based only on text responses to daily prompts? You don't go in looking for a date or hookup. You're trying to meet soul-to-soul. 'Only connect,' like *Howards End*. That's the spark of the Spark." She leaned back with a small smile. "Okay, Maya, now it's time for your origin story."

Maya gave a quick glance to Emme, who nodded encouragingly.

"Born in DC, raised in Prince George's County. The community I grew up in really believed in and emphasized Black Excellence—which sounds really good, except when it's kind of oppressive. Like the only way to be successful is make six figures, have multiple degrees, marry another Black person, then get a McMansion. Then have kids who will be doctors, or lawyers, or maybe an entrepreneur. And even if you don't have anything near that, you're supposed to want it—and I didn't want any of that, especially in 2009, when you see your supposed role models with their master's degrees working at Target.

"So I ran, went to the West Coast, and tried to become an artist. Failed. Went to Hawai'i to find a new dream, succeeded—for a while. Got a bachelor's in social work, had a great plan for afterward. That plan literally burned to the ground. So I'm here."

Taylor hummed thoughtfully. Emme hummed thoughtfully. They both opened their Notes apps and began typing. Maya shifted in her seat. This was eerie. Somehow, she'd gone from having a normal conversation to auditioning for some unspecified role.

She started fighting the urge to nibble on her newly manicured nails when *finally* Emme spoke. "So, we have notes," she said with a bright tone.

Oh shit. Maya watched Emme intently as she scrolled up through her screen of notes. She felt the sudden need to fix her posture and looked to Emme, then realized that her mentor was waiting for Taylor to start talking.

The shorter woman looked at Maya intently, her hands tented below her chin. "I want to give you three words: *reinvention, adaptability, creativity.* I know people hate putting stuff this way, but that sounds like your brand. When you tell your story, everything you say should push you toward those three words."

Maya nodded. It was her turn to hum thoughtfully. "But why?" must have been etched on her forehead.

Emme responded to her silent question. "Most of the people likely to offer opportunities to you are going to be Boomers—"

"And Gen Xers," Taylor interjected.

Emme assented. "And Gen Xers, especially ones who think they're cool. They all had or *have* the same bourgeois goals for their kids that you were running away from: go to college, make high six figures, vacation home in the Outer Banks. Even if they have 'Not all who wander are lost' tattooed on their calves. You don't want to make them question you or question their own choices—either way, that's bad for you. Leave off the negative motivation, stick to positive inspiration."

Emme drummed her fingers on the weathered wood of the table before she continued. "When your story is focused and short, people are intrigued. They'll seek you out like I did. Too many details, these people—"

"Muckety-mucks," Taylor interjected.

"They're easily bored. My goal is to get people excited about you, especially while you're shadowing me in the coming weeks. By the time we're done with the fellowship, I want people to know how talented and interesting you are. Then you're in high demand. You're a house priced below market for a bidding war. People are going to forgo inspection and pay closing costs."

A snort of ungainly laughter came from Taylor. "You can take the Vivant out of real estate, but you can't take real estate out of the Vivant." She settled back into her seat as she pulled a warm-looking black shawl over her shoulders. "Look, Maya, I know this all sounds wack as hell, but Emme helped me back when we were at GW, like she's helping you now." Taylor looped her dark hair behind her ears, revealing two lobes full of silver hoops. It was like she was silently signaling that she also had a bit of rebel left in her.

"Here I am, a native girl from bama-ass Waldorf, who now has my own company, a two-floor condo in this beautiful building, a doctor husband, and a geriatric pregnancy at thirty-eight. It's a beautiful life, and I owe most of it to Emme's timely advice."

Emme leaned into Taylor affectionately. "Thanks, big sister."

Taylor dropped her head against Emme's. "Thanks, baby sis."

Maya wanted this. She wanted their ambition and their connections. If Ant was a lovely fleece blanket that could keep her warm, Emme was a magic carpet, willing and able to take her places she never imagined. If all that took was a little personal branding, well, she was up for it.

"I hope you didn't bring me to Taylor's because you thought I was getting cold feet. If I didn't run at the blonde locs, I'm not running at all."

Her mentor gave a little shrug. "I didn't doubt you, but I just encouraged you to do something very hard with Ant. I want you to know that *I* know that. And I want you to see that it will be worthwhile."

Maya gave a half smile; she actually liked it better when they were pretending that situation was okay. But a little vulnerability wouldn't kill her.

"Thank you for considering that. I know that Ant and I will get our full friendship back one day. The hardest thing is dealing with the random fallout." Maya shivered as a breeze grazed the back of her neck. "Anyway, what I need to do now is focus on my goals. I'll know I've made it when I have my job and my own apartment. Living with my parents has been going much better than expected, but I've gotten my heart set on moving out as soon as I can find a place I can afford."

"Why wait, Maya?" Emme exclaimed, shaking her head. "Know you've got a friend with real estate connections!" She pointed to herself with alternating fingers.

Taylor rumbled with another laugh. "Oh, you've unleashed the beast now."

Emme gave a shrug that said "you're not wrong," then gave Maya a smile. Suddenly it felt like the sun had come out again on the chilly roof. "I know I can find a Vivant apartment that fits your needs. Leave it to me." She immediately reached for her phone and began typing.

"Okay, Emme, if you can make me over, I'm sure you can make over my housing situation."

Emme clapped happily. "Let's talk about your needs and maybe schedule a couple of apartment showings."

Taylor gave Maya a pitying look. "You should really go home and get some rest. If I know this one at all"—she pointed to Emme—"she's somehow going to schedule a dozen apartment showings for you tomorrow."

Emme sat up straight and slid her gaze from Taylor to Maya. "She's exaggerating. We'll probably only see eight places tomorrow, ten max," she said, smiling encouragingly.

Maya smiled back and wondered if she could convince Emme to let her wear her Crocs one last time. Her feet screamed at the idea of apartment hunting in her stylish, but pinchy, new flats.

Texts from Ella to Maya, September 18, 2021

Ella:

Momma sent me the video of your living room fashion show

How did YOU end up with a whole new wardrobe
That's 100% Neutrals?
When have you ever worn beige?!

Maya:

First of all, my accessories are providing pops of color

And second, I know that my sister with her turtleneck collection is not coming for my clothes!

Looking like a Black Theranos

The Avengers Guy, with the snapping?

No! The fake Steve Jobs lady

Ella:

Elizabeth Holmes?

Maya:

Yes

I don't only wear black tho

My turtlenecks are a beautiful rainbow! So are my tights

Anyway the reason for the neutrals is so I can add in my own pops of color

The look is supposed to say that I'm creative, adaptable, and adept at reinvention

What do you think?

You look like you went from being an art teacher in a public school to being an art teacher at a posh boarding school in Sweden
That's a compliment

Good

Maya:

because Emme had me trying
on clothes for 3 hours

Ella:

And she's still alive?!

Well, I'm getting paid so I thought of
it as slightly better than coal mining

But this look needs to work because
I am never doing that again

Okay you've suffered enough

but I'm gonna send you some tights
For your sweaterdresses
A colorful cornucopia of tights!
If you don't wear them I'll know Emme
gave you a lobotomy

Seriously though, what did
Ant say? You must look like the
antithesis of Hawaii Maya

. . .

Maya:

Ant and I aren't really talking right now

Ella:

WHAT?!?!?!

Yeah, I think he might have taken a job in Virginia to get away from me

THE COMMONWEALTH?!

Okay, we're doing a video call right now and you are telling me everything

9/27/21

Hey Ma,

Here's a postcard from my new temporary home.
I'm working on a Christmas tree farm for my new
job. They're housing me and giving me a bonus for
taking it. I couldn't say no.

   I live in a tiny house on a Black-owned farm
in Centerville. On paper it's only 20 miles from
DC but it feels like a world away.

   Hope things aren't too wacky at the hospital.
Have you announced your big news yet?

   Love,
   Ant

   P.S. Do you like the photo? It's my view of the
farm. I thought you'd like a peek!

Ant

Ant sat on the steps of his tiny house, exhaling slowly. It was the first time he'd seen his breath in years, and he was fascinated. He'd woken up early to catch the sunrise over the neat rows of pine trees dotting the adjacent hills. Even though they'd scratched him, made his hands sticky with sap, and deposited endless pine needles down his shirt (and pants, and somehow socks), Ant couldn't think of anything better than starting the morning gazing out at the trees.

In a few weeks, one-third of the field would be stumps, cut and distributed to church parking lots, firehouses, and other tree lots across the region. Remy, the farm's manager, called that "the time of chain saws." The accompanying glint in his eye was mildly terrifying, but now Ant chuckled at the memory.

He reached for his phone and was about to text Maya when he remembered—he'd asked for space, and she was giving it to him. Rationally, he knew that wasn't fair to Maya, but his feelings were happy to war with his brain until he pushed all thoughts of her to the side. Between packing up, moving out, and settling in at his temporary home on the farm, Ant had kept himself good and distracted. He thought of Maya no more than five times a day.

At least he didn't have to hear about Emme Vivant, pretty much ever. Out on the farm, no one seemed to have heard of her—another reason he was grateful to be here.

Once he got his fill of the morning, Ant went back inside to where his french press of coffee was steeping, plunged it, and gazed out the window. The fog had settled like a crocheted blanket over the baby pines, their little green tops just visible through the low cloud. Almost without thinking, he slipped the screenless window open and took a few photos, selecting the most aesthetically pleasing one for Instagram. There was a less-than-perfect one that reminded him of a foggy day in Honolulu.

Since he'd decided he needed space from Maya, he'd begun reaching out to other people in his life. The results had been mixed. On the one hand, he got (lovingly) cussed out via text message. Now he made sure to never again send anything to Pua until after 5:00 p.m. so he didn't accidentally wake her in the middle of the night. On the other hand, he had the Ace Space DC's Discord server, where he shared photos whenever he wanted. Mira had basically created it for him when it became clear he needed more people to talk with.

࿇

It took Ant a minute to recover from his second snap decision since following Maya to the mainland. But once he was able to take a breath and look around, he was charmed by *everything* at the Donwell family farm: the fall colors, the tree-lined two-lane roads, the bunnies that seemed to have the run of the place. Yes, he might have gotten a little click-happy with the camera conveniently in his pocket, but who could blame him? Autumn was astounding, and this was his first one in the continental US. There were so many more apples involved!

Ant expressed his enthusiasm by posting an embarrassing amount on TikTok and somewhat more reasonably on Instagram. When he hoped for an immediate reaction, he sent photos to Mira. Somehow a selfie with him, a baby goat, and a tiny pumpkin drove her over the edge.

I've made a The Idle Chatter forum for posting random thoughts and adorable photos.

When you have an impulse to send me cutesy stuff, please put it there.

You can send me funny things but don't expect me to text back, like, immediately. Nothing beautiful or touching—and not too frequent, can't risk you falling in love with me.

Ant waited, expecting to see the ellipsis of continued conversation. None came. He frowned and blinked at the phone. *Offended* wasn't the right word, but he definitely felt a way. Ant responded with a very dignified text message to reassure her that he didn't going around falling in love with *all* his female friends.

Mira sent him a FaceChat request and greeted him with lavender-toned hair and a solemn expression. "Okay, I sense that I sounded out of pocket, so let me try some direct communication. Can't have that, you're a Taurus moon—y'all love to get clingy." She tucked a lock of wavy hair behind her ear and continued. "For me as an aromantic person, my life is easier when I keep my boundaries clear. I wasn't trying to say that you fall in love willy-nilly, but me personally, I don't like to give romance soil in which to germinate. I'm speaking your language, plant man, so you get me."

He raised a skeptical eyebrow in response. "Go on."

Mira continued. "I'm a single woman, which means I've had my fair share of dudes projecting their romantic fantasies on me—allo/ace, cis/trans, most women have to deal with this. Because I'm *never* gonna reciprocate, I try to nip that stuff in the bud.

"To me, the difference between a friend and 'friend who could become something romantic' is how much intimacy you allow. We're still in the acquaintance / new friend space, but you're texting with me like we're dating. Even if the tone is platonic, it's boyfriend texting. I need you to dial it back."

That made Ant sit up. He'd made a point to try and spread his texts around, and he was still doing too much. "But Maya and I were like this all the time. And that was before I even knew that I . . ."

Mercifully, Mira spared him from finishing the sentence. "I figured. It's one of the reasons I thought it would work out with you and Maya. From everything you said, you both had been tilling very romantic soil. You sounded thoroughly enmeshed."

He was struck dumb again, taking in Mira's words. *Enmeshed?* That wasn't too far from codependent. Irritating as he was, maybe FLoridaMan1979 was right: Did he fall for Maya because he didn't give himself a choice?

"I'm not sure I know how else to be. Like I have to relearn how to be friends with people without Maya around."

Mira shrugged. "Obviously I'm not going to give you any more advice, but I will say that right now, midpandemic, we're all relearning how to be. Don't feel too awkward about it."

Before she could say more, her phone made a noise. "Oops, sorry, gotta go. I'm making someone platinum blonde today. Take care."

And then Mira was gone, leaving Ant with his thoughts. It didn't take long for him to realize that she had a point. That's when Ant decided that, even after he learned to think about her and not want to cry, he needed to learn not to need Maya so much. Even if it hurt them both, he needed to step back from their relationship. He needed to get un-enmeshed.

∽

It took a couple of days of thinking, but once he did, Ant had one big question for himself: Had he really followed Maya because he couldn't imagine staying in Hawai'i without her or because he didn't want to figure out how to be on his own? Being around Maya was easy. She was funny and smart and had a joke for every awkward silence. She made it easy to be social, even though he was the bigger extrovert.

He liked people almost too much, never shaking the need to make friends fast and hold on tight that was either an only-child thing or a military-brat thing. After his quick but revelatory talk with Mira, Ant's annoyance with Maya turned on himself. Whether he'd been using Maya as a social crutch or playing her sidekick, neither was healthy.

He did need space from Maya, but the space was *for him*—not really *from her*. He had a lot to figure out. And he had plans to make. He was going to fire up the Spark and find meetups for Virginia asexuals, or new Hawai'i transplants, or just nice people who wanted to go apple picking. He had all fall to enjoy, and he was going to do it on his own.

Hopefully by the time winter came around, he could figure out how to be Maya's friend again.

Texts from Emme to Maya, October 3, 2021

Emme:

> Good news! The carriage house is finally ready. It's redecorated and has brand new air filters in every room.

Maya:

> Awesome!

> So since we're both boosted
> + the air filters
> How would you feel about working unmasked

> I think that sounds okay

> Oh good! We're going to be doing a lot of meetings on Zoom next week so it would be great if people could see as much of your face as possible

> Happy to follow your lead

> Also, Taylor loved you and wanted to know if you'd want to
> come over for sunset yoga on her roof

Maya:

Say less! That sounds awesome

Emme:

Great! I'll have more info on Monday

See you then! I'm excited to
see the carriage house!

Maya

There was a pumpkin-shaped Post-it on the front door of the little stone house behind the Vivant family manse.

Come on in and get yourself camera-ready.

Maya chuckled and pushed open the door. *Hopefully I don't have too much more to do.*

She'd made sure to look the perfect balance of interesting and professional for this week of Zoom meetings. She wore her tortoiseshell glasses to look intellectual and had made a point of doing a face mask the night before and an eye mask this morning so she'd seem fresh and awake.

She stepped just inside the carriage house and gaped at the whitewashed stone fireplace on the opposite wall. It didn't scream "office." In fact, looking around, Maya was surprised by how cozy the space was. She'd expected white, marble, and chrome everything, with silent TV monitors on every wall. Instead it was like she'd slipped into a ski chalet with barnwood-clad walls and oak floors. The kitchen gave the impression that it had been stolen from some unsuspecting Swiss grandma. It also took up a full third of the Tardis-like little house, so much more than the small break-room nook she'd been imagining.

Tugging at the sleeves of her blazer, Maya stepped back with a start when she caught sight of the small but undoubtedly genuine Alma Thomas on the opposite wall—a welcome spot of warm color in the cool-toned room. It took her a moment to notice their work spaces, which sat alongside a wall of windows. The desks were positioned so they faced each other, with ten feet between them. A bookshelf was positioned behind each Eames chair, probably full of all the finance stuff Emme would want her to read.

But that was a problem for future Maya. Today she was going to spend most of her time on Zoom getting introduced to the businesses Emme had invested in and hearing from them about their work. She opened her new laptop and found the camera app to put on her makeup: mascara, a swipe of eyeliner, and red lipstick.

Her mom used to say her keys to beauty were good skin and Ruby Woo, despite the conventional wisdom that it looked slutty/clownish/ugly on Black women. And though Maya hated to admit it, the main reason she wore her new glasses was to temper that impression. If Emme hated it, she'd take it off.

Maya finished applying her lip liner, then the lipstick itself. She was checking her teeth for stray color when the door opened.

"Hope you're warm enough. We've got a corn stove for heating this place, so we can always start a fire if you're not comfortable—ooh!" She broke off. "Is that Ruby Woo?"

Turning from the laptop, Maya smiled. "It sure is! My mom's favorite."

Emme smiled a little sadly. "Mine too! Another thing we have in common." She smiled over her shoulder on the way to the kitchen. "Do you want coffee?"

Maya went to rise, but Emme stopped her. "No need to get up. You like cream, no sugar, right?"

"I *like* cream and sugar, but I'm trying to cut down on my sugar, so cream only is wonderful." Maya chuckled.

Emme clinked and stirred in the kitchen, ultimately plopping a beautifully fragrant mug of coffee at the desk Maya had chosen for herself.

"Please get caffeinated, get settled, and strap in. We've got video meetings straight through noon. I really want you to listen to everyone's stories, make observations, and take notes."

༄

After seven and a half meetings (numbers two and six were interrupted by off-screen emergencies) Maya's face ached from maintaining a restrained smile, and her fingers were cramped from taking copious notes on her laptop. Emme came over from her desk and peered at Maya's screen.

"Jesus, Maya! I heard you clacking away over here, but I didn't realize you'd pretty much transcribed all our conversations."

Maya laughed. She'd always been a fast typist, probably influenced by watching *Populaire* in her French-immersion middle school days. It had imprinted on her, weirdly making her think that typing really fast was cool, and bestowing a preference for sarcastic yet brooding types.

"You can add 'types like a demon' to my list of skills." Maya flexed her fingers and scrolled to the top of the document, relishing how long it took to get there.

Emme shook her head with an indulgent smile. "Now, Maya, we didn't do all this so you could end up in the secretarial pool. Keep that as a secret superpower for as long as you can."

Maya nodded, trying not to feel stung. She was here so she could avoid being another Black office manager who planned all the office parties. If the key to being great was hiding her basic skills, then she'd keep her ninety words per minute under her hat. Emme thought she had potential; Maya was determined to fulfill it. For now, it was probably a good time to change the subject.

"I noticed that all the people you're working with are pretty local: educational games folks were in Silver Spring; the chocolate company is on South Dakota Ave in Northeast; and the folks making a 'common application' for summer camps were in Falls Church."

"It's true," Emme replied, heading for the pale-periwinkle couch at the center of the room. Maya followed her and sat, enjoying the feel of the suede. "I try not to have business too far from my dad. I get a little antsy if I can't be home in time to read to him before bed."

Maya couldn't help leaning over and squeezing Emme's arm. "You're such a good daughter."

Her mentor shrugged. "We've been all each other had since my mom died. As long as I have my dad, I'm gonna take care of him." She shifted and swallowed. "It sounds like a sacrifice, but it isn't. My closest friends are here—especially now that Nico's moved back to DC— and the Vivant name means something here that it doesn't north of Baltimore or south of Richmond. I don't mind being a bigger fish in a little pond since it's the best pond in the world."

"I think it's cool that you're actually doing something to help people. You could just care for your dad and call it good, but here you are putting your money to work for other people's dreams."

Emme stiffened her posture and spoke in a strange *New Yawk* accent. "Money is like manure; it's not worth a thing unless it's spread around, encouraging young things to grow." She dropped the persona with a giggle. "I was in *Hello, Dolly!* in high school. It's still one of my favorite musicals."

Maya smiled at her warmly. She loved seeing this side of Emme: a little sweet, a little goofy, living proof that becoming the most successful version of herself didn't mean becoming less human. It was these little moments that made Maya feel that she'd made the right choice in trusting Emme when her dad would ask, "How's your friend Bug doing?"

She'd chosen Emme's wisdom and Emme's world, at least for now. "So, what's next?"

"Would you grab the coffee and cookies that the Edmondses left? Then we can discuss the boring part of all this: combing through all the local newspapers, magazines, and news stories, looking for small businesses that want to grow."

They set the snacks on a side table, and then Maya followed Emme to a large closet that Maya had thought was a bathroom. The floor was stacked with magazines. Emme had apparently been raiding every dentist office, spa waiting room, and fusty rich-guy barbershop in a ten-mile radius. They stacked the sizable coffee table with piles of *Washington Post Magazine*, *Washingtonian*, *Washington Business Journal*, the *Afro-American*, and alumni magazines from every college in the region. Maya guessed that there were eight redwoods' worth of paper in this little room. And Emme was convinced that somewhere in these piles was her next big thing.

"I know it seems tedious, but often this stuff isn't super searchable. The people who are just getting their projects off the ground aren't the folks profiled in the cover stories. They're folks with a short blurb that won't surface on search engines. Trust me, I've seen it from the other side with the Spark. But you get the most bang for your buck by getting in as close to the ground floor as possible and helping a small company build. That's why we're doing things the old-fashioned way."

Maya grabbed a handful of magazines in one hand and a highlighter in the other. "There's a lot to be said for your methods. Give me this type of research any day over sitting hunched at a computer getting eyestrain." She opened up a February 2020 issue and scanned the table of contents. Then she paused and reached for a second highlighter. "I'll be on the lookout for trends, too, problems begging for a solution."

Emme nodded at her warmly. "Good thinking, Maya! I love how you're always full of ideas." Before she could say more, her phone buzzed. Emme stood quickly and left the room, chatting cheerily to whoever was on the other end.

Maya did her best to immerse herself in the magazine, wielding her yellow highlighter for interesting businesses and her blue highlighter for emerging markets. "Emerging markets." She tried the phrase out loud. "That sounds like a real thing. I like it."

She happily researched for the rest of the afternoon, fueled by Loretta the chef's delicious cookies. She was so deep into research that she almost missed Emme practically bouncing into the room.

"I have an awesome surprise for you!" She practically sang the last word. "All I can say for now is: tomorrow, wear the houndstooth tunic sweater with the shiny black leggings and white sneakers." After a moment's consideration, Emme added, "It would also be a good day for your red lip."

Maya set her highlighters to the side and looked up at her mentor. "Would it be possible to have *any* context?"

Still entirely too pleased with herself, Emme shook her head. "You're too clever!"

Maya shrugged; she'd just have to be surprised. She stroked her Cupid's bow thoughtfully and was hit with another thought. "Septum piercing or no septum piercing?" She turned to Emme and tapped the current rainbow ring there.

Emme tilted her head. "Wear your dainty silver one. And no more questions or I'll think you're digging for clues, and we can't have that. Just arrive at ten a.m. tomorrow—it's going to be a long day."

Maya

"Good morning, lightbearers! This is Reverend Gina with today's good word . . ."

Maya waved to her dad as he drove on to his school. Since Emme was so emphatic about her looking nice, it seemed like a bad day to commute by bike. It was a beautiful day, however, for a stroll.

She gave a contented sigh as she started the climb up the very long and still steeper driveway. Before the pandemic she'd been a faithful person. She'd found a church in Honolulu that marched in the pride parade with a music ministry run by two openly gay men. (Many church music ministries are run by gay men, but most keep their talent in the closet.) Maya was deeply involved in congregational life, helping out with the nursery and playing guitar with the worship band. Though she'd grown up Baptist, she really enjoyed the whole liturgy thing. It was comforting to think of people all over the world saying the same thing she was saying or reading the same thing she was reading.

That feeling of unity was what drew her to Zoom services when the world was forced inside. But ever since losing her home, her work—everything she'd built for herself in Hawai'i—she hadn't been able to connect to her faith. And despite an hour of yoga each morning, Maya didn't feel very spiritual, either. That's why listening to Rev. Gina's YouTube meditations had felt like waking from a deep slumber all those months ago. Emme's connection to Rev. Gina was what first had Maya looking at her as more than "the girlboss." Though she'd probably never know it, Rev. Gina had changed her life.

So it was all Maya could do not to keel over when she arrived at the carriage house to find her internet guru sipping coffee on the lacy wrought iron patio furniture.

"It's you!" The words tumbled out of Maya's mouth before she could think of something less embarrassing to say. "Sorry. I'm usually not a giant fangirl. Hi, I'm Maya, Emme's protégé."

"Maya," she said, stretching her name and making it a greeting all by itself. "Glad to know you. You are absolutely stunning. I'm Gina Elton-DiMarco: she/they, Italian-Jamaican. I always tell people, so they don't have to ask."

"That's smart." Maya was still frozen in place, willing her subconscious to make her say something clever. It didn't help matters that Rev. Gina was hot—and hot in a way that felt specifically tailored to her: older, with a sardonic aura that she sweetened with a sharkish smile. The pansexual motto may be "hearts, not parts," but that didn't rule out having a type. And for some strange reason, Maya's type (in women, enby folks, and occasionally even cis dudes), was Mr. Rochester.

The older woman had the look: a close-cut fade that let her dark curls spill over her forehead; tight black jeans; a matching button-up shirt. The top three buttons were undone, of course, revealing a sliver of bronze-toned skin. Taken together, it was as if Prince (RIP) from *Purple Rain* had decided to become the cool music professor.

She raised her thick eyebrows and strolled lazily in Maya's direction. "So what are we doing? Tapping elbows? Standing and waving? Or are we finally back to shaking hands?"

Finally getting a grip on herself, Maya extended her bent arm. "Let's do an elbow bump—I actually like those. Elbows are woefully underappreciated."

Rev. Gina gamely stuck out an elbow. "Better an elbow bump than a key bump, right?"

What's a key bump? Don't ask her, you're too old not to know, just laugh.

Maya did so, a little stupidly to her own ears, and tapped her elbow to Gina's. She'd look it up later.

"I was listening to you on my walk up the driveway. I actually do it every day." Maya lifted the earbuds she'd been shaking like dice this whole conversation.

Dammit! I still sound like a fan.

"Glad to be part of your day." She nodded, then seemed to catch a glimpse of Maya's spark tattoo. Before Maya could do anything but gasp, Rev. Gina traced the four inches of ink admiringly with a fingertip. "Nice work."

The jolt that simple touch sent through Maya's arm must have short-circuited something in her brain, because she immediately blurted out, "You touched me!" Like she was a fourteen-year-old meeting Harry Styles. "I mean your work has really touched me. I was not in a great place spiritually, and all the stuff you do really helped me revive that part of myself."

Nice recovery, Maya; you are not making a fool of yourself.

"Stories like yours are why I do what I do, sweetheart."

The conversation lapsed there. It was Maya's turn to say something. Emme, wherever she was, would probably want her to be networking. She thought back to her college career center and tried to remember some good questions.

"What brings you to DC?" *Or basic questions, those are fine, too.*

Rev. Gina raked a hand through her hair before she spoke. "I'm on duty, officiating my brother's wedding. He was supposed to get married last year . . ." She trailed off with a knowing laugh. "Anyway, back when Emme shouted me out in her TED Talk, I reached out in her DMs, and we've been promising to meet. How do you like working with her?"

Phew. Thankfully Gina had chosen an easy subject. "We've only truly started this week, but I can already say that she has been considerate, extremely generous, observant, and everything you could hope for in someone helping you develop your career."

Rev. Gina shoved her hands in her pockets and nodded with a gentler version of her shark smile. "I'm real glad to hear that, Maya. I had a good feeling about Emme, but there's so much you can't know from just chatting with a person. So glad we're getting the chance to hang today."

They were perilously close to falling into another lapse of conversation when both their phones chimed with a text.

> Join me by the koi pond for smoothies and conversation.

Maya looked up to see Rev. Gina looking at her expectantly.

"I'll lead the way." Maya started walking, all the while racking her brain to remember where the koi pond was. She'd only glimpsed it during the whirlwind tour of the grounds during her first day.

How did Emme put it? "Carriage house, greenhouse, pool house, koi!" She turned back to Rev. Gina with a sincere smile. "It's on the other side of the main house. We can cut across the driveway."

They crunched up the carriage house's gravel driveway, walking slightly uphill until they reached the circular driveway in front of the fairy-tale house.

Rev. Gina gave a low whistle. "It's incredible that a place like this could exist in the middle of a forest, in the middle of a city. It's multiple levels of improbable. Could we take a peek inside before we go to Emme?"

Maya shook her head. "Sorry, Emme lives with her elderly father, so she's being extra cautious about the plague."

Rev. Gina nodded solemnly, and Maya continued walking around the house until they encountered Emme herself sitting under a stately Japanese maple before a tray stacked with pitchers, large glasses, and metal straws. After a few more steps, the pond fully revealed itself, topped by a Japanese bridge. Maya took in the scene and instantly knew the Vivants must really love Monet.

They joined Emme at evenly spaced wrought iron chairs with generous cushion-topped seats. Emme hopped up and began pouring their smoothies from an ornate glass pitcher into large matching tumblers. Both were notably opaque. Maya wondered how disgusting the stuff looked if Mrs. Edmonds was going to such lengths to hide it.

"Gina, I told our chef that you're keto, so she made sure this is low carb and high protein, while tasting like a cloud." She got up and took the smoothie over to her guest, who accepted with a broad smile.

Emme brought Maya's smoothie over and set it on the side table with a wink. "Surprise!"

Maya didn't know how to respond. Gina was here—for her?!

That notion was even more confusing than the Rev. Gina's presence. Maya was thunderstruck by the good reverend herself—and a little horny, if she was honest. Speaking seemed ill advised, so she resolved to stick with gulping down the smoothie for now. She took a tentative sip and was instantly reminded of the first time she got drunk. She was hanging at the playground near home and a friend brought bottles of Orangina that were half vodka. Naturally, she didn't remember much except for her attempt to climb in (or out?) of the neighborhood baseball field, her failure, and somehow ending up with a mouthful of fresh-cut grass.

This smoothie tasted like that entire night, down to the mouthful of grass *and* her Dr Pepper–flavored lip balm. Maya put her glass down and tried to make her face neutral. She looked over at Rev. Gina, who was happily regaling them with the many and surprising benefits of sea moss gel.

Maya

Smoothies by the koi pond led to lunch (outdoors, of course) in Woodley Park, at one of the few places Maya remembered. Her family always ended up at Open City after their trips to the National Zoo. Momma was addicted to a cleverly named milkshake called the "George Washington Carver," which unfortunately was no longer on the menu. Maya had the mussels frites and hot apple cider instead.

"So, Maya, Emme tells me you're helping her understand TikTok." Rev. Gina took a big bite of her veggie omelet. "Personally, I'm terrified of it, but a lot of my fellow creators on YouTube think we have to get on board or get run over."

Emme paused between bites of her Cobb salad. "Maya is a TikTok expert, and don't let her tell you otherwise."

Maya smiled bashfully. Emme was so wonderful at validation, even when she was doing it casually in front of people Maya admired. "What I will say is that I've spent years with true TikTok experts: the teens that came to the youth center where I worked. I learned a ton, and their parents loved it because their kids would talk my ear off and not theirs."

The good reverend gave a hearty laugh. "Back in divinity school I somehow got suckered into filling in as an assistant youth pastoral intern at this bougie-ass Episcopal church in Dallas. Even though it was only two months, it was all I could do not to quit."

"It truly was not your ministry," Maya added with a laugh, feeling something besides awkward for the first time today.

Eventually, Rev. Gina left to take a breather in her hotel, but not before Emme invited her to join them for rooftop yoga later in the week.

"Later, Emme. Later, stunning." Rev. Gina pointed and winked in her direction. Maya managed to squeak out a goodbye.

As Emme called for the check, Maya finished her cider and tried not to scream "WHAT THE HECK WAS THAT?" Instead she composed herself and turned to her mentor. "I'm going to need, like, seven explanations."

Maddeningly, all Emme did in response was smile as she signed the check. A crisp autumn breeze ruffled her loose copper curls. "Let's walk to the zoo and talk. It's just a few blocks away."

She was usually a big fan of "playful Emme," but introverted Maya was still chafing from hours of polite conversation with a hot stranger. She couldn't simply enjoy the mystery. (Rev. Gina's hotness actually made things more awkward; it was hard to stay professional.) But clearly letting a millionaire direct her life couldn't be all makeovers and rooftop dinners. Maya remembered that technically she was being paid, and swallowed a sigh as she stood. "Okay."

If she didn't get anything reasonable out of Emme, at least she could see some pandas. She slipped on her new blue winter coat and started walking. Emme clasped her hands behind her back and began asking Maya questions as they walked.

"What if today was simply a reminder that you have to be ready to meet cool people and make the most of it? I hope I get the opportunity to introduce you to many more people who impress you or inspire you. Everyone you meet can be a connection. Every connection can help you get where you want to go. I can't give you talent—you already have that—but I can offer you access to people you may want to know."

"Huh." An ambulance screeched by, giving Maya a little more time to take this in. She could accept the idea of having a persona ready to meet strangers and even charm them—she'd worked a lot of service jobs, after all—but she had no idea how to turn the people she met into the *connections* she apparently needed.

"So I guess the obvious question would be, How did I do?" Maya glanced around as they continued uphill, not quite willing to catch Emme's eye until the verdict had been delivered. Woodley Park was a cuter neighborhood than she remembered. The city's height restrictions capped buildings at ten stories, so they were elegant but not imposing. Most of the restaurants and cafés had expanded their seating from their front doors to a sidewalk square off the curb. Though there weren't a ton of people around, it made the block feel like it was bustling.

"Six out of ten," Emme declared. She'd taken so long that Maya had forgotten her question. Her mentor didn't sound upset, though, even if she'd barely passed this pop quiz. Emme continued. "You were a little diffident at first, but you made an impression. By the end, I think Gina was intrigued by you. That's a good start."

Maya turned to face Emme with a confused frown. What was she starting with Rev. Gina? She didn't want to be a social media manager for a YouTube star. First, she was wildly unqualified; second, nothing about that sounded like a stable, reliable career. She wanted to do interesting work, but she was done with freelance, spec work, or anything that paid in exposure. "I'll be honest. I don't see the vision, but I'm gonna trust you."

Emme gave her a small, warm smile. "And I will make sure it's worth it. Let's go visit some animals."

✑

For both Maya and Emme, going to the National Zoo was like cuddling under the same childhood blanket.

At the Panda House

"I was six when Ling-Ling died. It was my first experience of death," Emme said quietly as they stood together before the glass of the enclosure. "I took it really hard. The only way my mom could get me to sort of settle down was to promise that we'd visit Hsing-Hsing every week—and we did until he died. Those were really special times, just her and me. If I ever really needed to talk, it was when we were visiting Hsing-Hsing. This is where I come when I want to remember her."

Near the Ape House

Maya set the scene: "So my entire eighth grade is back on the buses waiting and waiting, and our teacher is yelling at us—even though we're on the bus. He's all, 'Now you got Principal Walker running around looking for one of y'all little behinds. We can't take y'all anywhere! It's disrespectful, this is inconsiderate.' Blah, blah, blah. Suddenly, here she comes, supporting *a limping* Principal Walker, and she's like, 'Sorry, guys! I tweaked my ankle taking a picture of orangutans on the O-Line. MiKayla saw me struggling and helped me up the hill.'

"Mr. Hines got real quiet and sat down for the rest of the ride. He apologized to us all on Monday—it was the first time I got a real apology from an adult."

It went like that for a couple of pleasant hours, trading anecdotes and enjoying the animals. They were taking in the magical underwater view of the sea lions when Emme's phone chimed. Maya watched her brighten as she scrolled.

"Okay, I have one more surprise for you today—I promise it's not nearly as stressful as my first one."

The zoo must have had healing properties, because Maya surprised herself by laughing and not seizing up with anxiety. "Okay, I'll follow but . . . no hints?" She injected some hope into her tone. "I think I'd handle surprises better with hints."

Emme smoothed her hair and rose. "I think surprises should be surprises. Let's get walking."

Soon they were in Emme's car speeding up Connecticut Avenue. Maya thought they were headed back to the carriage house for a Zoom meeting, but instead of taking the turn that would have led them through Rock Creek Park, Emme kept driving up Connecticut into a part of DC Maya wasn't sure she'd ever visited before. If Woodley Park was a little quaint, this part of town was practically a village.

The apartment buildings were all at least forty years old, tall but with a lot of charm. The sidewalks were narrow. The storefronts were decidedly unfashionable. A CVS, a gym, a pedestrian grocery store. The defining feature was the towering trees that seemed to leap from behind the apartment buildings, all bursting with fall color.

They stopped in front of a building with a large half-moon drive-way and lobby that had probably looked like the future in 1962. It was an aesthetic Maya had learned to love because Honolulu also had a ton of midcentury architecture. "This building is super cute," she said as Emme punched a code into the call box.

"I'm glad you think so." The door buzzed, and in very little time they were standing in a small, light-filled studio apartment. Emphasis on *small*. The place was the size of her parents' living room, and she didn't grow up in a big house. But the studio also had gleaming wood floors and a small but functional kitchen separated from the rest of the place by a french door. There was also a bathroom with a tub (essential) and a radiator. Much like the neighborhood, it was unfashionable but had its own beauty. Maya couldn't help smiling. Emme materialized beside her.

"What do you think?" Even with her mask on, Emme was so obviously pleased with herself that Maya almost didn't want to say how much she loved the place. But she didn't want to risk losing it for a second.

She bumped Emme's shoulder with her own. "I think I like your surprise after all." Maya did a slow turn. "But I'm not going to let myself fall in love until you tell me how much the rent is." She raised her eyebrows.

Emme gave a little shimmy in response. "It's thirteen hundred with utilities."

"Be for fucking real," Maya blurted out before she could stop herself. The largest room in most group houses went for the same price, and that was without their own kitchen and bathroom.

"Well, obviously this is a Vivant building, and all Vivant employees living in our buildings get the friends-and-family discount. That's what takes it down from fourteen hundred fifty, which is still decent for a four-hundred-square-foot place in Northwest DC."

It wasn't far off from Honolulu prices, either—which felt outrageous since her DC place wouldn't come with drive-up beaches and a warm ocean. But rent was out of control everywhere. The point was that Emme had found Maya her own place—something she'd never had in the entirety of her life! Something she wasn't sure she'd *ever* have. It felt like a miracle. Maya had only two questions left: "Where do I sign, and when can I move in?"

Texts from Maya to Ella, October 16, 2021

Maya:

I'm ecstatic!
Emme found me an apartment

And it's a 15 minute bike ride
to Emme's place in the park

Ella:

That's amazing!

Send me pictures!

Here's the listing
Willow.com/covingtonhousea_17482

This is a perfect little hobbit hole
of an apartment! Where is it?

Forest Hills
Like 10 blocks south of Chevy Chase

In the city! Wow.

Ella:

It's pretty far from everyone though
Even Ant's in Takoma Park, right?

Maya:

He's in Virginia remember

Oh right, sorry

I think he's fine with the distance

Why?

Well he texts me one sentence replies
And his IG feed is full of all
the cool stuff he's doing

That's rough. Wish I could hug you

I wish you could, too

But you don't need him or Emme
To enjoy DC
You've always been the
best solo explorer
When we were kids you were
always running off we'd lose
you in museum, the aquarium,
Red Lobster that one time

Maya:

The lobster tank
was very so entertaining, tho

Ella:

💀

All I'm saying is you'll have less
time to miss Ant if you do some
stuff you like on your own

Honestly I can't remember what I like

Well, take it from someone who
spent the summer in lockdown

Make any good memories while
you can because you never know
when you'll get stuck inside

An email from Taylor to Maya, October 20, 2021

Meeting Invite Events Team Confab

CC: Emme Vivant

Maya,

It was such a pleasure having you sit in with the Spark Event team! We are definitely going take your suggestion and pilot "Sparks on Ice" (love the name, BTW). I'll send you the invite for the next Events team meeting. Hope Emme can spare you.

Thanks,
Taylor

Black Girls Love Paramore Chat, October 26, 2021

—EmmeVP: Did you see? Gina shared a video of you doing a headstand during sunset yoga.

> —Signs&1nders: Oh God! I didn't know she was filming
>
> Can she take it down?

> —Signs&1nders: I'm on private for a reason. I don't have the energy to be queer, fat, Black, and a woman for the consumption of the general internet right now

—EmmeVP: but the caption she wrote is so beautiful and inspirational!

> —Signs&1nders: Okay
>
> . . .
>
> . . .
>
> —Signs&1nders: Emme, this video isn't of me It's of you taking a video of my sirsasana I'm barely in it

—EmmeVP: What, really?

—Signs&1nders: Oh! I see. She used the picture you took of me at the end of the reel, but it's like 3 seconds of this 30 second clip

—Signs&1nders: I'll live. I'm backlit in your photo anyway so Gina's million followers can't really see me

—EmmeVP: I'm looking at the post
And it's not what I expected. Gina said "I got a great video of you and your protégé"
I assumed she'd be highlighting **you**

—Signs&1nders: . . .

—Signs&1nders: Okay, Emme. I've been waiting but I still don't see the vision with Rev. Gina. All she talked about when we were together was her podcast idea

—EmmeVP: "Holy Moolah: mindful investing"

—Signs&1nders: As a Christian, respectfully 🤢

—EmmeVP: As an atheist, disrespectfully

😱😱😱

—EmmeVP: She's been emailing me constantly, too. I think she wants me to cohost. I would have blocked her if it wasn't for you

—Signs&1nders: Please explain.

—EmmeVP: I thought she was interested in you, okay.
—EmmeVP: I knew how hard it was for you to give up Ant—even though it was definitely the right choice
—EmmeVP: I wanted to reward your trust by connecting you with someone who shares your trajectory.
—EmmeVP: Gina, even with her questionable ideas podcast, is into you. And she is going places fast

—Signs&1nders: You are so sweet to see and believe in my beauty but No. just no. She is not remotely interested in a fat girlfriend.

—EmmeVP: But she flirted with you a lot. Outrageously

—Signs&1nders: It was "fat friend
flirting" Once I stopped being
so starstruck I could see it.
People flirt with us outrageously because
"everyone knows" it can't possibly be real.
—Signs&1nders: Especially when the fat
woman is also a Black woman 😒
Like remember when people thought Harry
Styles was dating Lizzo?

—EmmeVP: So Harry was never into Lizzo
at all?

—Signs&1nders: Oh, honey.

—EmmeVP: I'm kinda devastated

—Signs&1nders: Me too. I thought
you were getting me a job with her

Email from Maya to Nico Vasiliou, November 2, 2021

Subject: Green Roof Idea

Good afternoon Nico,

Have you considered reaching out to Donwell Family Flowers for the new green roof initiative? I'm pretty sure they have a great reputation among tenants. And they do garden education workshops. Just a thought.

Best,
Maya Davis

⁂

Texts from Maya's mom to Maya, November 5, 2021

Momma:

> Block off your calendar we are seeing A Strange Loop together for my birthday November 22nd

Maya:

Gigi told me about that show!
It sounds amazing
Very Black and Very queer

Momma:

I want to make sure I do some
fun things before winter
These new variants keep
getting scarier and scarier

✍

Email from Nico Vasiliou to Maya, November 7, 2021

Subject: RE: Green Roof Idea

Good morning Maya,

Thank you for reminding us of them. We will definitely be reaching out.

Best,
Nico Vasiliou

Maya

"Well." Maya's dad chuckled as he set the bowl of popcorn down on the basement coffee table. "I can definitely say that I did not have this on my pandemic bingo card."

Maya laughed. Even though everyone she knew had made some version of the "bingo card" joke these days, he was right. While she'd accepted that her parents had both lowered their brows in terms of TV intake, she never thought there'd be a day where three of them would be getting ready to watch a Black-biracial elementary school teacher find love on *The Bachelorette*.

Her mom had tried to entice her into the world of *90 Day Fiancé*, but she found that show depressing, and the ugly American behavior unwatchable. Since she'd officially given up, tonight Mom was hopping on the *Bachelorette* bandwagon, and was less than thrilled about it.

"I'm only here to see what all the fuss is about."

"Think of yourself as doing this for work," her dad offered. "I would bet at least fifty percent of the young white teachers at your school watch this show or know enough to have some opinions. Gives you something to talk about besides the weather."

"It's like modern art—you don't have to like it," Maya added. "From what I can tell online, most people are watching to pick it apart intellectually or straight up roast it."

Momma crunched down a handful of popcorn and Reese's Pieces before letting out a throaty laugh. "That's good to hear, because the trailers make it look boring as hell. Popcorn, baby?" She rattled the bowl in Maya's direction. She took it with a smile. When was the last time they'd all settled to watch something together?

Even though Maya had been home since spring and was actually enjoying her parents, the three of them hadn't done something like this since they were all home for Thanksgiving during Ella's last year of college. Maya was suddenly overwhelmed by the loveliness of it all— probably because she needed to tell her parents that she had an official move-in date. And she would. She'd do it tonight (probably), but not right now.

"Let me catch you up, Momma. There's only two guys we need to worry about: her high school crush, and the tall guy who looks like an f-boy but isn't."

Her dad snorted. "We don't agree on that."

Maya rolled her eyes.

He snorted again. "How he gonna be on TV looking all rumpled in that cater-waiter suit? Anyone that swag reliant (1) didn't come to impress the bachelorette and (2) knows women like him no matter what." He spread his arms as if to say "I rest my case."

Momma adjusted her glasses and looked at the screen. "And all these other dudes are playing for time?"

Dad shrugged. "The music teacher at my school said most of them get recycled into other parts of the *Bachelor* universe, so this part is one long audition for their other shows."

This made Momma sit back thoughtfully. "So this is basically *The Mole* but with kissing."

"And no official cash prize . . . ," Dad added.

"And many moles," Maya concluded.

Her mom tapped her upper lip thoughtfully and then signaled for the popcorn. "Okay, I'm interested now."

⚮

"So, how are you feeling at work now?" Maya's mom asked from her side of the couch. "Settled in?" She leaned forward and turned to her. Her dad muted the TV and did the same. Apparently they were very interested. Fortunately, the work had been good lately.

"I've really enjoyed doing the initial round of research for Emme's next investment. Not to toot my own horn, but I found a truly diverse crop of businesses from here to Baltimore that should be on Emme's radar. What I've been doing is creating profiles on all of the potential projects: size, sector, financials, blah blah blah. Once she sets her budget for next year's work, we'll be ready to do some outreach."

Her dad raised his eyebrows. "Wow, Maya, where'd you learn to do all that?"

She gave a little laugh. "I was the Ohana Center's unofficial grants manager for like four years. I flipped and reversed the process I used to find funders. This side of the money is a lot nicer."

"I know that's right!" Momma laughed.

"The most important thing," Maya added, "was finding a connection from Emme to the candidates. Basically, who in Emme's sphere can facilitate an introduction? The worst thing you can do is cold-call someone in need of funding and then drop them."

To prevent this, Maya had sorted through Emme's Instagram mutuals, her useful Visitation alumni, useful GW alumni. The goal was no more than three degrees of separation so the introduction could be made with an appropriate level of faux casualness. In the before-times, this would have been followed by a series of coffees, lunches, and dinners, first to see if the people themselves passed the vibe check, then to learn exactly what they needed.

"I hope Emme appreciates how diligently you've been working on this," Dad added, obviously trying and failing to keep the frown off his face.

"She does," Maya quickly replied. She took a breath. This was as good an opening as any. "She helped me get an apartment in Northwest. I can move in December 1."

An almost spiritual silence followed. Maya noticed that *The Bachelorette* was back from break and wondered if she could distract her family with whatever extremely awkward activity the contestants would inevitably be forced into next.

Her dad leaned over and wrapped her in a hug. "I knew it was gonna happen sometime but was hoping to have you until Christmas." He followed up his words with a tight squeeze.

Maya's eyes filled with unaccountable tears. He'd meant it; they'd meant it. No advice or questions, only support. She leaned into her dad's embrace and felt her mother squeeze her hand.

"Emme takes two weeks off for most of the holidays, so you'll still have me around for most of it. I'm gonna need at least a week in the kitchen to make my fancy cookies. I make them instead of Christmas cards now."

"Like the ones they do on Food Network?" At her nod, Maya's mom put her hand to her chest and gasped. "And why haven't *we* received a fancy-cookie Christmas card?"

Maya shook her head, blonde locs bouncing. "Because I was pretty sure y'all would get a box of crumbs! Don't worry—you'll be sick of my beautiful cookies by the time I'm done this year."

Her dad was probably about to say something when the screen caught his eye. "Ring the alarm, Rumpled Suit's got a solo date! This is all they're gonna talk about tomorrow."

❧

"Mom and I were cracking up when that five-foot-seven blond dude turned up on the date and Michelle looked madder than Nayte did." Angie chuckled while applying a glittery, sheer orange to Maya's nails.

"Not five foot seven!" Maya laughed. Angie was fun to chat with when she stuck to one topic. It was her tendency to bounce around that could drive someone (like Emme) nuts.

"Mom said, 'That white boy's about to get squashed like a bug!' I said, 'No, Ma, the tall brother is Canadian, he's too polite.' Then she said, 'Well, let Michelle squash him then.'"

Both ladies enjoyed a chuckle as Angie put Maya's left hand under the UV light to dry. "You and your mom should have your own *Bachelor* podcast, Ms. Angie. Listening to you talk about it is more fun than the show is."

Angie put another coat of orange on Maya's right hand and carried on with the conversation. "I like the way you think, Maya. My niece Jazzy could put us on YouTube. She knows how to do everything."

Maya smiled politely. She'd met Jazzy only once, at last week's session of rooftop yoga—which had turned into rooftop hot chocolate and sympathy once Emme and Maya realized they were too cold and Taylor said she was "too pregnant."

Jasmine, as she'd introduced herself, was a beautiful brown-skinned woman with high cheekbones, dimples, and close-cropped hair that showed the last remnants of pink dye. She smiled up at Maya when they were introduced, but she had the kind of strained, pinched face Maya recognized. It was one she'd seen in the mirror when her life was falling apart in Hawai'i. For most of their rooftop hang, Jasmine was also quiet and withdrawn. Maya couldn't think of a way to reach out, and Emme seemed to be triggered by her presence.

It was weird. It was also, she supposed, none of her business.

One side effect of this encounter was that Emme was more focused on finding next year's project than Maya had ever seen her. Emme was scrolling through the spreadsheet Maya had made with one hand, while dictating texts to the phone in her other. Occasionally, she could hear Emme muttering to herself, doing an odd European accent, "'*Jas* is immensely talented, Emme; she just needs help.' Like I'm not literally taking care of my father with dementia, Nicky. 'The pandemic took away everything *Jas* worked for.' But I'm silly 'cause I want to help someone in a similar situation."

Yeah, Maya was leaving *that* alone.

∽

As Maya's right hand went in the UV light dryer, Angie began packing her tools back into her pink wheeled suitcase.

"Maya," she began quietly, "how did things go with your friend—with the cute chunky boy?"

"Could we maybe go back to talking about *The Bachelorette*?"

Angie made a sympathetic face. "Did you send . . ." She nodded in Emme's direction. "Or did you try and close the door quietly?"

Maya sighed and rested her chin on her hand. "I tried to close things gently, but I think I caught a draft and it slammed anyway."

Angie gave her own sigh and finished packing up her things. Her phone buzzed. "That's my Uber." She set the suitcase down and wheeled it toward the door but stopped to rest a reassuring hand on Maya's shoulder. "Where there's life, there's hope. Hang in there, baby."

ENTER OMICRON

Maya

Everyone Maya knew was freaking out about this new variant, and with good reason. It spread fast but seemed just as powerful as the original recipe. At least they had the vaccine now, but you could still get really sick. Over Thanksgiving Emme gave big bonuses to staff who volunteered *not* to visit their families and stay in town. This looked really smart the week after the holiday, as the increased travel led to a spike in cases that put a whole lot of people in the hospital.

Dad's school had so many staff and subs call in sick that he and the other vice principal covered seven classes over that week. Momma was threatening to get the teachers' union involved to let her work virtually because she was at high risk for COVID. Ella had been sounding the alarm on Omicron since mid-November and was vowing that she would not be alone in London for another lockdown.

In the middle of it all, Maya had gotten the keys to her new apartment. A few days before Thanksgiving, she and Emme had gone by her building (the Covington, a Vivant property), where Maya signed the lease and did a little dance in the lobby. Now was the time to start moving in—slowly. Since Emme's place was a short bus or bike ride away from her new place, Maya planned on bringing a few things over before work, starting with her bike.

This meant starting her commute at the butt crack of dawn, when it was pitch black outside, which was harder to get used to than the

December chill. There was something somber about the month that would have been unbearable if it weren't mitigated by the millions of Christmas lights, which made her nostalgic and hopeful at the same time.

Holding on to her handlebars, Maya gazed out the windows of her red line train, watching the sky lighten from black to a velvet blue. She hoped to glimpse a bit of the sunrise before her train went underground. It was jarring to catch her reflection in the window when she was in her work clothes; she should be used to it, but she still didn't recognize herself.

At least this version of herself had her own apartment for the first time in her life, so that was something.

∽

When Maya and her bike got to the Covington, she made a point to savor every first: First time buzzing herself in with the metal-plated fob. First time greeting the building receptionist. First time locking her wheels away in the building's bike cage, which looked like a cross between a subway turnstile and modern sculpture. It was all thrilling. She practically skipped down the hall to the door of her ground-floor apartment. She wanted to take some pictures using her winter coat for perspective. As she opened her door, Maya heard someone call her name.

She looked down the hall and blinked in surprise.

"Nico?" It *was* him, looking drawn and distraught as he jogged toward her.

"Thank goodness, Emme said you'd be here." He paused to catch his breath, doubly surprising until Maya realized he was struggling not to cry. Up until now she'd thought Nico had only two emotional settings: sarcastic and annoyed. Now he was simply devastated; things had to be bad.

"Oh God, what's happened? Is Emme okay?"

Her Own Happiness

"Emme is . . . as well as can be expected. Her father has been hospitalized with COVID." He swallowed hard. "It's not looking good, Maya."

Her keys fell from her fingers in shock. Nico scrambled to grab them, probably as much to collect himself as to retrieve them. He stood and straightened his jacket. "She wanted you to know right away since you're living with your family. If you want to stay in a hotel until you've had three negative COVID tests, we'll cover it, no questions asked."

Now it was Maya's turn to swallow hard. She hadn't had a chance to consider the full implications of Nico's news until he laid it out so plainly. On the one hand, she'd been careful. She was vaxxed and boosted, and was never with more than five people except when she was on the subway. On the other hand, Omicron didn't seem too interested in how "careful" people were. Emme's dad pretty much lived in isolation except for the house staff and visits to his doctor.

"I think . . . yes, I'd like to do that, thank you. I'll make my own arrangements." She looked at Nico, who seemed so wilted it made her heart ache. "May I give you a hug?" She tugged at her face mask and waited until Nico's brief hug to hold him close. He was tense at first but hugged her back after releasing a shuddering breath. Maya let him go after a long moment. "Please give Emme my very best."

Nico nodded, sliding on his leather gloves. He extended his hand; Maya slipped her wool gloves on and took it. "I will. I'm glad to know she has such a good friend in you."

Maya squeezed his hand. "She has her best friend in you, Nico, and she knows that. It's why she trusts you above everyone."

He swallowed hard again. "It just kills me to see her hurting so." His eyes filled. "She means so much to me."

Maya pressed her lips together and blinked back her shock. Nico didn't seem like the type to cry at all, let alone in public. But Emme seemed to be his soft spot.

He turned to start down the hallway, then paused. "And of course, everything else is on hold until hopefully Emile is back with us. Salary

269

and benefits will continue as normal." And with another short wave, Nico was gone.

Maya reached for her doorknob with shaking hands. She'd been clinging to the belief—or the hope—that enough mask wearing, enough vaccination could at least slow COVID down. That if they got everyone to do the right things, they could get back to normal somehow. It was like she had suddenly remembered they'd all been trying very hard not to die. She felt her knees go when she stepped into her apartment and dropped to the floor. Her body was simply unable to deny how fully overwhelmed she was.

Maya was conscious of the feeling of the patterned floor under her hands. She felt like she should pray but couldn't get anything more out than "God, please help."

Still on the ground, she instinctively started spreading out her winter coat, comforted by the softness of the fleece lining. Then Maya stretched herself into child's pose and tried to breathe until it stopped feeling like the world was caving in.

Texts from Maya to her parents, December 8, 2021

I know you won't get this for a couple hours but I want you to know what's going on

Emme's dad is in the hospital with COVID
Emme might have it too.
They got me a hotel room out of an abundance of caution.

I'll quarantine for a bit and come home
As long as I test negative.

Don't panic! I feel fine
Just don't want to bring
The Rona home to y'all

✑

Texts from Maya to Emme, December 8, 2021

Emme, I'm so sorry

I've got my hotel room and between my grocery order and room service I'm set

Please don't give me another thought

Maya:

I'm seriously praying for
you and your dad

Emme:

Thank you, I'm so scared
I hate being alone

Nico is on his way, Emme
I know he wants to be there for you
let him, okay?

Okay. He's so good isn't he Maya? He's
bossy but he's so good.
He's always been so good to me

⌘

Texts from Maya to Ella, December 8, 2021

Hey baby sis, can we
FaceChat when you get
This?

Having a crisis
That's sparking a different
existential crisis

You know I hate freaking out alone

Maya

Maya hadn't given much thought to armchairs in hotel rooms before. And after spending an hour or so sending texts, she realized that no one else did, either. The chair was stiff, overstuffed, and looked like a recliner but instead uselessly rotated ninety degrees in either direction. But despite the many things wrong with the chair—including its noisy curtain-style brocade upholstery—it was either that or the floor. Though she was emotionally and physically exhausted from the day, Maya was not about to lie down in the much more comfortable king-size bed. She was too scared that she wouldn't get out again.

She could feel the tentacles of "the octopus" brushing her legs, that hopelessness that had nearly sucked her down in the spring. She'd do anything to not feel that way again, including staying in this chair that made her back hurt from *sitting*. (Was that a thirties thing?)

Hopefully she'd hear from her sister soon. She needed to talk to someone who'd just listen. Her finger had hovered over Ant's number at least ten times since she checked in to her hotel, but she didn't even know if they could pick up their friendship again now, when she needed it the most.

Instead she fell into a TikTok wormhole for a couple of hours. The app's algorithm had caught on to her need for validation and was offering her one sincere stranger after another with mantras and words of affirmation. A beautiful Black woman with perfect eyeliner—or a perfect filter; Maya couldn't tell—asked, "When was the last time you believed in yourself?"

She was spared the burden of responding by a chime from her phone: Ella.

> I'm here! I'm here!
>
> . . .
>
> **Ella Davis has sent you a video chat**

"Oh, thank God." Maya sighed, connecting the call.

She spent an hour spilling all her fears to her sister, not just for her health but for the future. She and Emme had been doing real work for only about a month. It didn't feel like she'd built anything yet.

"I'm trying not to be a bitch, but I've made two professional contacts. One is about to be busy with her new baby, and the other . . . Anyway, I don't see Emme being up for anything but caring for her dad or mourning him after this. Now I'm gonna be flipping Eliza Doolittle after the big ball: all dressed up for a new life with no way to get there. And I have a lease!" That last thought made Maya sigh hard.

Her sister was visible from the torso up, looking concerned—but also firm. Ella raised her index finger in a way that made it clear she had several points. "So, first: even though it ended early, you have a DC position on your résumé; second, you have some savings now; and third, don't forget about the bookstore. They loved you there! And I'm sure you said you left on good terms."

"I did but . . ." She trailed off, sadness creeping over her face. She saw Ella's soften in return.

"You're sad about Ant, aren't you?"

She nodded, looking away from her phone screen as her eyes filled with tears. "In all the ways I saw things going wrong, I never imagined a timeline where I ended up without him." She sniffled and wiped away a tear before it could slip down her cheek.

Maybe this whole thing had been inevitable. She didn't feel ready for a relationship, and they'd have to work out their boundaries as an allo/ace couple. But some part of her felt like she'd sacrificed the most beautiful thing in her life for a sense of stability that was dissipating like mist.

"Hey, hey, Mai?" Her sister was all concern now. "Do one thing for me? I have to go to bed soon. But I need you to change. Did you bring anything more comfortable?"

Maya blinked, coming back to herself and the conversation. Then she looked down. She was still in her work clothes.

Ella continued: "I'm looking at you in this chic camel jumpsuit, and it's like you dressed for your own funeral." She clapped her hand over her mouth with wide eyes. "I'm sorry, bad analogy for the current moment."

Maya snorted a laugh. It felt like the first time she'd laughed in years. "Okay, Ella Bella, clearly you need to go to bed, and I need to change."

Ella yawned and nodded, leaning heavily on her forearm. "Talk more tomorrow?"

"Sure thing. Not like I'm gonna have much else to do."

"Okay, go change. Love you, Mai."

Maya disconnected the call and joylessly forced herself up. It was time for next steps.

1. She was going to get changed like Ella suggested.
2. She was going to pour half a bottle of her drugstore bubble bath into her gigantic tub and stay there until she felt better.
3. She was going to avoid her bed until she absolutely had to get in it. She wasn't ready to face down the octopus again.

Her sister was right about one thing: once her elegant jumpsuit was in a less elegant pile on the floor, Maya felt ten times lighter. She tossed it into a corner while the water ran—and suddenly remembered one of the best things about having your own space: getting to walk around naked. Soon her undies and her good bra joined her jumpsuit, and she rolled onto the hotel bed. She pulled up YouTube on the room's TV and put on an undemanding playlist of Tiny Desk Concerts. By the time her bath was ready, Maya was dancing full-out to the cumbia coming from the screen, shaking her hips and shimmying to the bathroom.

It's fun to jiggle of your own accord. She smiled at her reflection, then stepped into the fragrant water topped with a pavlova of bubbles. Five days was a long time to be alone with her thoughts, so Maya tried to be present in the little moments as much as possible. She focused on the ways her locs felt in her hands as she twisted them into little buns on top of her head. She pressed her face into the bubbles and laughed at the resulting beard that made her look like Black Santa. As the water cooled, she felt the rippling of her hungry stomach. That was her sign to get out of the tub and go order some room service.

Ant

FYI, my taxi should be outside
in about 5 minutes

Ant swallowed and tugged nervously at the ribbed cuffs on his sweatshirt. This should be easy. This should be familiar. So why did he feel so incredibly weird? Who was he kidding? Ant knew exactly why—it was because he'd been letting the silence grow since autumn. He'd ignored all olive branches while refusing to make plans. He'd been "busy" and unavailable until she stopped trying. And now she was coming to the house, and he didn't know what to say.

Auntie Kay came down the steps and looked at him, taking in his nervousness. She met his eyes without pity. "I told you, no matter how awkward things are, you can't ghost your momma."

Ant's face fell, but he had to laugh; she had warned him. She'd happened to be in the room when he'd made the brief, awkward call to his mom saying that he wouldn't be coming back for Thanksgiving because of his new job.

⁊

His mom had hummed. "What would you like me to do with your stuff?" she asked with a calm that should have alarmed him, but he was tired. He'd spent all day getting ready for his move to Centerville. And honestly? He was too annoyed with the subject to notice.

"Can't your movers pack up my room like they have every other time? I know the navy moves you to your final destination when you retire."

There was a brief silence before Ant's mom responded with a measured, "That's true. But it could be a chance to say goodbye." Her voice softened slightly. "You kind of rushed out the last time."

Ant shrugged stiffly. "I don't think that would help me. Besides, I still hate flying. I needed a support human to come to the mainland."

He heard his mom perk up at that. "I could fly Maya out, too. Would that help?"

"That wouldn't help, Ma. Things are weird with Maya." From the dining room table, Ant could see Auntie Kay pause in stirring her red sauce, unabashedly eavesdropping. He rolled his eyes. "Besides, she thinks it's exploitative to travel to Hawai'i as a tourist now," he continued.

"We're not tourists. Antonio, you've lived here half your life—and not on base."

Ant shrugged again. "We don't have a home there anymore, though, so . . ." He trailed off.

"I see," was all his mother said in response. There had never been a more complete sentence. *That* he noticed.

"I'll come visit you after you're settled in Puerto Rico," he added, brightening his voice.

"Okay, *mijo*. We'll talk soon. Love you."

"Love you, too, Ma."

After he hung up, Auntie Kay tapped the pan she was stirring with her wooden spoon and turned around. "Whatever happens next, know you brought it on yourself."

That had been in September. A conversation he'd wholly forgotten until the red cab pulled into the driveway. Ant was on his feet and out the door before he could think too hard about it. Ma stepped out of the cab, and he suddenly remembered how short she was. As he ran to her, he noticed how tired she looked. "Ma!"

Her head whipped in the direction of his voice. "*Mijo!* My baby!" She opened her arms wide for him. Then they wrapped each other in the tightest hug imaginable, rocking together on the lawn. Then they were crying. *Both* of them were crying. Ant hadn't seen his mother cry since the dark two years after his father died. It was like she'd used up all her tears—or didn't think there was anything else worth crying about.

Ant stood back, pulled the sleeve of his sweatshirt over his hand, and tried to dry her tears. Before he could, Ma grabbed his hand and held it to her face. "I really missed you, baby boy!" Her voice was rough, but it still felt miraculous to hear it in person.

"I missed you, too, Ma." He wiped at his own tears. "So much!"

Ma sniffled. "Why wouldn't you come see me then?" She looked up at Ant without a frown, but sounded so sad he couldn't be anything but honest.

"I was mad at you," he blurted out.

"So be mad at me but come see me! That's what family is!" Ma laughed, looping her arms around his waist.

"Okay, Ma." He kissed the top of her head.

They both were rocked sideways with the impact of Auntie Kay, coming to hug them both. "Yay! That went so much better than I thought it would."

Ma laughed. "Well, I finally watched *Encanto* before I flew out here, so I was softened up. I think I'm my family's Bruno."

"Come on, you softies. I promised my good sis some warm apple cider when she got back to this coast, so it's waiting for us on the stove."

Ant and his mother followed Auntie Kay inside, hand in hand. He felt like they were ready to do anything, as long as it was together. They crossed the threshold and let Auntie Kay shoo them to the couch so she could serve cider in peace. Ant turned to his mom and frowned slightly. "Do you want to take a nap, Ma? You've gotta be jet-lagged to hell and back. Especially if you got in so late last night you needed a hotel."

His mother chuckled and shook her head. "Honey, I've been in town for five days and three negative COVID tests. I just assume that I've had a close contact when I get on a plane and quarantine for five days after I land."

That made Ant step back. "So, what did you do, stuck at the hotel for five days? That sounds like your nightmare." He watched his mother drum thoughtfully on her chin.

"Funny you should ask. I've been hanging out with Maya."

Maya

Daylight poured in through a gap in her room's blackout curtains. Maya groaned; December had no right being so bright. She let one eye crack open blearily. Last night Maya had ended her evening with two melatonin. She desperately wanted to sleep in since she didn't have anywhere to go, and morally, she wasn't sure if she *should* go anywhere. Did quarantine mean avoiding all shared spaces or only crowded ones?

"It's too early for ethical dilemmas," she groused through a yawn. Then she turned on the TV and watched amenities scroll by. "Oh hey, we get a free newspaper." She had a sudden vision of herself sitting on her hotel balcony, drinking coffee, and doing the crossword—like a real adult. It appealed to her much more than lying in bed and worrying about Emme, her future, then Emme again. Sitting up, Maya reached for the hotel phone and ordered coffee with the yogurt parfait she saw on the screen. Then she got out of bed (still naked) and went to her emergency duffel.

After her encounter with Nico, Maya had taken a Lyft back to her parents' house and quickly grabbed some essentials, including the "go bag" she kept in the garage; ever since her first earthquake in Oakland had made her fear nature, Maya had a "ready to flee" bag for emergencies packed with easy-to-wear clothes, plenty of underwear, food, and cash. She'd finally got around to packing her East Coast version after

Montage Week—and the size of the guest room closet—made it necessary to move a chunk of her clothes elsewhere.

Maya knelt on the carpet and opened the unassuming navy-blue bag. Even though her big makeover had been only two months ago, seeing her old clothes felt like opening a time capsule, and everything reminded her of Ant. There was the orange maxi dress she'd worn on the great onion rings hunt, lying atop the T-shirt and leggings she'd worn when they got vaxxed in the Six Flags parking lot. She folded them away in the hotel dresser and kept digging: underwear, bralettes, another fleece-lined hoodie the size of a tent—and somehow, the line-a-day journal she thought she'd lost after neglecting her daily lines since September.

Maya opened the journal to an open entry and grabbed a pen from the nearby desk.

Dear God,

Long time, no see

I don't get this. I don't get any of this.

Would you cool it with the variants?!

Please help quarantining feel less lonely. Just get me through these next days.

Being merely yogurt and coffee, her order didn't take long to arrive, and soon she was sitting on her hotel balcony in her hibiscus hoodie, skull-printed leggings, and Crocs with socks, trying to think of a five-letter "teen tennis sensation."

"Maya, is that you?" a voice called from the adjacent balcony. A familiar but impossible voice.

"Adriana?" she called back incredulously. What was Ant's mom doing here? She put her newspaper aside and gaped at the woman standing on the neighboring balcony.

Adriana clapped her gloved hands, delighted. "It's so nice to see a familiar face! I like the blonde—it's really unexpected."

Maya was surprised by the surge of happiness in her chest. This was like an answered prayer. "I thought I wasn't going to see another soul for the next five days. I'm quarantining because my boss has Schrödinger's COVID and I don't want to bring anything home to my parents. My mom has asthma and my dad has diabetes."

Ant's mom nodded. "Same. I'm here to visit my Antonio and my best friend, Kay. But I know better than most folks how hard-core Omicron is going. Since Thanksgiving, every third person that canceled an appointment because they probably had COVID was *just* with their family—on another island or the mainland. When I made my trip, I assumed half the plane had COVID."

Maya couldn't help herself at hearing Ant's name. "How is he?" Her voice sounded a little high and tense to her own ears, hopefully not as desperate as she felt. Her heart sank as she watched his mom's face fall. How badly had Maya hurt him? Or had something worse happened?

"I wish I could tell you," Adriana replied, looking at the hotel's rear lawn. "He's barely been in touch since the fall, besides a postcard telling me he was in Virginia and some texts here and there." She sighed. "It's the reason I'm here. When he told me he wasn't coming home for Thanksgiving, I booked my flight here. I want to get us back on track before I go to Puerto Rico." She gave a dry laugh. "My life can't be all angry relatives."

Maya gave a little laugh of her own in sympathy. "Ant hasn't really been talking to me, either. I can't tell if he's mad, embarrassed, or simply doesn't want to see me."

Adriana's head snapped back to her. "What could have broken up the Wonder Twins?!"

Maya could only offer a sad sigh in response.

Adriana held up placating hands. "It looks like we're gonna be neighbors for the next couple days. If you want to tell me about it, we have time."

∽

Maya knew that she'd always liked Ant's mom, but she was shocked at how easy Adriana was to hang out with. They found each other on *Mario Kart* and trash-talked through their shared hotel wall. They ordered their meals at the same time and ate on their respective balconies in winter coats. They talked, a lot—and found it surprisingly easy since neither of them had to explain much.

Maya knew the contours of Adriana's story from Ant, and had been in her orbit as long as she'd been in Ant's. The older lady was there with her when she first saw the Ohana Center burning on the news. She'd brought her a blanket while Maya sobbed on the couch. It was easy to be honest with someone who'd seen you at your worst.

On their last night of quarantine, Adriana sprang for a big dinner for both of them from the Michelin-starred Japanese place down the street, which had only reluctantly started doing takeout for their economic survival. It was spectacular. They dined alfresco, eating beautiful sushi and drinking sake as they watched the sunset.

"Tomorrow, I go to an uncertain welcome from my son, and then to an even more uncertain welcome from my family in Puerto Rico—except for my fellow outcast Tío Herman, who owns a drag bar in San Juan. And on to a new job, where I will probably spend the first few months saying 'Yes, I am Dr. Gabriel.'" She rolled her eyes. "And of course, the joys of trying to start a brand-new life at fifty-two. But even with all my struggles, and those yet to come, I'm happy to be alive."

Maya swallowed a bit of scallop nigiri with a laugh. "Sounds lovely. Can't relate." She had demolished a good bit of the pickled radish roll before she felt Adriana's eyes on her.

"What do you mean by that, Maya?"

Oh no, she'd offended her—and they'd been getting along so well. She had even listened to everything that had happened with Ant without (obviously) taking either of their sides. Maya couldn't lose another member of the Gabriel family, and immediately tried to apologize. "I'm so sorry, Adriana. That came out much more disrespectful than I intended . . ."

She trailed off as the older woman put her hands up and shook her head. "You weren't rude, Maya. But . . . are you not glad to be alive?"

Maya set down her chopsticks. Her throat was suddenly dry. The answer throbbed in her head, but it was too big to say out loud, so she shook her head instead, swallowing again as a rogue tear ran down her cheek.

"I mean, I'd never *do* anything about it because that would destroy my parents. But if it was left to me . . . it would be an easy no to having been born." She looked to the flaming orange-red of the winter sky and waited for Adriana to say something. On the other balcony, the older lady had picked up her chair and come as close to Maya as her balcony would allow.

"Sweetheart," she began, sitting to face Maya again. "I think you need to talk with someone about depression." Her voice was gentle, coaxing, like Maya was a frightened mare. It seemed a touch unnecessary, to be honest.

Maya shook her head. She knew what depression felt like. She remembered "the octopus"—the heavy limbs, her parents' worried faces over her in bed—and she'd been doing everything she could to avoid it. This was not that. The world was just . . . gray. Things were sad, or hard, or even pointless, but sometimes life was like that.

"I get up every day. I go to work. Actually, I was doing a pretty great job before everything happened this week." She was starting to sound defensive, and she couldn't say why.

Adriana's face was blessedly neutral. Maya didn't think she could look at her if she saw worry (or worse, pity) there. "Please hear this from someone who grieved heavily, thought I was done, and then realized I very much wasn't. Just because you're functioning doesn't mean you're okay. The world tells Black women that our pain doesn't matter. They say we're strong, so it's easy to ignore our hurt. They say it so much, we often ignore it ourselves. But I'm listening to you trying to say it's nothing even as I hear how much you don't want to be alive. Is that true, Maya?"

Maya twisted in her seat, blinking rapidly. Oh God, she was going to cry again. She nodded, wiping the tears away with both hands before they could course down her cheeks. Rationally, she knew that depression was a combination of brain chemistry and circumstance. So why did she feel like she'd failed somehow? She had God, and yoga, and people who loved her, but somehow, she didn't want to be here anymore.

"Okay, honey. I need you to promise me that you'll talk to someone soon. And we can drop this whole conversation."

Maya nodded again. "I promise." She stood. "Thanks for dinner, Adriana. I think I'm emotionally tapped. I'm gonna lie down and watch *The Great British Baking Show* or something to bring me down." She cleared her table and headed toward her door. "Thank you, by the way. This was hard, but I think it was really important."

Adriana nodded. "Hopefully we can see each other again soon."

Maya gave a little half smile and went inside. They both knew that entirely depended on Ant.

Ant

The morning sky was still dark, but Ant was already on the bus headed to work. He'd gotten suckered into delivering poinsettias for three days running because he kept making the mistake of bringing his car to work. Man alive, did people like their poinsettias around here, especially the churches. Ant was used to seeing them in rows of sizable bushes in front of the UH Agricultural Science Facility. He was still working on seeing the plants as "holiday" themed, despite their being featured on Christmas cards and holiday banners. December would apparently be the month Ant spent readjusting.

∽

It had started with his mother's arrival, which shocked him into instantaneous reconciliation on Auntie Kay's front lawn. He found it impossible to hold on to the scraps of his anger about her renting out the house. And once he stopped being mad (and pretending that he wasn't), Ant seriously listened to the terms of the lease.

"The lease is up in 2026, without the option for renewal."

They were in Auntie Kay's kitchen trying to re-create Abuela Nena's *asopao de pollo*. Kay had taken them to the local international market so they could get the *sofrito*, *sazón*, and plentiful cilantro the stew required. Then she left them to cook and talk.

Ant shucked the corn thoughtfully. "So 2026, as in five years from now . . ." He trailed off into a thoughtful hum.

"Yup," his mom confirmed, arranging chicken thighs on the cutting board. "For your five-year plan. I listen when you talk, you know." She elbowed him playfully. "But seriously, I had my mind made up about leaving Hawai'i for a while. I considered you, but this move was all about me."

12/11/21

Dear God,

I know I need help now. Please help me ask for it.

Thanks,
Maya

Texts from Maya to her parents, December 13, 2021

Maya:

Hey Momma, Hey Daddy
I had a third negative test!
I can come home!

Momma:

That's wonderful, baby!

Daddy:

I can come get you after work

Check out is at 11, so I'll just take a Lyft
home and crack the windows.

Momma:

Okay, I'm working from home
today, so I'll be ready to give you
a big hug once you're home

I can't wait!

Maya

Maya gave her phone a small smile and tossed it on her bed. She had two hours to make the most of her final hotel day. She needed some room service, and she needed to have one last bath in the hotel's pond-size tub. Hopefully, between now and when she left, Maya could find the words to ask her mom to help her find a therapist without sharing how scary things were in her mind sometimes.

She didn't want to frighten her mom, and she really didn't want her mom to blame herself. Maya rubbed her temples and sighed. Why did it seem so daunting to talk to her guidance counselor mother about her mental health? Maybe she needed to practice. She did the mental math, realized it was a reasonable time in the UK, and pressed the phone button on her FaceChat app.

Ella materialized from the neck up, not wearing a turtleneck for once. Maya couldn't help her beaming smile at the sight of her sister. *I just miss her so much.*

"What's up, buttercup?" Ella half sang. She was leaning against a beige wallpapered wall, probably in a hotel or something.

Maya adjusted her hotel robe. "It's my last day in the hotel, and I've realized something about myself while I'm here. I'm pretty sure I've been dealing with depression the whole time I've been back. It's kinda coming to a head now. But I don't know where to start looking."

Ella nodded thoughtfully. "Well, I love my online therapist. Going online let me get real specific: I wanted a Black American ex-pat living in Europe. My lady lives in Italy and runs a pretty solid virtual practice. It was a lifesaver when Will and I started living together during lockdown."

Maya felt her jaw drop. She'd had no idea Ella was in therapy, and they talked about everything. "How long have you been seeing her?"

Her sister raked her fingers through her short, curly pixie cut and made a horsey noise. "Since I finished grad school. My mentor said I would need one to survive being Black *and* a woman in engineering. I needed to be ready if they tried to Meghan Markle me."

"Huh." That's all Maya could say. "I was just over here, trying to figure out how to break it to Mom that I wanted therapy."

That made Ella snort. "After the last two years, if you aren't dealing with anxiety or depression, I find you highly suspect." That made them both laugh. "Seriously, though, Mai—tell our parents everything or tell them nothing. I know they're just happy to see you every day. The most important thing is your healing."

Maya didn't know why, but those simple words brought tears to her eyes. "Thanks, Ella Bella."

After practicing the whole ride over, Maya sat with her mom on the living room sofa at home and did her best to get the words out. Once she was done, her mom responded with a tight hug and about half a dozen kisses on her forehead.

"Give me a couple days. I've helped several of my colleagues find therapists over the last few years, so I have some ideas. Everyone comes to the guidance counselor when they need some help—it's helped to have some resources on hand."

Momma sat up and touched Maya's face. "I only have one condition for my services. I need you to let us care for you. Your father and I know our limits, emotional and financial. We aren't going to hurt ourselves by showing up for you. But I would feel better about whatever we do next if you promise to prioritize your healing. I know it's hard to pause, but nothing is more important right now. Let us take care of necessities, while you take care of you." Her mother stretched out her hand. "Do we have a deal?"

Maya took her mother's hand and shook it firmly. "Yes."

She had no idea what came next, but for the first time in months, Maya felt a spark of hope that wasn't tinged with desperation. It wasn't the relief that she'd felt when she handed her life over to Emme. It was something smaller, but brighter.

It was just a spark, but it was enough.

⟳

Things I'd like to do in December

1. Make Christmas cookies
2. Christmas lights at Watkins Park
3. Mulled cider
4. NYE parties
5. Reconnect with Ant

The last item stung, but for Maya push had come to shove and she had to figure out how to get him back in her life, however he wanted to be there. At this point she'd be happy to simply be his friend again; anything else was too much to hope for.

She sat at the kitchen table with her line-a-day journal, trying to remember other things she liked doing this time of year. It was helping her remember things she liked, in general. It was weird, but she'd been home for about nine months, and the only time she'd done things that she really wanted was with Ant. How did she always feel so free around him? And how had she thought she could throw that away?

Her thoughts were interrupted by a honk from outside. Maya went to the window and screamed. Standing outside was the only person she wanted to see more than Antonio. "Ella!" she cried, rushing down the steps and out the front door.

"Maya!" Ella screamed in return, stretching her name to three affectionate syllables. They hugged outside, walked up the steps to the house, and hugged again.

Maya froze at the front door. "Ella, have you had a chance to quarantine or anything?"

She didn't know what she'd do if her sister said no, but she felt obliged to ask. Thankfully Ella nodded with a little laugh. "I was quarantining in New York when you FaceChatted me. I had to find the one wall in Will's house without any art so you wouldn't know where I was."

Maya beamed. "Sneaky—I like it!"

Ella hung up her coat with a shimmy. "Speaking of sneaky, can you help me make a surprise dinner for Mom, like you did when you came back to visit my senior year of college?"

Maya blinked at her sister in surprise. "You remember that?"

Ella laughed. "Of course I do. You were awesome—and so was that pot roast. You've ruined me for other people's pot roast, and British people are really into them so it's a serious problem."

They sat at the kitchen table, where Ella immediately noticed the line-a-day journal. "Oh wow, you're still using it! That's so cool."

She handed it to Maya, scrupulously looking away from the pages.

Maya took the journal and reached for a nearby pen. "I was just trying to remember stuff I like doing this time of year. It's weird, but I'm struggling to remember what I liked in the olden times."

Ella drummed her fingers on her chin. "How about ice-skating? When we were kids we'd always go down to the ice rink on the Mall and you'd skate circles around me for an hour or so."

That brought a smile to Maya's face. Skating was the closest you could get to flying while still being on the ground. "You're here for me to skate circles around, so let's go!"

Ella sat up. "Now?"

They both looked outside at the setting sun. "Nah," they said in unison.

"How about tomorrow?" Maya suggested.

"Sounds perfect, just like you." Ella launched herself at her sister, wrapping her in a hug.

Maya couldn't help herself; she burst into tears. "I'm not perfect, Ella." She sniffed.

"But you're you—that's better than perfect."

They held each other just a little longer, then Ella urged them up. "Okay, let's look in the fridge and see what we can make."

"Sure thing." Maya stood and followed her sister into the kitchen. "Fair warning, we may have to harvest some meal kits."

Ella turned sharply. "Meal kits?!"

Maya has invited you to the Disappointing Black Girls Still Love Paramore group chat, December 18, 2021

—Signs&1nders: Hey, Emme, I'm so glad to hear that your dad is on the mend

—EmmeVP: Thank you, Maya! We had a pretty big scare, but he turned a corner

—Signs&1nders: That's wonderful!

—EmmeVP: But I have the feeling something else on your mind since you went to the trouble of making a new chat

—Signs&1nders: I've made a decision that you may find disappointing. I need to take my life back, Emme.
—Signs&1nders: I realized that I have some healing to do before I make any big plans
But my next steps have to come from me

—EmmeVP: . . .
—EmmeVP: You aren't being noble for the sake of my father's health, are you?

—Signs&1nders: No, this is a selfish decision. This is for me.

—EmmeVP: Then I'm going to miss you, Maya. I hope one day, when the plague is a weird memory, we can meet up at Velma's, and then go for bubble tea.

—Signs&1nders: I'd like that.

Ant

He was so happy to be home and pleasantly surprised to realize that DC was starting to feel like home. Every reunion was joyful, from his first hug with Auntie Kay to riding the bus downtown again. When he'd left DC for Virginia, the city was wearing a navy blazer. Now it had put on a tacky light-up Christmas sweater. There were banners on every light pole and Christmas lights in front yards, trimming windows, and wrapped around the stunted trunks of bare city trees in their planters. He couldn't help wondering which of the decorated trees in decked-out lobbies he might have been tending just weeks ago.

But even as he soaked in all the holiday spirit from his window seat on the bus, Ant couldn't get his mother's words out of his head: *"I considered you, but this move was all about me."*

Back in Virginia, Ant had been working to make himself the main character. He'd been keeping his distance from Maya so he wouldn't fall back into the habit of being her sidekick. But . . . what if his need to be more independent and his relationship with Maya were separate issues that he was conflating? Yes, he needed to be independent—but he'd also been making everything about him. His mom renting out their house had nothing to do with him. Mira's boundaries around the kind of texts Ant could send? That was about her—not him.

What if Maya's rejection wasn't about him, or about Emme, but truly about Maya?

He had about ten minutes left before his bus ride was over. That was just enough time for him to reread Maya's letter for the tenth time. He'd been keeping it in his backpack to remind himself *not* to pine after her. Now he tried to pretend Maya was a stranger and he'd found her letter on the street. If he wasn't looking for what it said about *him*, could he see what Maya said about herself? What if he *did* need to make her the main character, just to understand her a bit better?

He fished the letter out his backpack and read it again, giving it his full focus.

> *But a bigger part—a sadder but wiser part of me— knows that I'm not whole now. And I know you, Ant. If we got together, you would devote yourself to fixing all my broken pieces, whatever the cost, and that's not the kind of relationship I want.*

Ant looked up and swallowed. His fingers felt numb. How had he missed all Maya's pain? She felt broken and unlovable—and worried about being a burden. It was hitting Ant all at once. He may have pushed away his best friend, the woman he loved, precisely when she needed him the most.

Just like that, Ant went from wanting to avoid Maya to wanting to see her more than anything in the world. He had to work now, but he'd find time—he'd make time.

We just need to talk. If we talk, we can figure things out.

❧

It looked like Ant was destined to be visited by the ghosts of DC past today. He had come to work consumed with thoughts of Maya, then been asked to make an emergency delivery to the Smithsonian National Museum of Natural History—about three dozen poinsettias. Stepping out of the van, he saw his old boss Rhonda giving him a smiley wave from a safe six feet away.

"So good to see you landed well," she said as she signed for the plants.

"Thanks for making it happen," Ant responded with a wide smile below his mask.

"I only made the introduction!" Rhonda called back as she wheeled the delivery away.

Ant took his time walking back down the National Mall to where he'd parked the van. He was taking in the crisp air and the gray yet cheery day. His mind drifted back to Maya. There was no reason to wait. He pulled out his phone to text her—yes, it would be weird, but nothing could be better than seeing her again.

Then he heard a laugh tinkle in his ears. Ant froze and turned toward the sound.

"Maya," he breathed. She was moving gracefully in the middle of the ice-skating rink in the sculpture garden. It was one of the places she'd said she wanted to take him to back in the fall. He didn't know she could skate so well! But there she was, doing some pretty impressive stuff. Little spins and short jumps—even balancing on one foot. Ant moved toward the rink as if pulled by a magnet.

A figure behind her moved less gracefully. "I thought you said it was like riding a bike, Mai!" her companion shouted in laughing accusation. He had confirmation now, not that he needed it.

"I thought ballerinas were naturally graceful; turns out we're both wrong." Maya turned back and went to steady her wobbly skating partner despite her words.

Ant continued walking until his feet bumped the edge of the rink. You didn't have to believe in astrology to see that the stars had aligned for this moment. He took a deep breath, then waved. If she was happy to see him, that was all he needed.

Maya was back in the middle of the rink doing a slow spin. Her locs were blonde and shorter than they used to be. Maya herself looked slightly alien in her elegant winter coat. But she was wearing the hand-knit *Doctor Who*–inspired scarf he remembered her sister sending her several Christmases ago.

Ant noticed the moment she caught sight of him. She wobbled just a bit, but there was a warmth in her unfolding smile, a light in her dark-amber eyes that told him right now, in this very place, they were exactly where they were supposed to be. She skated over to him.

He remembered that he was still wearing his mask, and took it off, smiling so much his face ached.

"Hi, Ant." She looked up at him, happy but uncertain. Ant hated himself for making her doubt him. He had to fix that. Glancing down, he saw how they both gripped the metal rail between them with gloved hands. He reached out and took both of hers, lacing their fingers together.

"Hi, Maya."

She looked at their joined hands and then turned her gaze up at him, dark eyes shining with happy tears. The moment was interrupted by a cry of delight from across the ice. "It's snowing!"

Ant and Maya both looked up. Large snowflakes grazed Ant's cheeks. He looked at Maya, treasuring the way the flakes got caught in her eyelashes. It was impossible, but she was more beautiful than he'd ever seen her. She watched the sky for a moment more.

"This feels like a miracle." She gave him a shaky smile. He wasn't sure if she meant the snow or this moment, but he definitely felt it, too.

"I think the miracle is us; someone once told me there's a special magic in holding hands." Ant looked down at their joined hands and gave them a squeeze. When he looked up, all Ant could see was Maya's sunshine smile and brown eyes that warmed him in the cold. Then Ant kissed her—how could he not?

It was the best thing in the world.

First Day of Spring, 2022

3/20/22

Dear God,

Thank you for another year of life. Thank you for therapy, and Lexapro. (Please bless my grad school application, so I can be a good therapist, too.) Thank you for my parents, for my sister, and Ant's mom. Most of all thank you for giving me my Antonio. Thank you for the love we've found and for having him beside me through everything life throws our way.

You can handle more than you think if you have the right hand to hold.

Gratefully,
Maya

ACKNOWLEDGMENTS

Until the moment I hit "Send" on my final manuscript, I was pretty sure this book would do me in before it got done. It wasn't just the stress of writing a novel on deadline or trying (and failing) to write a book in a year. The main struggle with writing this novel was trying to do it during one of the most difficult and chaotic periods in modern history.

I launched into work on my second novel in October 2020. This was after seven months of confronting the unavoidable twin plagues of COVID and systemic racist violence (specifically the murders of Ahmaud Arbery, Breonna Taylor, and George Floyd).

Everything was harder, including writing. The external circumstances took a greater toll on my mental health than I ever expected. I realized that telling stories takes more than imagination; it requires hope. I had never felt more hopeless in my life.

Thankfully my husband noticed what I could not: that my "pandemic blues" had tilted into depression, and my "understandable worry" had become anxiety. I'm so grateful for his ability to always see me and his unconditional love. I want to also acknowledge my wonderful Black lady therapist, Sherry, for her listening ear, warm heart, and clear guidance in addressing my mental health needs.

☙

Between my first book and this one, I have been able to meet so many wonderful authors—most scribbling around their day jobs, like me. These women have been an incredible source of care and friendship: Denise Williams, my DVdebut mentor; my Montlake and Lake Union friends, Jennifer Bardsley, Sara Goodman Confino, Elissa Dickey, Paulette Kennedy, Priscilla Oliveras, and Mansi Shah; and my author friends beyond Amazon, Adele Buck, Preslaysa Williams, and Maan Gabriel.

Do yourself a favor and go buy their books!

Speaking of Amazon, I must thank the excellent team at Montlake—as well as Lindsay Faber, my developmental editor. She helped me polish this manuscript into a diamond, with her insightful questions and helpful suggestions. The biggest thanks go to my incredible editor Alison Dasho. Your kindness and astounding faith have meant the absolute world.

Thanks always to the anchor of my professional life, my agent, Michelle Richter. You are simply the best.

Finally, thanks to my loving mother, my darling daughter, and the best husband / sounding board / proofreader a person could ever have. It's not easy having an author in your life, but I'm so grateful for you and the many ways you inspire me every day.

ABOUT THE AUTHOR

Eden Appiah-Kubi, author of *The Bennet Women*, has been putting her spin on classic stories since third grade. She was born in Washington, DC, and raised in the Maryland suburbs, where she still lives with her husband and hilarious daughter.